PILGRIM SOLOMON

AND

JOHN SOLOMON, RETIRED:

THE ADVENTURES OF

JOHN SOLOMON, VOLUME 8

H . BEDFORD-JONES

PILGRIM SOLOMON
AND
JOHN SOLOMON, RETIRED

THE ADVENTURES OF
JOHN SOLOMON, VOLUME 8

H. BEDFORD-JONES

COVER BY
P.J. MONAHAN

STEEGER BOOKS • 2022

PILGRIM SOLOMON

CHAPTER I

THE STREET OF
THE WHITE CAMEL

JIM MAGRUDER sat frowningly at his desk, staring at the note and opened packet which lay before him. From outside, the babel of Cairo streets came with lessened force through the blinds, and the thudding steps of a column of Anzac soldiery went driving past the house in token that war was upon the land of Egypt.

The son of a missionary in Moslem lands, Magruder had found it both profitable and congenial to look after the interests of half a score of American commercial houses in Cairo, since the Great War had flung the eastern world topsy-turvy. Knowing several Arabic dialects and the ways of the East, Magruder had done well by his clients.

"This sure gets my goat!" he grunted, reading the letter once again. It had come by special messenger with the packet; but the messenger had vanished mysteriously. Magruder leaned forward and tapped a bell.

"*Effendi?*" A native house servant appeared at the door.

"Ali, where is the Street of the White Camel?" demanded Magruder in Arabic.

Surprise flitted across the brown face of Ali.

"*Effendi,* thy servant knows not these dens of iniquity—"

"Come, Ali! No evasions, please. Where is this street?"

The plea of ignorance having failed, Ali tried that of virtue.

"*Effendi,* I have heard of such a street. It is of very evil reputation. Allah preserve thy servant from knowing such places!

However, I have heard that if one goes along the Nahhassin Street to the market of the coppersmiths, and turns to the right behind the Beshtak palace, one comes to an alley wherein is but one house, and in this one house lives a woman of poor repute named Rahaba, who is rumored to be of great beauty."

"You have a good memory for gossip," said Magruder dryly. "Go!"

It was late afternoon; he would have to act quickly, if at all. Prompt six, the letter said.

For a space he considered that letter anew, wondering at it, studying it for some escaped clew, but finding none. The writing was very neat, and the wording was so comfortably phrased that everything essential was here, yet nothing additional. Magruder's fingers strayed to the packet and took from the small box a ring of silver. The ring was small for him, fitting the little finger of his left hand, but it would have been large for Arabs, he reflected.

Upon the flat face of the silver ring was graven a square, from corner to corner of which ran diagonal cross-lines. There was nothing else. Magruder was familiar with the design upon the ring—a design common to all Oriental countries under various forms, and known by tradition as the seal of King Solomon. He turned again to the letter:

> MR. JAMES MAGRUDER. *Square Suarès, City.*
>
> DEAR SIR: Are you willing to visit a country which few white men have ever seen, and to earn one hundred thousand dollars at some personal risk?
>
> If so, present yourself promptly at six o'clock this evening, at the house of Rahaba in the Street of the White Camel. Ask for Rahaba, and wear the inclosed ring. Your duties will be in all ways honorable, and are not concerned with the war in Europe.

The letter was unsigned. Magruder laid it aside and lit a cigarette reflectively.

A hundred thousand! That meant New York and his own country again, he mused; it meant a flying start in the world—

and all he wanted was the start. He had been here in the Orient for three years, engaged in commercial work. He was twenty-six, and unless he could pull out and go home in another year or so, he would have to stay here, resigning himself to expatriation and living the only life at which he could make fair money.

"And Joe Christmas, how I'd like to be home again!" he mused. "New York and Chicago, the University Club, the pretty girls on the Avenue, hat-check robbers—whew! For a hundred thousand I could afford to throw up this business, and whoever wrote this letter must have known it. H'm! Let's see again." He picked up the sheet of paper. "What country does the beggar mean? Tibet or Abyssinia or Arabia? No telling. Duties honorable—and a bit dangerous; that sounds interesting. Not concerned with the war in Europe—but how about the war in Mesopotamia or Syria? Well, I may be wrong. This thing is like you read in a novel—I've a mind to chance it! A hundred thousand iron men look big right now."

Why had that letter and ring been sent to him, of all men? The only thing that rendered him at all conspicuous was that he was an American, one of two or three left in Egypt; in these days of strife and turmoil, all tourists were rigidly excluded. And yet—

"Hang it, that's no explanation!" he muttered disgustedly, rising and getting his hat and stick. "And why should I go chasing to the house of some ungodly Egyptian woman? That letter was written by a white man, though. Well, no harm in taking a look-see, I suppose. If things show up off color, I don't need to buy chips in the game."

Since no taxicabs were left in evidence, Magruder walked over to the Place de l'Opéra and took a victoria, ordering it straight out the Mouski. Now he found himself in the ancient Fatimite city of the caliphs, and at the el-Ashraf mosque dismissed the victoria and struck north along the intersecting street on foot. He knew his way well enough, and was in no danger of confusion from the Kairene streets, which change their name unexpectedly at every few hundred yards.

Passing the towering hospital off Kalaun, Magruder struck on through the street of the coppersmiths. With the Beshtak palace ahead to the right, he paused, then turned into the cross street. At this hour there was little traffic, yet, as Magruder fronted into the dark maze of native lanes ahead of him, he was met by a towering figure which seemed to materialize from nothing—a rissaldar-major of Indian troops, his brown face lowering from beneath his heavy turban.

"Pardon, sahib!" was the curt greeting. "You have business hereabouts?"

Used as he was to Cairo in war time, Magruder looked at the officer in amazement.

"Eh? What the devil do you mean?"

"Sahib, I but obey my orders."

Magruder took out a cigarette reflectively. Had that letter come from some nest of plotters, who had been discovered and seized? If he told his business, would he not he liable to seizure as an accomplice? Trusting to his own innocence, he determined to go ahead.

"Yes, I have business hereabouts," he returned quietly, and lit a cigarette. "Am I headed aright for the Street of the White Camel?"

Now, as he held up the match, it chanced that the silver ring on his finger was presented to the sight of the Indian. Magruder observed that the subofficer's eyes were fastened upon the ring, then the soldier drew himself up in a stiff salute.

"Aye, sahib—at the second turning of this alley you will find the house, on a side alley of its own."

"Thank you."

Magruder strode on. He realized that the ring had passed him, but he could not yet understand why sentinels drawn from Britain's native army guarded this street and house—and the soldier had seemed to know that Magruder sought a certain house!

"Either they've nabbed a bunch of plotters," thought the American, "and are quietly grabbing every one who comes along—or else I'm in with the right crowd, sure enough."

An instant later, indeed, another man passed him; this time a white man, in the uniform of a captain of Indian lancers, who gave him a single keen glance and passed on without pause. The swift Egyptian twilight was closing down as Magruder, following his instructions, came to a large building on the left, in a tiny cul-de-sac all its own.

"So this is the Street of the White Camel, eh?" He gazed at the building and found it unlighted, gloomy of aspect. The fascination of his blind quest was strangely gripping and compellent; intrigue, soldiers, a scarlet woman of Old Cairo—and he, Jim Magruder, of Baltimore, the central figure of it all!

Chuckling at the thought, he came to the doorway of the house. Neither knocker nor bell presented itself to view, but as Magruder lifted his knuckles to the wood, the door opened suddenly and showed a bowing native.

"*Effendi,* whom seek you?"

"The woman Rahaba," answered Magruder in Arbi, extending the ring.

"Will you follow, *effendi?*"

Magruder stepped into a bare hallway, lighted by a dim hanging lamp. At the far end, a door gave him admittance into a long room where burned candles in high sconces. Divans, chairs, and taborets holding sweetmeats and cigarettes dotted the floor; the walls were hidden behind Bagdad weaves and kilims. The native servant had vanished entirely, so Magruder sat down and helped himself to an excellent cigarette. He eyed the hangings and appointments of the room with approval; not for nothing had he been handling the affairs of rug importers during the past year! He had never before been in a den of Oriental iniquity, and it was a distinctly pleasant sensation to find that the furnishings quite came up to the approved standard set by the Arabian Nights and other authorities.

Magruder's cigarette was half gone when suddenly a harsh voice split the languorous silence of the place—a voice midway in speech that sounded as if from some other room of which the door had opened abruptly:

"—cannot be done, sir! I will not issue such passports to any one. It is preposterous, sir, preposterous!"

The American's eyes widened in stark amazement, for he had heard that voice only the day previous, in a vain attempt to induce the authorities to lift the embargo on a consignment of goods to New York. It was the voice of the general who, as military governor, held Cairo between his hands in these days of war.

And then came another voice, softer yet equally and incredibly familiar to Magruder. It was the voice of a man who had been in his office a few days before this, making inquiries concerning some freight being sent to the States from Alexandria.

"Beggin' your pardon, general, but you're a-goin' to issue them 'ere passports, just like that! You may 'ave your choice, sir. Either you issues them passports 'ere and now, or by to-morrow night there'll be another military governor sittin' in your place! It's a-goin' to be a werry 'ard world, indeed, for you, sir, if you don't do just as I says—"

A door slammed, and the voices were cut off. Magruder laid down his cigarette, utterly astounded at what he had involuntarily heard.

The military governor here—in this house! That explained the sentinels, of course, and was not so incredible. But the other man—the little cockney who dared make such demands and threats—this was the bewildering, stupefying thing! Who was this man who could threaten the highest Anglo-Egyptian officers with removal?

Magruder mentally pictured the man, remembering him very well: but as he did so, his amazement increased. Solomon was the name, John Solomon, and for all his cockney evidences, Solomon had claimed to be an American citizen. A rather small, plump man, with gray hair, blank blue eyes, and features lined with age yet remarkably devoid of expression—such was the mental picture Magruder formed. The man was commonplace. In a crowd he would have passed absolutely unobserved. What authority, then, was his? What position, rank, or power that he was able to dictate to a British general?

Suddenly Magruder saw a kilim move, and he glanced up sharply. The hanging slid aside, and into the room strode a man—an Arab, clad in simple white burnoose, but wearing a look of indescribable pride and dignity upon his worn, brown features. He advanced and held out his hand, speaking in clearly enunciated English:

"Good evening. You are Mr. Magruder? Sit down, please."

Magruder obeyed, just a little overcome. The Arab met his gaze for a moment, then smiled faintly.

"I can explain only briefly and perhaps unsatisfactorily, Mr. Magruder, but if you decide to accept my proposition you'll learn more details later. I am not acting for myself, but for a friend of mine—an American, whose chief reason in seeking your help was that you also are an American. After investigating you, he decided that with your knowledge of Arbi and the ways of Arabs, you were the very man whom he desired."

"Thanks," returned Magruder dryly. "Who's this friend of yours—Solomon?"

The Arab started perceptibly.

"What do you know of Solomon?"

A flash of intuition told Jim Magruder not to bluff. In a few words he told of overhearing that scrap of conversation, and the little he knew of Solomon. The Arab smiled.

"Your guess was right, Mr. Magruder; he is the man, my friend. Now, have you decided to accept the proposition made you in that letter? Will you join us?"

"That depends on the work," returned Magruder cautiously. "What is it?"

"I cannot tell you; I do not know myself," was the surprising reply. "If you accept, I shall give you a certain mission, and Mr. Solomon will join you later. He has business which is dangerous, and upon which he wishes to embark with a companion who is reliable and efficient."

"Ergo, an American," and Magruder smiled. "What's the strange country mentioned in the letter?"

"Mecca and the territory adjacent."

A low whistle of amazement escaped the American. Mecca and the Hijaz—territory closed to all save Moslems for fourteen hundred years! The heart of Islam, close guarded by the most fanatical of all races! The last unknown country on earth!

"If you think I'm going to Mecca, nothing doing!" said Magruder grimly. "That twenty thousand pounds is a nice big sum, but I'm not after life insurance. I may be a reckless and gay young thing, my friend, but no one ever called me a damned fool."

The Arab frowned, somewhat puzzled.

"I do not quite get your meaning, Mr. Magruder. You refuse the trip?"

"Yes, I refuse. I'm a Christian, and Christians find the Hijaz mighty unhealthy."

The other smiled faintly. "You misunderstand, sir. As to your British passports, you have overheard part of a conversation relative to them—and I need say no more. They will carry you freely through all British territory.

"Now, then, as to the Hijaz! You will go under the highest authority in the Moslem world—that of the Sherif of Mecca himself. Instead of being an object of suspicion, you will be an object of honor. The silver ring upon your finger will secure you friends in the most unexpected places. There are few pilgrims now in Mecca; the war has stopped that."

Suspicion narrowed Magruder's eyes to steely gleams.

"If this is true, then why? If such an unheard-of dispensation is made in my favor, there must be a mighty good reason for it."

"There is." The Arab nodded gravely and hesitated. "Mr. Magruder, I cannot tell you that reason, but you will hear of it soon enough. In these days of the Great War, all the old customs are being overthrown: among others, those of my own race. A few years hence, and Mecca will be open—not to all men, of course, but to consuls and diplomatic relations. I can only say that you go with the authority of the Sherif of Mecca and need fear nothing from any Arab. The danger—for there certainly is danger—is from the Turks. As for coming through alive, you have my personal assurance that you have every chance."

"And who are you?" demanded Magruder bluntly.

"The Sherif of Mecca is my father. The Emir of Hail is my cousin."

Magruder leaned back, no longer in the dark about this business. Only that morning, while strolling through the bazaars, he had heard men gossiping about a rumored uprising of the Bedouin tribes of Arabia, under the Sherif of Mecca, against the Turkish power. The Arab hates the Turk more bitterly than the Turk hates the Christian; for the Turk is of Asia, an offshoot of the destroying wave caused by Timur the Lame, and the Arab of pure blood boasts his whiteness. Further, the Sultan of Turkey has usurped the caliphate, which by Moslem law belongs to the lineal descendant of Mohammed—the Sherif of Mecca. One object of the rumored uprising was to restore the ancient Arabian caliphate.

Knowing that the man before him must be extremely powerful, since the sherif's place in the world of Islam corresponds to that of the pope in the Occidental lands, Magruder thought hard. He was dealing with no ordinary people. The heretofore burning question, "Who is this Solomon?" dwindled into insignificance before the general situation.

"When do I receive that hundred thousand dollars?" he asked suddenly.

"The minute you pass your word that you accept our proposition."

So he was dealing with men of honor—men who gave a hundred thousand dollars upon a word! But, thought Magruder, he might have known it; these princely Arabs had supreme contempt for all things save honor.

"Very well," he said quietly, "I accept."

"Good!" With the single exclamation, the Arab reached under his burnoose and drew forth some papers. One of these he extended to Magruder. It was a certified check for one hundred thousand dollars, drawn upon a New York bank and signed by John Solomon.

"Here"—and he held out an unsealed letter addressed to "Miss Clarice Worden"—"is the mission of which I spoke. Do you remember the wrecking of the *Ægean?*"

Magruder nodded. Only a fortnight since, the China mail steamer *Ægean* had blundered into a derelict dhow in the Red Sea and had sunk in ten minutes. The survivors had been no more than a handful, and several Americans were among those lost.

"A few days ago we received word that Miss Worden, an American tourist, en route home from Australia, was picked

up by some fishermen and taken into El Shaja. There, fortunately, some of my own family happened to be, and took her on
to Mecca in safety. We are sending you to her with this letter,
largely to reassure her of her personal safety, and later we shall
intrust you with the task of conducting her out of the country."

"Oh!" exclaimed Magruder, feeling very much as though he
were living a dream. "So I go from here to Mecca? I'd like to
know how!"

"By rail to Suez. As you leave the train, a man will meet you,
and you may recognize him by the ring similar to yours. After
that, trust to him. If you get safely to Mecca, you will await the
arrival of Mr. Solomon."

"If I get there safely?" queried Magruder. "There's a chance
that I won't, then?"

The Arab shrugged his shoulders.

"Of course. Spies are everywhere."

Magruder failed to see how spies were concerned with his
present mission; but, sensing that the interview was over, he rose.

"And when do I leave?"

"You will receive your passports tomorrow morning and take
the midnight train to Suez to-morrow evening."

"Very well."

CHAPTER II

THE MISSIONARY

IF THERE were a German or a Turk left betwixt Nairobi and the steel line guarding the Suez Canal, the government certainly knew nothing of it. Egypt had been weeded for possible spies more thoroughly than England itself, consequently Magruder paid little heed to the curt warning given him by Solomon's friend.

"If there are any spies, they'll be natives," he reflected, "and I'll guarantee to handle any native alive with one hand."

Nor was this any idle boast, in view of Magruder's length, breadth, and general dimensions. On various occasions he had had to be able to take care of himself in primitive fashion, and he could do it in a most efficient manner.

On the following day, which was presumably to be his last in Cairo, he transferred all his affairs to the most capable of his French assistants, paid his debts, and otherwise wound up his affairs locally. Shortly before noon, the doorman Ali brought him the card of the Reverend Frank Logan, reporting the said gentleman to be an American missionary.

"Send him along," ordered Magruder.

Logan proved to be a rather large man, stoop-shouldered, who walked with a decided limp and carried a stick of large caliber to assist him. His full-featured face was solemn and earnest in the extreme, in sharp contrast to his black attire were his heavy-lidded eyes of keenest blue.

"I am pleased, indeed, to shake hands with a fellow coun-

tryman, sir!" he addressed Magruder seriously. His every word
seemed to carry a weight of thought. "I have been directed to
you, my dear young man, by the consul general here—*our* consul
general, perhaps, would be the correct phrase."

"Yes?" murmured Magruder wickedly. "Sit down. Have a
drink?"

"I—ah—presume you jest, young man," was the severe
response. "I do not touch spirituous liquors. It hardly becomes
the cloth, I believe. Not that I have not been sore tempted by
the terrible things I have seen—ah, the wickedness of men!"

It developed that the Reverend Mr. Logan had been a
missionary in Syria, had been through the Armenian massacres, had been rescued and conveyed to Egypt by a neutral ship,
and was now engaged in a harebrained project—namely, that
of engaging in missionary work in Jedda, the port of pilgrim
disembarkation for Mecca, within the very gates of the holy
land of Islam! Magruder smiled slightly.

"I understand, sir," went on Logan, "that you are unusually
familiar with the Arab tongue, which I myself use to some
extent. Therefore I have come to endeavor to gain your compan-
ionship and assistance, if possible, in this venture—"

"You'd better give it up," cut in Magruder. "It's a wild scheme,
to say the least. You would become a martyr in short order."

"That, sir, is a risk we all must run," said Logan piously. "A risk
to be entirely discounted, young man. I am quite prepared to
give my unworthy life, if by so doing I can lighten the heathen
gloom of Arabia."

"You wouldn't lighten anything," returned Magruder bluntly.
"You wouldn't convert a good Arab in a million years, and the
bad ones don't pay to monkey with, believe me!"

"At least I shall make the effort," was the dogged reply.
Magruder squared around.

"See here, Mr. Logan, you'd better come down to earth and
adjust yourself! No matter what you would or would not do in
Arabia, you can't go there. You have as good a chance of walk-

ing into the Prophet's tomb right now as of reaching Jedda. The
British aren't letting any one past Suez, much less American
missionaries who'll get killed and cause Washington to get a
typewriter all het up writing notes about it! So resign yourself
to the situation; or, if you want to die, go back to Syria. But quit
fooling around the touchy spots of Islam, because there's posi-
tively nothing doing!"

Once or twice, with some agitation. Mr. Logan endeavored
to break into Magruder's flow of words. Then, sighing, he drew
a document from his pocket and poised it before him.

"Here, sir, is my passport," he returned mildly. "I have minis-
tered to British troops along the northern border, and am not
without recognition in official quarters. I think, sir, this answers
your chief objection."

Magruder threw up his hands.

"All right. If you can do that much, I quit talking. What do
you want of me?"

"I am leaving almost immediately, sir, and, as I have been the
custodian of funds and other important matters connected with
the work in Syria, I am asking that you will assume charge of the
same until my return. It necessitates a familiarity with Arabic—"

Magruder did not pause to note that Mr. Logan used the
term "Arabic" instead of the word more natural to a speaker of
the language, "Arbi."

"Can't do it," he broke in curtly. "I'm leaving here to-night
myself. But I can turn you over to my assistant, who will now
assume charge of my interests—a young Frenchman whom you
will find excellent in every way."

"Do not ring for him, sir!" exclaimed Mr. Logan, with dignity,
as Magruder put forth his hand to the bell. The visitor rose. "If
you, as an American, cannot do this, I prefer to turn it over to our
consular offices for handling. You are also going to Suez, then?"

"I didn't say so," answered Magruder. "However, I am. And
perhaps farther."

"Oh, then I shall see more of you, since I also leave to-night!"

Mr. Logan extended his hand in a paternal fashion. "Farewell for the present, young man."

Magruder said farewell, without regrets. He was not attracted to the missionary.

At noon he departed for luncheon with his assistant, leaving Ali in charge of the offices. Returning after luncheon, Magruder was informed by Ali that the Reverend Mr. Logan had returned, had waited for twenty minutes, then had gone again, promising to show up later for some unexplained reason. Magruder nodded and forgot the man.

Reflecting that it was necessary to have confidence in his Arab friend, Magruder went over to the club for tea at four; and from there, although the promised passports had not arrived, went on to engage his passage to Suez. To his great surprise, he found that a through sleeper to Suez would be on that night's express, and he promptly engaged a compartment. He had anticipated changing at Benha, and Ismailia.

"I wonder, now, if this could be more of that confounded clever Solomon's doings?" he thought, while returning to the office. "If he could order the military governor around, he could have a through car put on the express for my benefit. Anyhow, thanks to fortune, I'll have a clear night's sleep!"

He was stopping at the Continental, which now charged bare *pension* rates and was thankful to get them; so, deciding to put in the evening at the club, he stopped in, packed in a hand bag what he considered the necessities of life, filled his pocket with pipe, English tobacco, and the royal "special" cigarettes of Egypt, and then took up his way anew to the office.

Ali handed him a long envelope, which had been left by a messenger an hour previously. Opening it, Magruder found within a passport, fully made out and sweeping enough in its scope to carry him anywhere between Saloniki and Bombay without question; indeed, he was described as being upon official business. That phrase put him in thoughtful mood.

"I wonder if this job *is* official business, after all?" He pondered the question. "It is more than likely the English and French are behind this rumored revolt of the Arabian tribes, which would be a shrewd blow at Turkey; and if they are, the revolt will succeed. I suppose the Senussiyeh have assented, in which case the caliphate will be revived in Arabia beyond question of a doubt. It's only a matter of pushing the thing through, and once it's done, the prestige of Turkey will be smashed good and hard. H'm! This is guesswork, of course, but I'll bet a dollar it's a mighty close guess!"

He turned to his desk, meaning to put the letter addressed to Miss Clarice Worden with his passport. He had left the letter on his desk that morning, together with a few of his own private papers.

"The devil!" exclaimed the American, as he ran through the pile of papers. "These aren't as I left them! And—and where's that letter?"

He was quite certain that the papers had been disturbed. And the letter was gone!

There ensued a very bad ten minutes for every one in the office. The result was nil. No one had noticed the letter; the only outsider who had that day set foot in Magruder's sanctum was the Reverend Mr. Logan. Him Magruder was inclined to suspect, but it quickly struck him that the suspicion was altogether absurd. On casting back, indeed, to their interview, Magruder remembered that Logan had sat across the room from the desk, and that he had purloined the letter during his noonday visit seemed too fantastic to be tenable.

"What's happened before must have happened now," concluded Magruder to his assistant, after sending Ali for a victoria. "Ali emptied my wastebasket this afternoon and threw out that letter with the trash; he probably knocked over the pile of papers. Well, let it go. If a letter with that superscription turns up, hold on to it for me, will you? Good-by, old man, and good luck in the job!"

Thus he left his office for the last time, smiling and carefree.

The instant he was out of sight, however, he leaned forward to the native driver.

"The Mouski—drive on to the Beshtak palace, and hurry! *Estagel!*"

The carriage dashed on at a brisk pace. It was a trifle after six, and Magruder had hopes of getting another letter without delay; the loss was not one which would cause any mishaps, he reflected, nor did it seem that a letter of introduction would be absolutely essential in the heart of a mysterious and unknown country.

Bidding the driver wait at the Beshtak palace corner, Magruder hastened down the narrow alley, and a moment later saw before him the house of Rahaba. At his knock there was some delay before the door was opened by a stupid-eyed native woman, half clad.

"Solomon *effendi*, and at once!" exclaimed Magruder, displaying his ring. To his stupefaction, the woman stared at it, lifted her vacant eyes to his face, and shook her head.

"*Ma nich fahim,*" she answered dully. "You have the wrong house."

"Nonsense!" snapped Magruder. "Does not Rahaba live here?"

"I am Rahaba."

"Well, where are they who were here yesterday?" queried the exasperated American.

"*Ana m'arafche.*" She gradually closed the door. "I don't know. They will not return. It is not allowed me to have traffic with white men, so go away—"

The door slammed, and through the lattice she flung a torrent of low abuse which brought the red to Magruder's cheeks. He turned and retraced his steps to his victoria, then reconsidered his course.

He might seek out the military governor and demand to know where Solomon was; but, since every one had vanished from Rahaba's house, such a course might cause unpleasantness to Solomon or his Arab friend. Besides, the game was not worth the candle. That letter was not vitally important, since it had been unsealed.

"I might just as well go ahead with it," thought Magruder. "It's of no particular moment to me, anyhow. The passport, fortunately, is safe, and it's the main thing."

So, dismissing the lost letter as of no consequence, he was driven to the Hermes, dined passably, and then betook himself to the club for the evening.

It so happened that Russian pool, an excellent game, which makes high demand upon the skill and attention of the players, had leaped into favor of late. Magruder engaged in a game with a trio of merry young Australian officers, and in the midst was called away by one of the attendants. A gentleman waited below to see him—no name had been given.

Magruder excused himself from the game for a moment and hastened to the reception room. It occurred swiftly to him that Solomon might have heard of his visit to the house of Rahaba and might have sent to inquire the reason. This thought, however, was at once banished by the funereal aspect of the Reverend Frank Logan awaiting him.

"Oh—ah—good evening my dear young man!" exclaimed Logan. "I trust I have not disturbed you at your recreations? I have called on a most embarrassing errand, I assure you, a most distressing errand, indeed!"

"Yes?" queried Magruder curtly. "I heard you were at the office this noon—"

"Yes, I dropped in to ask you about the Suez train. Fortunately I find that there is to be a through sleeper, and my preliminary troubles are settled. But, while I was in your office this noon, my dear Mr. Magruder, I occupied my idle moments in profitably taking down a few notes for a discourse which it is my intention to deliver the first Sabbath after my arrival in the holy city of the heathen, Mecca."

Mr. Logan stopped for breath. He looked embarrassed, hesitated, then continued:

"Late this afternoon, sir, I discovered that most inadvertently I had carried off one of your papers—an envelope which I had presumably gathered up with my notes. Here it is, Mr. Magruder, and it is my earnest hope that my distressful action has not been of any inconvenience to you—"

With an exclamation of delight, Magruder seized the extended envelope. He recognized the neat copperplate writing of the superscription immediately; it was his missing letter! No need to scrutinize the missive inside, he thought. He could read that later on, for as yet he had not read the letter of introduction.

"Bully for you!" he exclaimed quickly. "Yes, I'd missed this, and had noticed that the papers were considerably upset—"

"I am very awkward," and Logan made an apologetic gesture. "I remember now that I knocked some papers around with my elbow while writing—extremely careless of me, sir! And now that I have repaired my unfortunate action, I must excuse myself."

"Oh, stop a while, won't you? We're having a dandy Russian pool game upstairs, and there's all kinds of gossip going around about the raids on the canal—"

"Young man, I hope never to enter a pool room! No, pray excuse me, for I must go to my hotel and pack my few belongings." And with this severe response, Mr. Logan departed.

Feeling in high feather, Magruder returned to his game and thought no more of his American friend. At eleven he had a parting drink with the officers, took a victoria down to the Central Station, found that his passport gained him respectful salutes and a total lack of all quizzing, and went aboard the waiting car. Of Logan he saw nothing.

When Magruder awakened, Shaluf station was dropping behind, the gray dawn was breaking over the canal and low desert at the left of the train, and Suez lay close ahead. The American at once began to dress. Barely had he finished when the brakes of the train suddenly ground her down to a halt. They were just within the environs of the Arab quarter of Suez. A glimpse of khaki told Magruder that this was a military stop-page, for some unknown reason, and he settled down to wait.

Five minutes later, his compartment was unlocked and in upon him strode a colonel of some Indian regiment, with a curt apology for the intrusion.

"Your passport, if you please."

Somewhat surprised by the rank of this officer, who was followed by two aids-de-camp, Magruder handed over his pass-port. The colonel glanced at it, then passed it to the other two others with a low-voiced comment.

"I must request to glance at all your papers, if you please," he continued.

"Censorship?" queried Magruder, extending what other papers he had in his pocket.

The colonel did not respond, but, swiftly scanning the papers, opened the envelope addressed to Miss Worden and took out the letter of introduction. An instant later, Magruder found himself staring into the muzzle of a Browning.

"Raise your hands, please!" came the danger-clipped words.

"Eh?" Staring, Magruder complied. "Look here, what are you pulling off? I'm an American, and I'm on a special mission—"

"My dear chap, it's no bally use," broke in the colonel. "The bracelets, Morley!"

One of the officers stepped forward, jingling handcuffs ready. Magruder stepped back.

"Hold on a moment!" he exclaimed. "If I'm under arrest, for Heaven's sake give me a reason! I've done nothing that I know of—"

"Come, come, play the game! That's not sporting, you know." And the colonel smiled wolfishly. "I suppose you know why you're arrested, my dear chap? And what this paper will bear witness against you?"

"Upon my honor, no!" cried Magruder.

The officer gave him a keen glance and replied, with a complete change of tone:

"We were warned from Cairo to look out for you, my man—to look out for you, with your forged passport and neat little notes on the canal defenses! I presume you'll no longer deny this?"

With the words, he extended the letter of introduction, keeping it safely out of Magruder's reach. The astounded American saw that it was written in German script, and that it bore a small, neatly sketched map of the canal.

"Great Scott!" he exclaimed slowly. "Then—then—"

The aid reached forward and snapped the handcuffs about his wrists.

"Very simple, eh?" The colonel put away his weapon. "Oh, we'll give you a fair trial, of course, but a spy is a spy, you know. Sorry, old top. Bring him along, Morley."

Magruder followed his captors dumbly. Slowly comprehension grew upon him, and the realization that he was damned utterly and beyond hope. A spy!

All too clearly he perceived how he had been tricked. That conversation to which he had listened had been conducted for his benefit, to deceive him into thinking the military governor was at the house of Rahaba. His first suspicion had been correct, then! The house had been under surveillance, after all!

And that letter to Miss Clarice Worden! Magruder cursed softly under his breath as he thought of Logan. Had Logan been a government spy? More than likely. The man who was to have met Magruder at Suez would probably have taken charge of that letter with its damning contents, and would have passed it on into Turkish hands. The American would have innocently acted as a go-between—

"Yes, by thunder! Logan was a spy, and got me dead to rights!" thought Magruder. "And if I tell my story straight off, it'll look like a fairy tale. No wonder they were willing to hand over a hundred thousand bones for this sort of work! Looks like it's exit Jim Magruder, and no mistake."

CHAPTER III

SLAVES OF THE RING

FIVE MINUTES later, the train had passed on. Magruder, who seemed to have been the sole object of search, was seated on an upturned cracker box and enjoyed breakfast with his hosts. Two bearded Sikhs kept him under guard, and his irons were not removed; in all other respects he might have been a guest instead of a supposed spy.

The day was breaking in golden splendor. The military camp, which was strung out along the canal side of the railroad line, was already long since in action for the day; came thronging past the open-air mess long strings of camels, headquarters motor cars, Arabs who did not get past the sentries, and sellers of curios and sweetmeats from the town who had passes and were allowed free access.

It was a gaudy, shifting scene, aglow with life and color; Magruder found it hard to realize that he, in the midst of it all, was face to face with pitiless death. Early though the morning was, the native venders appeared to be doing a thriving business among the groups of overseas soldiers, hawking their wares with much chaffer and a babel of tongues.

"I suppose there's no use asking you to talk?" observed the colonel to Magruder, during a lull in the conversation. It was the only reference made to the American's plight.

"Not a bit." And Magruder smiled grimly. To relate his tale now would avail nothing; this would be much better done before the court-martial, when the American consular aid could be invoked and enough delay caused to properly establish the truth of his story, which must be done from the Cairo end. "I'll talk before the court quickly enough."

The colonel nodded. "You're a German, of course?"

"Not yet," retorted Magruder. "My passport covered me quite correctly, colonel."

The officer gave him a puzzled look and discontinued the questions.

Suddenly the American's attention was drawn to the tent street before him. Amid the throngs, a single figure had halted outside the line of sentries which guarded the tents from molestation, and was staring fixedly at the group of which Magruder was the center. It was a tall figure, this—an Arab, attired in extremely rich garments; but at sight of the dark features beneath the folds of the *kufiyeh* or head kerchief, Magruder involuntarily started with surprise. The face was that of the Arab who had interviewed him at the house of Rahaba—the self-styled son of the Sherif of Mecca!

The Arab caught Magruder's eye, lifted his finger to his lips in a swift gesture of warning, then turned away. For an instant Magruder was sorely tempted to denounce the man, but this intention was cut short by an exclamation from one of the officers:

"I say, sir! Look at that chap in the gay attire yonder—just turned around!"

"Yes?" The colonel glanced at the Arab, who was now speaking rapidly to another but less conspicuous native in the throng. "Looks like a sheik, eh what?"

"Jolly well so, sir!" was the response. "He's the son of the Sherif of Mecca; I saw him at Suez last week, and I had the guard of honor to bring him ashore."

There was an eager craning of necks, but Magruder was startled into silence.

So, then, this Arab had not lied concerning his identity! Yet Hussein, Sherif of Mecca, was a friend of and was backed by the

English, according to all reports. Why should his son be engaged in German or Turkish intrigues?

"I'm blessed if I can see any light on this confounded maze!" thought Magruder, in despair. "Anyhow, that chap recognized me and probably means to find some way of giving me a lift. Of course, I'll have to have it out with the authorities, and they'll be apt to deport me as a damn-fool alien. Quite right, too! I'm lucky if I escape a firing squad. Somebody sure has got me in bad!"

The Arab disappeared, with no further sign to Magruder. Five minutes later, breakfast over, the colonel rose and beckoned Morley, the aid.

"I wish you'd take this chap to the general, Lieutenant Morley. Better use one of the closed headquarters motors in order not to draw comment. You will, of course, take no chances."

The lieutenant saluted and sent off a Sikh for an automobile. The colonel, with a nod to Magruder which might mean anything, strode off down the company street. The officers remaining, while they obviously could not repress their curious glances, were careful not to say anything which might wound their captive. Magruder chuckled over this British trait. He was beginning now to think that he would come out all right, after all, provided he could gain time to prove himself by communication with Cairo. Impossible as his story at first might appear, it was susceptible of proof.

The headquarters "motor" turned up in due course, proving to be a taxicab from Alexandria commandeered for military use, the driver being a member of the Suez native constabulary. Magruder was ordered inside, and Morley followed. The taxicab veered off across the railroad and plunged down one of the streets of the Arab quarter, evidently heading for the lower town.

Two minutes later, the way was blocked by a file of camels and donkeys. As the brakes ground and the machine slowed down, there came a bursting report from behind and the car sagged to one side.

The driver leaned out over the side for sight of the burst tire.

As he did so, he seemed to vanish suddenly, as though pulled from his seat. At the same instant, the door was jerked open and a burnoosed Arab leaped into the car, shoving a revolver into Morley's face.

"Hands up, please!" he commanded. With an oath of surprise, the lieutenant obeyed.

Another figure leaped to the driver's seat, and the taxi darted off anew, recklessly sluing into a side street and pulling up with a mad jerk. The Arab who was crowded against Magruder leaned forward, searched the officer's pockets, and drew forth the key of the handcuffs that confined the American.

"Get out, Magruder! Quickly!"

The whole affair had been so swiftly run through that Magruder barely realized this must be a rescue when the command came to get out. A doorway stood open in front of him, and another Arab met him with upraised hand. Magruder saw the silver ring that matched his own and allowed himself to be drawn inside.

"Follow me, *sidi*," came the soft words in Arbi. "There is no time to lose."

Dazed by the remarkable manner in which he was being abducted or saved, he hardly knew which, Magruder stumbled through a dark passage into a lighted room. Here his guide and two other natives awaited him, and with them was the son of the Sherif of Mecca.

"Do not talk, please!" said this last in swift English. "Let these men dress you."

"But, see here! I don't want to be rescued," began Magruder. "Get things straightened out—"

"We are risking a good deal to save you in our own way," broke in the other curtly. "Time means a great deal to every one, particularly to us. You have taken our money—now keep the bargain and earn it as you agreed."

Having uttered this disagreeable truth, the speaker stalked from the room and Magruder saw him no more for that time.

Over his own khaki clothes Magruder now found the Arabs arraying him themselves, his handcuffs having been unlocked and flung aside. His head was bound with a gay kerchief held in place by a fine Cashmere shawl twisted around and made to conceal his face. Over his body was flung a white cotton *quamis,* or long skirt; over this a belt with two daggers and revolvers, and a fine striped burnoose, or, more properly, *abba,* over the whole.

"My name is Hamid," said the Arab who had displayed the silver ring—a fine, smiling man with direct eyes. "Come with me, brother, and let us fool these Englishmen! True, they are our friends, but sometimes our friends are very clumsy and costly to possess. Come!"

Almost with the words, it was shown that in this instance the British were anything but clumsy, for a thunderous hammering reverberated from the front doorway. With a confident smile, Hamid led Magruder through another narrow passage, through a court gay with flowers and orange trees, into a dirty alley, and two minutes later into a street through which a file of soldiers were passing at the double. Hamid chuckled at sight of them.

"Not jackals, but eagles, must catch the prey this day! Come, brother!"

Unquestioning, Magruder accompanied the Arab. By this time, innocent or guilty, he was in so deep that there was no drawing back. He could only trust that somehow he would be extricated from his difficulty before it became too late.

By dint of using alleys, private residences, and several shops for his thoroughfare, Hamid attained the water front at a speed that fairly amazed Magruder. As they emerged on the boat landings, the Arab caught Magruder's arm with a muttered exclamation:

"Look! By the Prophet! *Ya Gharati*—oh, my shame!"

"What is it, then?" cried the American, staring at the water.

"Look at that boat going out past Port Ibrahim! What son of an unhappy father has wrought this misfortune upon us? There lay our refuge and escape—by Allah! There is no time to waste standing here. Wait, my brother."

Across the low shoals where the small boats plied over to the canal entrance, Port Ibrahim, Magruder saw a finely lined schooner standing out under her auxiliary power, the English flag at her peak. Even as he watched, her canvas began to flutter out and she sped down the Suez Gulf like a bird in flight, and was gone.

Her departure had plainly disconcerted Hamid; however, the Arab spent no more time in lamentation. He hastened to the landing stairs, where a red-bearded Afghan sergeant and four men acted as guards. For a moment he spoke with these, then went on to the landing stages below, where an immediate babel of tongues arose in evidence that there was no lack of idle boatmen.

Hamid came back, cast a rapid and reassuring glance around the vicinity, whither as yet no clamor of running soldiers had reached, and came to Magruder.

"Show thy ring to this dog of an Afghan, who will let thee pass," he said rapidly. "Below, a boatman will beckon thee. Step quickly into his boat and go with him."

"And you?" Magruder scrutinized the man with momentary suspicion, which rapidly vanished. Hamid, he concluded, was playing fair.

"I will rejoin you to-morrow night; the boatman has instructions. You may trust him fully, for he is no boatman, but one of us, and his name is Wali ibn Kasim the Hazrami."

Now, there is among the Hindus a saying: "If you meet a viper and a Hazrami, spare the viper!" It expresses a great deal that is left unsaid, but it is unjust. The men of Hazramaut are Arabs of the Arabs, proud and with a talent for fighting; they are the soldiers of fortune of the East, swaggerers and roisterers, never cowards. So Magruder, as he went down to the landing stage, felt instinctively that he was a step deeper in now that he had a Hazrami for a companion.

He was by this time beginning to enjoy himself, and had to a large extent regained his innate self-confidence. True, he understood nothing of what had passed or was passing, and knew not whether he was in the toils of a German-Turkish intrigue or a catspaw for some other band of plotters; but the keen zest of this life-and-death game, at which his friends and slaves of the ring seemed to hold all the cards, was thrilling and uplifting. The very mention of that boatman who was no boatman was like a clipping from the Arabian Nights.

Passing the Afghan sergeant, he held out his hand. To his quick surprise, the Afghan saluted, and on the brown skin glittered a ring like his own! Once more was Magruder startled beyond words. Either he was at sea in his entire diagnosis of the intrigue, or else the Afghan was a traitor to the Raja—a thing absolutely incredible!

At the foot of the stairs stood Wali ibn Kasim, clad, like himself, in a white *abba,* but wearing the green turban which tokened that the wearer had made the holy pilgrimage. The other boatmen lolling around displayed no interest. Magruder showed his ring; Wali grinned and beckoned, and a moment later the American was stepping into a large launch.

If Hamid had somewhere slipped up on his calculations, the Hazrami straightway showed that where he was concerned there would be nothing amiss. In fifteen seconds the launch was darting out toward Port Ibrahim, and in fifteen more it was shooting south into the gulf at the rate of a good ten knots, without interference from the gunboats or destroyers that swung idly at their anchors.

Wali ibn Kasim, who was a tall, sinewy, bold-eyed fellow, lost no time in settling what he believed to be social differences. Lashing the tiller and letting the launch drive south before the following seas, he joined Magruder amidships and transfixed the passenger with a reflective glare.

"Where are we going?" demanded Magruder, getting in the first blow.

"To Jedda, O Egyptian—for I perceive you have Egyptian boots. Now, since there is work for two men here, give me thy name and that of thy patron saint, that I may issue orders as to a man and not a dog."

"*Hazrami harami*—the Hazrami are ruffians!" Magruder quoted the proverb, with a laugh. "Worse still, O Wali, I see that they are triple fools and utterly devoid of sense or eyesight. Do you expect to use such a tone to *me?* Have you never seen Americans?"

He swiftly disclosed the khaki beneath his *abba*, and bared his face. Wali was thunderstruck at finding his passenger to be no Arab, but an American; for a moment he stared at Magruder in blank dismay, then put out his hand in greeting, with a slow grin.

"*Al nar wa la'al ar!* May fire seize upon me, but not shame! We are comrades, then, and friends of Solomon, and between us shall be no strife. Eh, brother?"

"Agreed, brother!" said Magruder, and shook hands, meeting a grip like iron.

Jeb el Ataqa, the "Mount of Deliverance," with its high, rocky passes, girding the African coast, dropped behind, together with Port Ibrahim and Suez itself. The palm-fringed Wells of Moses, on the Arabian side, dipped into the horizon, and ahead the gulf widened, as Wali held the launch down the Arabian coast.

In vain did Magruder endeavor to extract from his companion some information in regard to the mysterious intrigue now under way. The Hazrami professed to know nothing save his immediate orders, which were to lie up that night at one of the islands in the Jobal Straits, at the entrance to the Red Sea, and there await the coming of Hamid, who was to fetch enough petrol to take the launch down the coast to Jedda. Wali appeared to view the hazardous trip in the launch as a thoroughly enjoyable adventure, in which opinion Magruder could not concur by any means.

Regarding the equally mysterious John Solomon, however, Wali was much more communicative. He stated bluntly that

Solomon was a lineal descendant of the Hebrew king of like name—an idea which Magruder afterward found very prevalent in Arab circles—and shared the wisdom and supernatural power of the Hebrew.

What was more to the point, it seemed that Solomon, while not a renegade, yet held a position of tremendous influence in the Eastern world; that the silver ring was a symbol used by his organization; that this organization extended through every walk of life, and that Solomon made or unmade rulers and empires. That he was firmly allied with the English and that Turkey had set a huge price upon his head Wali believed implicitly.

Joining this information to his slight knowledge of the pudgy, blue-eyed little man who spoke with such a cockney accent, Magruder deemed Wali a fluent liar and let it go at that. But if Solomon were using him as a cat's-paw for a pro-Turk intrigue, why was Wali so certain about the English alliance? Was the Hazrami deceived in his master?

"Everything I learn seems to tangle the thread of things still further," concluded the American, in despair. "What about Miss Clarice Worden? I wonder if she's an invention of a fertile brain? Anyhow, I seem to be on the way to Mecca, whether to find her or to be offered up as a sacrifice to Allah remains to be seen!"

The great, outstanding salient fact, to Magruder's mind, was that he had been paid a hundred thousand dollars, which was now safely stowed away in the bank, and that he was expected to fulfill his end of the contract. Until he found, beyond all shadow of a doubt, that Miss Worden did not exist and that in making the contract he had been outrageously deceived, he was fully determined to keep good faith. So he resigned himself to await events and did not broach his suspicions to Wali ibn Kasim.

The launch was well stocked with food, and, despite the intense heat, Magruder found the trip enjoyable. Toward the heel of the afternoon, a destroyer, nosing up through the straits, drove down alongside and remained long enough to allow

Wali to hold up his silver ring, at which the British lieutenant in command sheered away at once. This incident, anew, gave Magruder food for startled surmise; surely that symbol was accepted as a passport by the British—yet why, if it were the symbol of a pro-Osmanli conspiracy? Or could it be that Solomon and his friends were playing a double game?

Of the auxiliary-power schooner Magruder could descry nothing further. She must have possessed huge speed, for she had slipped down the gulf and away from the ten-knot launch without the slightest difficulty.

At sunset the launch was snugly rocking at the shore of one of the bare little islets that nestle under the nose of Cape Mohammed and out ahead lay the fabled Red Sea.

"I've sure had one eventful day!" chuckled Magruder, as he stretched out on the clean white sand beneath the stars and lit his pipe, while Wali prepared supper. "Arrested as a spy, caught with the goods, rescued, snatched away from under the very noses of the poor Britishers—and now Africa is behind, I'm on the soil of Asia, and ahead lies the greatest adventure of all, unless that Arab chap lies. Mecca! By George, if I pull through it safe, I'll sure have something to brag about! But I wonder, now: Is there a Clarice Worden, or not? If there is—"

Later, when, with his *abba* about him, he stretched out on the sand beside Wali, it occurred to him that he was alone with a half savage upon a desert island in the most barbarian end of the earth. He fell asleep with his lips curved in a grim smile.

With the sunrise, a cranky Arab dhow came lumbering up and anchored beside the launch. The natives aboard had been sent by Hamid, they said, and in token thereof delivered to Wali two large drums of petrol. Hamid had not come with them, for the excellent reason that some person unknown had inserted a knife between his ribs, and whether or not he would live was problematical. At hearing this, Wali turned to Magruder with his perpetual grin.

"Well, brother! It seems that we run no bootless errand, and one that is like to send many men to hell. Shall we go on to Jedda?"

"Where else?" returned the American, and climbed aboard. "Your master, Suleiman, seems to have some very efficient enemies, O'Hazrami!"

Wali chuckled. "That proves his greatness, O infidel!"

CHAPTER IV

LOGAN REDIVIVUS

TWO EVENTLESS days ensued—two days of blazing heat, which in the mornings made even Wali ibn Kasim crawl beneath the tiny awning in sickly fashion; two days of chugging into the south, with never a ship to be seen on the lonely sea. For two years no pilgrims had sought the holy shrines. The Red Sea was deserted save for transports and British mail steamers, and these held afar from the old steamer lanes.

The unhandsome Yambo, port of Al Medina as Jedda is of Mecca, slipped behind. At noon of the second day, Wali swore by his father's beard that they would be in Jedda that night; but for once the sacred oath proved false. The gates of uncertainty were now fast closing upon Magruder, and that afternoon they clashed upon him and he learned the truth of the strange things which had come to pass.

It came about in this wise: Cape Hatiba was looming against the horizon, with promise of Jedda beyond, when over the sea rim ahead came slipping a schooner. At sight of her Wali came to his feet with a hoarse cry of rejoicing.

"By Allah! There, brother, is the ship of Suleiman, come forth to meet us!"

As the schooner came closer, Magruder saw that her masts were bare and she was under power; she was, in fact, that same schooner which had left Suez a few moments before him. Straight for the launch she headed, as though to prove the Hazrami's words.

Half a dozen Arabs crowded her bulwark, and at the head of her lowered gangway ladder stood a tall figure in a deep red *abba*. Wali peered up with a frown as he headed in.

"That is a man I know not!" he muttered, as he caught the rope flung down. "However, there can be naught amiss. Up with you, brother! I follow."

Magruder sprang to the ladder and mounted swiftly, without premonition of disaster. As he went over the rail, an unseen body hurtled into him, sinewy hands caught his arms, and he was borne to the deck beneath a crushing weight of men.

"That man below is Wali ibn Kasim!" cried an Arab voice. "He is true, *sidi!*"

"Nay, he has sold his master, Suleiman!" vibrated powerful tones, whose strangely accented Arbi and familiar cadence struck Magruder, struggling as he was. "He has sold his master—fire!"

A straggling burst of shots rang forth. Then from the waters below came up a voice below which Magruder knew as that of the Hazrami:

"Ai! Allah curse thine ancestors, O traitors—"

Magruder felt his wrists firmly tied behind his back, and he was dragged to his feet, helpless, by the Arabs around him. A glance over the rail showed the figure of Wali limply dropped across a thwart of the launch; a thin trickle of blood was crimson in the sunlight.

"Take this infidel to the cabin!" That same vibrant, powerful tone caused Magruder to whirl. It was the man in the deep red *abba* who was speaking, but his face was hidden from sight and Magruder could not quite place the voice. "Cast off that launch and return as we came. Summon me before we land at Jedda."

Magruder was dragged across the deck and flung, panting, into a cabin richly furnished. Even as he attempted to regain his footing, the man in the red *abba* followed, locked the door, and turned to the bound American.

"Evil communications corrupt good manners, young man!" he said, in a sepulchral tone, and flung back his face covering.

Magruder stared into the laughing features of the Reverend Frank Logan!

At that sight, astonishment overwhelmed him. And now he saw that Logan was the same, yet not the same. The stooped shoulders had become wide and straight; the features had hardened, the blue eyes had become cold and bitter.

"Now, for a moment, think about your situation," went on Logan coolly, watching Magruder, with a smile that was half contempt. "Try to beat your brains out against the cage, and you're gone. I'll be back in a minute, and we'll have a straight talk."

He unlocked the door and departed. On his finger glittered the silver ring of Solomon.

Magruder sat down in one of the cabin chairs and tried to get some order out of the chaos which had so suddenly engulfed him. This ship and crew presumably belonged to Solomon the mysterious; both Hamid and Wali ibn Kasim had known it as a refuge. Wali had been mercilessly shot down—why? Had he sold out Solomon, as Logan's shout indicated?

Why he himself should be a prisoner, Magruder failed to see. What made most immediate appeal to him, however, was the parting speech of his captor. He determined swiftly that but one course lay open to him, namely, to lie low, bide his time, and strike when least expected. Meanwhile, he must untangle the skein, if possible.

"Logan will probably straighten things out," he reflected. "Who the devil is he? I thought he was a British spy, but he talks Arbi with the accent that clings to every German tongue that ever tackles the language. Is he a German, then?"

His meditations were cut short by the return of Logan, who entered, pulled up a chair close to that of Magruder, and bit the end from a cigar.

"Now, Mr. Magruder," he said, holding a match to the weed, "we'll talk. I'll admit that when I heard you were coming along after me it was a stiff shock."

"How did you hear?" queried Magruder, feeling his way in the darkness.

"Wireless. I got to Jedda about sunrise this morning, and my first job was to put the wireless there out of commission. During the night word had come in that you were on the way, and I had quite a job explaining the mix-up."

Gone were all the affected manners of the pseudo missionary. Magruder now found him a powerful, cool, and evidently reckless fellow.

"It was a near thing, too," went on Logan meditatively. "You see, the Sherif of Mecca began his little revolt ahead of time. He threw ten thousand men on Jedda night before last and shot the last Osmanli in the place. When he moves on Mecca I don't know yet."

This gave Magruder some light. Jedda captured by the Sherif of Mecca! Therefore the rumored revolt was become actual fact. Warily, fearful to disclose his ignorance of what was forward, the American cloaked himself in silence and let Logan do the talking with which the latter appeared quite satisfied.

"So you destroyed the Jedda wireless?" Magruder asked craftily.

"Yes—they never will discover who did it!" Logan laughed to himself. "And in just the same fashion, my friend, I've knocked Solomon and his fine intrigues into a cocked hat. Sorry I had to get you into a hole, but I really needed that letter of introduction to Miss Worden, which was written by Solomon himself. It helped out my forged passport immensely, and quite established me as James Magruder among the rebels in Jedda."

Magruder nodded sagely, inwardly hugging himself at this information. Things were clearing up, indeed!

"Guess I can see through this glass wall," he thought to himself. "Logan is a German spy who's attempting to take my place with Solomon's friends. He snagged me badly there at Suez, and I'll pay him out for it—later!"

"Well?" he said aloud. "You're playing a lone hand in this? Or aren't you?"

"You're a cool one, you American!" Logan grinned. "No, I've as pretty a little organization as Solomon himself, Magruder. Part of it's back in Suez, and more of it's ahead. Just at present I'm alone, however. Now, listen to me."

He leaned forward and eyed Magruder with gimlet gaze.

"You've probably surmised that I am a spy, playing a lone hand, as you say. I've covered Egypt pretty thoroughly, and now the chance has come to take part in a larger game—the same that you're playing. I know that you've been hired by Solomon to help him in this revolt of the Arabian tribes; I know that England is backing this revolt; and I, if I can get to Mecca under your name, intend to crush this rebellion flat. I want you to realize fully that I am powerful and that you're on the losing side."

Again Magruder nodded. "You're a German?"

"No," was the reply. "Austrian. You'll never know me by any other name than Logan, however. Well, I'm through posing as yourself. I am established in Jedda. I told these men aboard here, who are, of course, Solomon's men, that you were an impostor coming to assume my name and so forth—you understand? They knew the man with you and shot him because I said he had sold out to you. Well, he died like a man."

"And you'll pay for that murder before I'm through with you," was Magruder's mental comment. Aloud, however, he only said: "How did you get that ring you wear?"

"Had it made, after seeing one on your hand and guessing it was a symbol." Logan's frosty, cruel blue eyes lightened in a laugh. It was not a pleasant laugh, however. "That brings us to date. Solomon is nobody knows where, but probably back in Egypt. The Sherif of Mecca is in Mecca; one of his sons is in Suez, the other two are leading the revolt."

"What's the sherif doing in Mecca, then?" Magruder frowned. "Isn't that in Turkish hands?"

"Exactly. He's safe there, because none of these Moslems,

Turk or Arab, would lay a finger on him; a holy man, you know, descended from Mohammed and all that. His sons have captured Jedda, as I told you. Well, I am going to get into Mecca by their aid, posing under your name, of course; and once I get into Mecca to take charge of things, that supremely important city will never fall into the hands of the rebels. Now do you get the situation?"

"Why—I'm beginning to," said Magruder slowly. The other puffed his cigar alight.

In fact, Logan had made the situation exceeding clear. Magruder now understood the position of this Austrian spy—evidently a man learned in Arab ways and tongues. Logan had played the desperate game of establishing himself as James Magruder and intended to play it a little further.

This spy must be an important man in his own way, thought the American, and no ordinary espion. Logan meant to take command of Mecca and to hold it for the Turks; therefore he must have authority unlimited, to say nothing of his boasted "organization." He certainly had crippled Solomon's party in a ruthless method, and his face and eyes now held the hard, unflinching efficiency of the trained Teuton.

That the rebels could and would capture the holy cities of Islam from the Turks was a practical certainty. If this man Logan once reached Mecca, the certainty would become a very doubtful possibility, as Magruder saw at once. Logan was not the type to fail.

"One thing I don't quite understand," went on the American, determining to maintain his careless pose, while inwardly he was registering a goodly score against Logan. "Why did you scruple to shoot me down with Wali ibn Kasim? Why bother to capture me when I could so easily undermine your status as Jim Magruder?"

"You'd have a job to do it," and Logan chuckled. "I'll be frank with you, Magruder. You're a mercenary in this game, hired to do certain work; clever in many ways, and, as I can see, a man to be depended on. I captured you in order to make you a proposition."

"All right, make it," said Magruder promptly.

The Austrian eyed him coldly for a moment. In those blue orbs Magruder read no pity, only a grim determination, a ruthless certitude of action.

"I wouldn't trust your word, of course," said Logan, with a calm air that infuriated Magruder more than his words. "I'll keep you safely confined until I'm through the rebel lines and into Mecca—that is, if you assent to my offer. I'll see that you don't talk. Well, once safely in Mecca, I'll meet any price you name to join me and take charge of things with me. You'd be invaluable to me with your knowledge of Arabic things, and I'll trust you to stick to your bargain once we get nicely started on our private war. Eh?"

Magruder was taken aback by this offer, although his face remained impassive. He saw that Logan considered him one who would sell his sword to the highest bidder; also, Logan needed his assistance.

"If I refuse your offer?" he queried.

"You'll be shot before we sight Jedda," was the cool response. "I'm taking no chances, of course."

The American restrained the hot words that rose to his tongue, and forced himself to look at his position with some degree of calmness.

There would be no profit in getting himself shot, and a live dog is better than a dead lion. Accept the offer, of course, he could not; he felt himself bound to Solomon now more than ever. But if it could be done, he was at perfect liberty to trick Logan.

"When we reach Mecca, do I take charge of Miss Worden?" he asked.

"That depends on the lady herself." And Logan laughed evilly. "If she happens to please me, my friend, you'll do exactly as I tell you to do."

"And how much will you pay, then?"

"Name your price. Half when we reach Mecca, and half when the work's done."

"Solomon offered twenty thousand pounds," said Magruder doubtfully.

"All right. I'll double that offer."

Whew! This Austrian seemed to have unlimited capital! Magruder dropped his head, apparently in thought—in reality to keep the Austrian from reading the hatred in his eyes.

"I don't know," he said slowly. "If—I tell you! I don't want to be shot, that's sure, Logan. Suppose you defer action till we reach Mecca? I'll answer you then."

For a moment Logan scrutinized him, then the man's lips curved sardonically.

"Done, Magruder! Until we get there, I'll answer for you; once we're inside Mecca gates, you're even more completely in my power. Just remember that, if you're tempted to butt out your brains."

"If you're going to keep me tied up," retorted the American, "do the job more decently. This behind-the-back stuff is unendurable. There's no sense in torturing me."

Logan nodded assent. Then, leaning forward, the spy deftly went through Magruder's pockets, appropriated all the latter's papers, rose, and left the cabin. He returned in a few moments with two Arabs, whom he addressed in that same burring Arbi. Despite fanciful story-tellers, no Teuton alive, for some mysterious reason, is able to obtain a perfect pronunciation of the tongue of Islam.

"This is the infidel dog who dared to call himself one of Suleiman's men! Here, loosen his bonds and put these upon his wrists!" He held out a pair of handcuffs to the Arabs, then drew forth an automatic in silent menace to Magruder.

"Take that ring from his finger and give it to me."

The orders were obeyed. Magruder had been previously stripped of his weapons, and he now saw Logan pocket Solomon's silver ring. His wrists were brought around to the front, and he surmised that the spy held the key of the handcuffs which clicked his hands together.

To attempt telling the Arabs of the true situation of affairs would be folly, he realized at once. He could not prove his words, and Logan had too well established his own position. Five minutes later, he was left alone in the cabin, which he found luxurious but efficiently barred against escape, and with some difficulty he filled and lighted his pipe, then settled down.

"For the present, I'm strictly up against it," he reflected dismally. "Unless I can find some means of escape before we reach Mecca, this devil Logan will do for me; he has no more pity than a wolf, and I sure won't join in with him! Yet, even if I do escape, what will be the result? I'd be game for either side. The only man who could reinstate me as Jim Magruder is that chap Solomon, and he's apparently out of it just now."

It was not, to say the least, a comforting prospect. The astute Logan was playing a masterly game.

An hour later the schooner came to anchor. As the engines stopped and the anchor chain roared out. Magruder went to the porthole. The ship lay a mile offshore, a swarm of small craft being on the way out to meet her; and orange-yellow in the sunset light lay the crumbling city of Jedda, touched by distance into picturesque softness.

After a half-hour wait, Logan returned with food and drink, watching Magruder while he ate, but saying nothing. Then, calling two Arabs, he curtly ordered Magruder brought ashore, with him.

That night the American, having seen Logan received with the utmost honor by jubilant rebel leaders, slept upon a rug in a corner of his captor's room, chained to a stout ring in the wall. In the morning he had the pleasure of watching Logan receive the two sons of the Sherif of Mecca, who led the rebel forces, and of hearing all arrangements made for a swift journey over the forty miles to Mecca. The chieftains knew nothing of Solo-

mon, their local wireless being damaged beyond repair; and
Magruder admitted to himself that Logan knew how to handle
these sons of the desert.

Also, from the conversation, he learned that Solomon had
gained the assent of the dread Senussiyeh to the establishment
of the caliphate; that Solomon had, with British aid, supplied
ammunition and arms; that by Solomon's orders two armies
sent by the Emirs of Hail and Riadh, independent states of
interior Arabia, were converging on the holy cities of Medina
and Mecca, and that the railroad from Damascus had already
been cut.

Logan was playing a desperate game, but with Medina and
Mecca in his hands he would hold the trump cards. And Solomon, as Magruder began to realize, was very much the man
that Wali ibn Kasim had represented him to be. But Logan was
playing a faster, harder game.

An hour before noon, Magruder was haled forth to the street,
was mounted on a horse whose bridle was fastened to another
beast ridden by Logan, and, amid yells of execration and not
a few stones from the assembled throngs, the American rode
through the gates of Jedda toward the hills beyond.

"Logan's taking no chances, right enough," thought Jim
Magruder, eying the stalwart Austrian at his side. "But one
thing is sure—Clarice Worden exists!"

They were escorted by fifty horsemen, headed by one of the
sherif's sons. Magruder found it difficult to realize that he was
now treading ground which even the consuls in Jedda found
forbidden—the sacred road traveled each year by a half million
pilgrims of Islam! After seven miles of sandy plain, the road
struck into the hills, protected on either hand by a string of
small forts, which had been seized by the rebel Arabs. None of
these seemed to evince any reverence for the hallowed ground:
to them it was an old story. They were too much engaged in the
business of revolt to bother any infidel intruder who was under
the protection of the future Caliph of Islam.

The heat of the day was passed at one of the hill forts. Magruder found himself closely watched by Logan, but no speech passed between the two. The Austrian, indeed, was anxious to take up the road again, finally persuading the Arabs forward; and late in the afternoon the party arrived at Bahreia, the halfway station to Mecca. This village, with its large adjacent fort, was also in Arab hands.

"We'll be in Mecca by midnight," said the Austrian, joining Magruder and squatting in the sand. "The city's not invested, and I'll have no trouble entering. Once inside, watch Logan Pasha produce his credentials from the Porte"—and Logan tapped his breast pocket—"and inject life into those lazy Osmanlis! They're good soldiers, if well led, and I'll promise you that not a rebel sets foot in Mecca."

"Eh? You seem pretty confident of that," said Magruder. "I don't see—"

"Terrorism, my dear fellow," was the patronizing response. "I seize the sherif and kill him at the first shot; ergo, there will be no first shot! My Turks will back me up when they see my authority, never fear. Then I expect to put you in charge of the civil city while I take the military side. If it comes to fighting, I'll destroy the Kaaba and the city, so we can be pretty safe in saying the rebels won't attack. They reverence the place too much."

Magruder did not reply. Suddenly there had come to him a plan—a plan so amazing, so desperate, so ironically simple that he mentally stood aghast before its possibilities. Then, as he glanced at Logan, he knew that with audacity it would succeed.

"All I need is the chance!" he thought exultantly.

CHAPTER V

MAGRUDER REDIVIVUS

UNDER A brilliant full moon the march was taken up that night and pressed forward rapidly. As they were passing two large pillars of white stone, the sherif's son drew abreast of Logan and called the Austrian's attention to them.

"Those pillars mark the boundary of the holy land of Mecca," he said in excellent English—for he, like his two brethren, had been educated in Europe. "Presently you will make out ahead the Jeb el en Nur, or Mountain of Light. When we come within sight of Mecca itself, you will be met by certain of my father's men and I will leave you."

So, then, Logan was to be conducted into Mecca by the sherif's men, not by the Turks; as the friend of Solomon, not as the Austrian come to command the holy city! Magruder nodded with satisfaction. If his desperate plan should succeed, this circumstance promised to aid him mightily. He could see that his passive air had quite deceived Logan, who had to some degree relaxed his careful watch of the prisoner. The Arabs all understood that Magruder was being taken to Mecca to be kept there until Solomon arrived to punish this false friend, as the American was deemed. Logan had done his work craftily.

Now the famous conical Mountain of Light towered above them, its entombed crest glittering silvern in the moonlight. On they wended through the sandy hills, Logan ever inciting the Arabs to make better speed—"for the business of Suleiman is urgent!"—and spurring his beast mercilessly. Magruder rode in silence; he found it most difficult to comprehend that thus easily, under the seal of one John Solomon, he was crossing land where for over fourteen hundred years no Christian had dared to walk openly. Truly, as the sherif's son had said, the Great War was sweeping all the old customs of men away.

Two riders darted out ahead and were lost to sight. Ten minutes later, the valley swung sharply to the left—and Magruder found himself at the very gates of Mecca!

There before him lay the deep valley, from which the city ran up to the crests of the great, stony hills around; half revealed in the flood of moonlight stood the Haram, the great sacred inclosure in which stood the Kaaba, the holy of holies of Islam. To the left, a hill overlooking the city was crowned by a great fort, and directly ahead Magruder made out the new barracks, long, rangy buildings which seemed capable of holding a large force of troops.

This, then, was Magruder's first glimpse of Mecca, the holy city of Arabia for hundreds of years preceding Mohammed's time. As the cavalcade came to a halt on the high valley elbow, the Cimmerian darkness to the right gave birth to a dozen Arabs on foot, who came forward with a soft salutation. These, it proved, were the men sent by the sherif. Their leader joined the sherif's son, and both Arabs came to Logan's side, disdaining the presence of the American and probably being ignorant that he understood their speech.

"My father's palace is on the opposite side of the city," said the great man's son. "To take you through the streets at this hour of night would cause notice, *sidi*. It might be best to wait here until dawn, especially as Yelniz Pasha, the Osmanli dog who commands the troops here, is to-night at the barracks near the gates and his men will be on the alert."

This evidently did not please Logan. The Austrian dared not delay an hour in getting into the city and there forming a junction with this same Yelniz Pasha; for the longer he remained in his character of Magruder among Solomon's allies, the greater was his danger.

"Haste is imperative, my brother," he rejoined slowly. "Could we not at least find shelter in some building for the night?"

The sherif's son spoke with the leader from the city, then nodded.

"Yes. This man owns one of those houses adjoining the barracks, and can give you shelter there for the night. About this infidel captive—shall our friends relieve you of his care, brother?"

"By no means," returned Logan hastily. "Let me alone be responsible for him."

No sooner said than done. By Logan's orders, Magruder was swiftly seized and gagged; the sherif's son, promising that within a week Mecca would be under siege, said farewell and turned about with his party into the darkness. Logan and Magruder advanced on foot with the dozen Arabs who had come forth to meet them.

Magruder strode along with the rest, a dagger point at his back. Without an alarm being raised, they approached the barracks, slipped along in the shadow of the buildings, and filed into a door that opened to receive them. This was the second house from the barrack buildings. Once inside, candles were lighted and Logan autocratically ordered the front room cleared for his own use.

"Leave this captive with me!" he commanded, gesturing toward Magruder. "Bring our breakfast here at sunrise, and waken me then. By the way, fetch me a rope now and tie this infidel by the chain of his handcuffs to one of the window bars."

As Magruder reflected, it was little short of amazing to watch these proud Meccans obey the orders of a white man—whose sole protection was the seal of John Solomon!

With a thin but stout rope of camel's hair passed between his wrists, Magruder was securely bound as ordered by Logan. No sooner were the Arabs' backs turned upon him, however, than with a quick movement he got his hands inside the open front of his *abba* and twisted his right hand into the pocket of his khaki jacket. There, overlooked by the Austrian, was a small penknife. An instant later, the American held it in his fingers, and had no difficulty in opening a blade. The thin rope parted.

The door of the room slammed shut behind the last of the Arabs. From a pile of rugs in one corner, which served as a bed, the Austrian picked up one and advanced toward his captive. A single candle, placed in a wall niche, lighted the room.

"Well, I suppose you have gathered that the end of the venture is at hand?" said Logan, flinging down the rug before Magruder, with a thin sneer. "In an hour I'll slip out to the barracks, establish myself with Yelniz Pasha, and before dawn Mecca is mine! When those rebels show their faces, they'll find a surprise awaiting them, eh? What answer do you propose making to my offer, Mr. Magruder?"

Magruder shook his head wearily.

"You promised forty thousand pounds—half cash?" he returned, simulating a wary and greedy look. "Let me see the color of the money and I'll tell you."

Logan laughed harshly and turned away. He did not see Magruder's sidelong movement, nor did he see the wrists that swept toward him; as he turned, the handcuffs struck him with all the American's weight behind him—struck him squarely behind the ear.

The spy dropped senseless like a pole-axed bull.

"Hope I didn't kill the beggar!" thought Magruder, in swift alarm. "No—he's breathing, all right. By George, I believe the scheme is going to work!"

In a fever of excitement, he knelt over the unconscious Austrian. In the latter's pocket he found the key of his handcuffs, and in another moment was free. He put the bracelets upon the wrists of Logan, retaining the key, gagged the spy effectually, and tied his ankles with the camel's hair rope; then made a thorough search of his erstwhile captor. With a deep breath of relief, he pocketed two excellent automatics, with spare clips of cartridges, drew Solomon's ring upon his finger, then went to the candle to examine a sheaf of papers.

A low exclamation of joy broke from him. There was his letter of introduction, which he found very brief and to the point and signed by John Solomon; with it Logan's forged passport and his own authentic paper; then, and of the highest immediate importance to his audacious plan, a parchment written in German and Turkish, making Logan Pasha military commander of the Hejaz, ordering Yelniz Pasha and other Osmanli chiefs to obey him without question, and signed by Enver Bey and the sultan himself.

"Now, Jim Magruder, hop to it!" muttered the American grimly. "Get settled in an hour and then sleep, you lucky beggar!"

Pinching out the candle, he opened the door. The passageway outside loomed dark and empty. With cautious tread, Magruder advanced to the front door, pulled down a huge bar of wood, opened the door, and slipped out into the moonlit night.

Without hesitation, he struck off across the open, straight for the barracks. When the gateway loomed above him, a very efficient-looking Turk infantryman stepped out from the shadows with ready rifle and a sharp command to halt.

"A friend!" returned Magruder in Arbi. "I must see Yelniz Pasha instantly!"

"Ho!" The Turk laughed. "You are more like to see the gates of paradise, dog! Be off!"

"Call your officer," snapped Magruder harshly, "or by my beard you shall hang ere the sun rises! Call your officer, dolt!"

With a volley of profane threats, the soldier sent a low call over his shoulder, and a moment later an officer emerged from the shadowed gateway, flashing an electric torch on Magruder. The latter held out the parchment, showing the signature of the sultan.

"Do you know what this is?" he demanded. "Waken Yelniz Pasha and take me to him on the instant, if you value yourself!

My business is for his ears alone, and if you presume to keep me waiting you shall face a firing squad before another day!"

From the Osmanli officer broke an astounded exclamation as he recognized the seal and signature. He saluted stiffly, issued a sharp order, and a file of soldiers came scurrying forth.

"You shall not be delayed, *effendi*," he said in Arbi to Magruder. "You must give his excellency a chance to dress—"

"And you work to do," broke in Magruder curtly. He turned and indicated the house he had just left. "Call out fifty men and surround that house—do it quietly! You will find a man bound and gagged in the front room; bring him to Yelniz Pasha instantly. Bring also every one else in the house; they are Arabs of this place and must not be harmed. My authority for these orders will be confirmed by the pasha."

"At once, *effendi*. If it please you to enter—"

Magruder nodded and strode on into the barracks. Another officer appeared, and at the head of a file of running men passed out to obey the commands just issued.

Ten minutes later, the American, abruptly dismissing the clustering officers, stood alone with Yelniz—a fat, heavy-jowled, crafty fellow, half awake and barely half dressed. Magruder silently handed over the parchment, which Yelniz Pasha read without visible surprise.

"I expected you, Logan Pasha," said the Turk in guttural English. "I do not speak German. We were advised by telegraph, just before the rebels cut the lines, that you would come. The will of the padishah is my pleasure."

Clapping his hands, Yelniz summoned servants and ordered rooms to be prepared at once for Logan Pasha. Magruder invented a plausible story of his arrival, described Logan as a British spy whom he had circumvented, and found the crafty Osmanli prepared to obey any orders that he might give.

"It might be best to detain these Arabs for a day or so," he went on. "They should not be injured, however, for they are presumably prominent citizens and we must not infuriate the townsfolk."

"That is wise, *effendi*," and the Osmanli nodded his head in approval. "The spy—"

"Imprison him for the present," cut in Magruder. "Now, *effendi*, do you not think it best for me to remain in the background and issue orders through you? Many of these Meccans might take it amiss that I, an unbeliever, should be in command of their city; further, I have no desire to supersede you in your dignities. It is my business to fight, yours to govern—"

"My son, you have a heart of gold! Embrace me!"

Magruder submitted to a greasy embrace on the part of the crafty governor, who was only too delighted at this soft speech, where he had doubtless expected harsh autocracy. Even as he submitted, Magruder wondered what Logan would have said in his place and grinned covertly at the thought.

"Now, I pray you," he said, "let me get some sleep. At sunrise I must be up, for it is necessary that I have an interview with the Sherif of Mecca without delay. Can you in your wisdom arrange this for me?"

"Son of mine age," quoth the delighted pasha, "give command, and I will rebuild the universe for thee!"

Twenty minutes later, "Logan *Effendi*" was sound asleep upon a soft couch.

His move was not so mad as it appeared, and this exact and complete reversal of the tables on Logan was sweet revenge. Magruder knew that he could not expect to pose as the Austrian for any length of time; the organization of which Logan had spoken would doubtless find him out.

However, the American was now savagely determined to prove himself in this affair. After all, the destiny of empires lost perspective on close approach until it became no greater than the destiny of men, and Magruder intended to play a strong hand swiftly. If he could throw Mecca into the hands of the rebels, he would be well worth his salt! Nor did he lose sight of Logan's benevolent intentions toward Miss Clarice Worden.

Shortly after sunrise, Magruder was awakened by a slave, bathed, and dressed, and his breakfast was brought in on a tray. He had barely finished when Yelniz Pasha sought an interview, preceded by two slaves who bore an immense water pipe.

"Good morning, my son!" exclaimed the pasha paternally. "Ah! Seldom do I arise so early; but to honor thee—well, let us try this pipe, Logan Pasha. It holds the finest black Jabalil unmixed with Syrian adulteration—"

"I've no time for smoking now," said Magruder curtly. "Have you arranged for me to see the sherif? If so, I must leave immediately."

The Osmanli shrugged his shoulders. "Go, then, for all is ready. A guard of honor awaits thee at the gate. But I do not see the necessity of this unseemly haste."

"Perhaps you don't know that the rebels have taken Jedda and that three armies are converging on this city?" demanded the American.

The Osmanli stared in startled dismay, for this was news indeed. Without stopping to discuss the matter, Magruder turned and sought the gateway.

Here he found waiting for him a spruce officer with twenty horsemen and a fine steed saddled and ready. Magruder saluted, imitating the German manner as well as possible, and the salute was punctiliously returned. At this instant, however, one of the soldiers who crowded about the gates sprang out with a loud cry.

"That man is not Logan Pasha!" He pointed to Magruder excitedly. "He is not Logan—"

"Seize that madman and throw him into a cell!" ordered Magruder coldly. A dozen men flung themselves on the soldier, who was haled away forthwith. Magruder mounted and rode off with his escort; but inwardly he wondered when more of Logan's men would crop up. There was no time to lose in shifting camps, he decided.

They clattered through the streets and along the bazaars that bordered the Haram—streets and bazaars alike desolate and empty, for the pilgrim trade had ceased and all the Meccans who could afford it had removed to Taif, a resort city three days' journey away. And so, without further incident, they came into the northern suburb.

"There is the Mab'da, excellency," and the officer at Magruder's stirrup pointed ahead. "You will retain us at your side, I presume?"

"No, I go in alone."

"Then look well to yourself, excellency!" was the warning. "These Arab dogs cannot be trusted. At the first suspicious sign, fire a revolver, and we will enter."

Magruder nodded. They came to a large gateway, which was opened without question by a native, and rode on up a drive through fine gardens. Ahead was disclosed a huge building, white-washed, with large wooden balconies. This was the Mab'da, or palace of the sherif.

Servants came running from the entrance, but Magruder alone dismounted and gave them his horse. A tall Nubian slave greeted him in Arbi with word that the sherif awaited him, and, with a salute to his Turks, he followed the Nubian into the palace. Then, in truth, he found himself transported to the days of Harun-al-Rashid and the Arabian Nights!

The American's first impression was of a large hall, adorned with the most magnificent rugs and tapestries, the walls ranged with gilt armchairs and immense Nubians armed with gilded weapons, while a white silk punkah hung from the ceiling. Upon a raised dais immediately in front of him. Magruder perceived a large chair in which sat a gray-bearded man plainly clad— Hussein, the Sherif of Mecca. Behind the sherif were armed Arabs.

"Logan Pasha," said the sherif, in good English. "I have received your orders and have admitted you to an interview at this unusual hour. Speak!"

Evidently Yelniz Pasha had admitted the supposed Logan's authority, thought Magruder. He smiled slightly, for the air and voice of the sherif were bitter in the extreme.

"Sherif Hussein, I pray you grant me a private audience," he said slowly. "Both with you and with the young lady named Miss Worden, who is in your care. I must speak with you both instantly and in private, therefore I have come alone, leaving my guard outside."

As he spoke, he lifted his hand so that the silver ring showed plainly.

One startled whisper of amazement passed about the hall. The sherif rose—a tall, dignified figure of a man—and for a moment stared at Magruder in unconcealed surprise. Then he turned to the Arabs behind him, spoke for a moment in a low voice, and stepped from the dais, extending his hand to his visitor. Magruder shook hands smilingly.

"Come with me, sir."

The American followed through a doorway to the left, and found himself in a book-incased study. Sherif Hussein seated himself before a gigantic desk of oak carved with verses from the Koran, and motioned the American to a chair opposite. Magruder, before seating himself, laid all the papers taken from Logan upon the desk.

"You might glance over those, sherif," he said briskly. "They will serve to prove my story and to explain it as I go along—"

He looked up, and caught his breath sharply. In the doorway stood Clarice Worden, gazing at him.

MISS WORDEN did not look the part of a castaway, for she wore a gown of white serge that spelled "Paris" in every line. After a smiling handshake, Magruder sat down with an indistinct impression of hair like raw, red gold, bewitching features, a slender figure that held the lithe grace of a fawn, and withal an amazing self-possession. Magruder had not quite gotten over the fact that he was actually in the city of Mecca; but this girl seemed entirely at ease.

With her eyes upon him, and the grave sherif studying papers and man alternately, Magruder told his story in detail.

"I don't know just what Solomon wanted me to do here," he said, in conclusion, "but the chance has offered to pose as Logan, even as he posed to your son at Jedda in my name. I'm in too far now to back out; it's swim or sink, and I don't intend to sink.

"If this chap, the real Logan, ever gets loose, he'll sure raise trouble for you, sherif." Magruder leaned forward earnestly. "I propose that while we have the chance, you send for your son from Jedda, or your two sons, and seize this city."

The Arab nodded gravely.

"Yes. But you should kill this Austrian at once, my brother."

"I'm not a murderer." Magruder flushed. "Every hour may be of import. Will you send off at once?"

"We can do better than that," returned Sherif Hussein, a twinkle in his deep-set eyes. "In the event of a siege, the chief menace to the town is that southwest fort. There and at the barracks, Yelniz Pasha has three thousand men. I have eight hundred waiting outside the city and can add two hundred to the number from my own retainers. If you will set the time, we may be able to seize the fort and hold it until my sons arrive."

"Not so bad." Magruder frowned in thought. "How soon can you launch the attack?"

"In an hour."

The American saw that his story was not doubted openly, if at all. He also knew that every moment was potent with disaster, for even now he might have been denounced to Yelniz Pasha by members of Logan's "organization."

"And when can your sons arrive?"

"A messenger will start at once. By to-morrow's dawn they will be here."

"Send the messenger."

The sherif clapped his hands. One of the Nubians appeared at the door, and him Hussein addressed in a dialect strange to Magruder. The slave bowed low and withdrew.

"It seems to me, Mr. Magruder," put in Miss Worden suddenly, "that in this matter you are entirely overlooking your own safety."

"Not a bit of it!" And Magruder grinned. "I haven't come to that part yet, that's all. Now, can your thousand men reach the fort from the rear, sherif?"

Hussein nodded silently.

"Good! Then at noon I'll have Yelniz conduct a review of all the troops, leaving a few in the fort for appearances. So put the time at sharp noon. Now, as Miss Worden has just said, what about us? Logan intended to seize you as a hostage, and Yelniz won't hesitate to do that if any trouble develops."

"I shall be with my troops." Hussein's white, strong teeth flashed in a grim smile. "I am no straw leader, sir! My family have already been sent off to safety. As to Miss Worden—" He broke off and paused for a moment. "Frankly, madam, I dare not send you elsewhere, for except in the care of myself or my sons, your life would not be safe a moment."

"Well, then"—and the girl glanced at Magruder with a sparkle of excitement in her golden-brown eyes—"I'll go to the fort with you! And how about you, Mr. Magruder?"

"Looks like a clear case all around—the fort for me! I'll join you somehow, and from then onward I'll quit being Logan Pasha. By the way, sherif, where is this chap, John Solomon? Also, what is he?"

"As to where he is, I cannot tell you. He is like the wind—here to-day, gone to-morrow. But"—and the Arab's deep eyes warmed swiftly—"he is a most remarkable man, sir! Among my people he possesses great influence. Christian as he is—"

Hussein launched into an enthusiastic panegyric of Solomon; but Magruder's interest had waned. The American was thinking that the eyes of Clarice Worden were like the rich golden brown of the Burmese topaz; that behind her wondrous eyes there flamed a soul rarely mellowed with the worthy things of life. No wonder she had escaped the *Ægean* disaster? Such a girl as this, so instinct with the vital forces and strong impulses that spell character, would have escaped from anything. She was the type that passed like a pillar of fire through epical events, the type whose name was burned deep into the memories of men, the type of Helen and Judith and the dear lady Heloise, the type—

Magruder suddenly felt those eyes searching into his and he rose suddenly.

"I must be off. All set, sherif? I'll hold a grand review at noon, and you'd better time your attack to the dot. No telling what may be sprung on us. Say, I'd always thought that these tales of Oriental intrigue were far-fetched; but, upon my word, after what I've engaged in during the past week, I'll believe anything I read! Good-by, Miss Worden. I hope to see you safe at the fort."

"And good luck to you!" she said gravely, shaking hands. "I'm afraid you'll be the one to need it most, for I'm sure I don't see how you expect to join us."

"I don't, either—yet," laughed Magruder. "But I shall. Good-by, sherif."

For the moment he forgot his Eastern manners, so busy was his mind with the girl beside him, and breezily caught the hand of the sherif in a firm grip—that hand which men counted it an honor to touch with the lips. Hussein returned the pressure, smiling slightly.

"At one o'clock this afternoon, Mr. Magruder, you will be an emir—the first emir of the new caliphate, when the green standard of the Prophet waves above Mecca in place of the detested red ensign of Osmanli rule! Farewell, and may Allah protect you!"

Magruder departed as he had come, save that before his mind's eye lingered this girl with the soul of flame, as he mentally termed her. His appearance visibly relieved the anxiety of his escort.

"By the beard of Osman!" swore the officer. "I had begun to think you murdered, excellency! Gained you any news of import?"

"Aye. To the presence of Yelniz instantly!"

They struck into a gallop, four men riding ahead to clear the streets. Upon reaching the barracks, Magruder found Yelniz, attired in full uniform, anxiously awaiting him.

"You are come in good time, my son!" cried the Osmanli. "A scouting party reports the southern passes guarded by rebels—Jedda is in truth captured!"

The American dismounted and lighted one of Logan's good cigars. He was quite cool and was now praying only for time.

The prospect of being an emir rather appealed to him. He was at present a pasha, and to be the holder of these titles, hitherto drawn from fantastic tales and the breathings of romance, was an amusing novelty. Also, he could imagine the laughter in the topaz eyes of Clarice Worden when they stood on Fifth Avenue together—

"Confound it! I'm not there yet!" he exclaimed.

"Where?" queried Yelniz Pasha, looking rather bewildered. Magruder caught himself up with a round turn.

"Why, in Jedda. I'm considering its recapture, you see. First, however, I have learned that the rebels will fall upon Mecca within a week. Your sending out scouts was an excellent idea, Yelniz! Now, I'd like to hold a review of all your troops—those here and those up in the fort yonder. Can this be arranged for noon?"

The Osmanli grimaced, for the noon hour was hot and he was stout.

"As you wish, my son. Before the noon prayer, or after?"

"Before," said Magruder. "Let the noon prayer be said in ranks. What force have you?"

"A thousand cavalry, two thousand infantry—of the new army," was the answer, not without pride. Magruder felt a touch of compunction at thought of how he was planning to betray these men; but this was war, and Logan Pasha must play the game.

"Very well," nodded the American. "Then suppose we send off five hundred cavalry at once toward Medina. There is a garrison at Taif, I suppose—"

"Five hundred infantry, under Janat Bey."

"We must communicate with and warn them at once. Will you make the dispositions as I have suggested, or have you other plans in view?"

"It is as you wish, my son."

The Osmanli was plainly very much perturbed over the news given him by Magruder. He summoned his aids-decamp and obeyed the American's instructions to the letter, ordering a grand review of the troops at noon and sending half his cavalry off toward Medina. But Magruder, noting a battery of excellent 4.7 guns parked in the barracks square, and seeing that they could soon knock the fort to pieces, suggested to Yelniz Pasha that in the event of trouble his artillery would be better housed

in the fort itself; they were at once ordered to limber up and
proceed to the fort.

These things took time. It still lacked half an hour of noon
when Magruder, satisfied that the trap was completely set,
bethought himself of the Austrian. He was then discussing a
light luncheon with Yelniz Pasha before setting off to the review,
and, taking for granted that Logan had been imprisoned in the
fort, requested that he be strongly guarded.

"He is safe in one of the barrack cells," returned the Osmanli
complacently. "Shall we get him out and have a little sport with
him, my son? And it might be well to put this sherif under lock
and key. *Le vieux farceur!* It will make the people angry; well,
then, let us shoot a few of them, also!"

Obviously the pasha was getting well aroused. Magruder
raised the question of the sherif's holiness, at which Yelniz
scoffed, declaring himself a free thinker and cursing all Moslems
together. He wanted, indeed, to give over the whole city for
pillage and slaughter.

"Well, send for the spy and release the Arabs," conceded the
American. "We may get more information from him, at least."

A faint thrill of bugles came down from the fort. Magruder,
realizing that the end was now approaching, hitched his automatics around on his belt and prepared to face Logan. But a
moment later the aid reappeared with the startling news that
the spy had escaped!

While Yelniz stormed at his officers, Magruder walked
quietly to the barracks door, and, listening to the reports, looked
at the fort. The garrison was already filing down toward the
plain, and, company by company, the troops in the barracks
were marching out.

From the reports of the officers, it appeared that the guard
had been changed an hour since and that Logan had vanished
with his guard, who was doubtless one of his organization. Thus,
considered Magruder, there was no time to lose. An hour would

have given Logan time to get his handcuffs filed off and to prepare to strike swiftly. Magruder turned to Yelniz.

"See that this man is found instantly!" he snapped. "I shall ride forth to meet the troops from the fort. Send two of your officers with me."

At a word from Yelniz in Osmanli, two of the aids sprang to join Magruder. All three passed outside and mounted, and Magruder sent his horse at a canter down the road to the fort.

The American perceived immediately that he had been none too quick in making his "get-away." A moment's delay would have been ruinous. Approaching down the wide street that led into the heart of town, was a little squad of horsemen, in the center a rider wearing a deep red *abba*. Magruder recognized that garment at once and dug in his spurs.

The troops from the barracks were forming on the parade ground outside: those from the fort were partially down the hill. Magruder saw that Logan and his little squad of horsemen were plunging forward in the endeavor to intercept him. Even as he put spurs to his horse, Logan threw up a revolver and fired, the bullet passing uncomfortably close.

"An assassination!" cried Magruder in Arbi, catching the cue instantly.

"Back to the barracks!" shouted one of the two officers, wheeling their horses.

Instead of seeking that refuge, which for him would be no refuge at all, the American bent low over the neck of his horse and urged his steed onward. His left hand holding the reins, his right crept to his waist and gripped an automatic.

Before his horse had pounded off ten yards, Magruder saw that he would be intercepted. The troops on the parade ground were in confusion, evidently not knowing what was forward. Being well away from them now, Magruder whipped out his automatic and let fly at Logan's band. He fired twice.

At his second shot, the horse bearing Logan plunged downward, sending the Austrian asprawl in the dust. Half the men with him drew rein and crowded around; but four shot out of the mass and drove on to cut off Magruder; four Turks, cavalrymen, who yelled wildly and began a spattering fire from their carbines.

"This," muttered Magruder, digging in his spurs until his maddened horse thundered along at racing speed, "is one hot day, so here goes for it!"

With two shots he dropped two of the Turks—a feat significant of skill, for it is hard to shoot straight from a galloping horse. Then, as the remaining two spurred down upon him, aid came most unexpectedly. The shout had passed through the ranks on the parade ground that Logan Pasha was being assassinated, and no sooner did the intervening distance give them a fair chance than with a ripping crash a line of Mausers spat fire. The two men who rode at Magruder went down under a perfect hail of lead.

Shoving away his automatic, the American sent his thundering horse straight at the garrison of the fort—a full regiment, completely blocking the rear, its officers hurrying to the front. Magruder drew rein before them.

"Hurry!" he ordered in French, knowing that they spoke it like their mother tongue. "Hurry, for there is a plot to assassinate Yelniz Pasha! Make way for me!"

For a long moment, as the troops began to file past him at the double, Magruder thought that his amazing audacity would pull him through unhalted. His ear, and his alone, caught a faintly muffled rattle of shots from the fort above—Sherif Hussein had struck! The Turks were too intent upon the parade ground below to hear that muffled firing.

But the real Logan Pasha, unhurt by his fall, had wasted no time. Mounting behind one of his men, he had dashed up to the barracks, and in fifteen seconds the words of his Osmanli men had put Yelniz Pasha into a fuming rage. Logan delayed not for questions. Before Magruder was half through the files of infantry on the hill path, the Austrian and a hundred Osmanli cavalry were spurring after him like madmen.

In desperation, Magruder yelled at the column ahead and sent his horse headlong at them. They parted before him; amazed, bewildered, understanding nothing of what was going on, the Turkish ranks opened out and let him through, then burst asunder as Logan and his horsemen came thundering up the hill slopes.

After these, Yelniz had launched other squadrons of cavalry, and the perplexed garrison of the fort went scrambling to either side the road. Magruder, however, had a clear start of a hundred yards, with the fort thrice that distance away, and it was this start which saved him. With the bullets humming around like bees, he held straight for the gates of the fort, and he was within a hundred feet of them when his horse went down under the bullets.

The American fell, rolled over half a dozen times, and came shakily to his feet—in time to see a wonderful sight, a sight which few men of modern days have beheld. Somewhere in the towering fort above him, a machine gun began to buzz, then another, sweeping the pursuing cavalry away like flies. At the same instant, a heavier gun boomed, and the shell burst slap amid the troops on parade.

The succeeding two minutes was an inferno. With dreadful surety, the Arabs who had seized the fortress got its cannon into action. Two shells converted the great barracks into a flaming ruin, while gun after gun swept death down upon the Osmanli ranks. Then, as the green banner of the caliphate swung up above the fort, the Turks scattered and sought safety in disordered flight.

Magruder entered the fort with a dozen Arabs crowding jubilantly around him, and over the hubbub of voices and the din of rifles blazing away at nothing in particular Magruder heard the name "Suleiman!" on every lip.

"Solomon's emissary comes in for a share of Solomon's glory, eh?" he thought. "Let's see how many wounds I got."

To his surprise, he found himself bruised but practically

unhurt; three ragged holes through his loose *abba* bore testimony that his escape had been a narrow one.

Following one of the giant Nubians who came to guide him, Magruder crossed the wide parade of the fort to the flagstaff, where the tall figure of Sherif Hussein, clad now in the sacred green of Islam, awaited him. The Arabs, Magruder noted, seemed to understand their business fairly well and were excellently armed; they had dispersed about the walls and gun emplacements, while the battery of field guns which Magruder had dispatched from the barracks was being disposed for immediate service, if required.

Hussein, his severe features aflame with delight, turned to meet the American with extended hand—a familiarity which brought a murmur from the Arabs roundabout. But this the sherif disdained to notice.

"Truly Suleiman chooses not men, but jinn to serve him!" cried Hussein in Arabic. "No man could have gained this place alive, O jinni! What was that promise I made thee this morning? See, now, how the caliph remembers his words! Let the fact that you are an infidel be forgotten in the sight of all true believers, for in the name of Allah I give you the rank and name of emir under me!"

A great yell of applause swelled up. Not knowing what he was expected to do, Magruder chuckled and spoke out in English:

"I'm much obliged, sherif—but would you mind setting that down in writing? When I get back to New York, my commission as emir will be a grand thing to hang over the fireplace—"

"I knowed it!" spoke out a voice, before which the other voices suddenly hushed—a voice that struck a familiar chord in Magruder's memory. "I knowed it! Titles is all werry well in their place, but in New York their place ain't on the front door, says I. Werry 'appy I am to see you lookin' so well, Mr. Magruder, sir!"

As Magruder turned amazedly, one great shout of "Suleiman!" swelled up from the crowd, and the American found himself gripping the hand of a fat, blue-eyed, grinning Arab.

CHAPTER VII

COMPLICATIONS

JOHN SOLOMON it was, and no other, clad as an Arab. As Magruder inspected the pudgy little man whose blank face showed only the lines of great weariness, he found it hard to realize that behind those innocent blue eyes lay the brain which had labored so keenly to give birth to this moment of triumph—this moment when the caliphate of Arabia was a fact! Yet he knew that the journey hither and arrival in Mecca, where Solomon had been least expected by Logan, must have been a very epic in itself.

There was no further time for talking, however. The force of Yelniz Pasha—or, rather, for the Austrian Logan, who must now be in command—was still a factor in the game. Magruder hastened to the walls with the sherif and Solomon, and as he did so he remembered that now the Sherif of Mecca was no more, for Hussein was the caliph and had assumed that title.

Half an hour of observation and reports from spies who hurried from the city was sufficient to seal the triumph of that day. Broken and disorganized, not knowing what had happened or how they had been tricked, with no artillery except a few machine guns, the Osmanlis sullenly drew out upon the Medina Road and marched away. Logan was not so mad as to fling his men uselessly against the high fort.

"I was afraid," said the caliph, watching the dust of the retreat through a pair of binoculars, "that he might cut the conduit, shut off the water supply, and invest the city. Evidently, however, Allah has put it into his head that he is vastly outnumbered."

"That's about it," chuckled Magruder. "He thinks your sons have struck." The American turned to the pudgy figure beside him. "Well, John Solomon, I'm glad to meet you on your own ground! By George, that day you came poking into the office, I little dreamed why you were getting a line on me!"

"The ways o' Prowidence is werry mysterious," and for an instant the wide blue eyes twinkled. Then they clouded over. With an expression that might have boded anything, Solomon drew forth an old clay pipe and began to whittle tobacco into it. "Smokin' ain't allowed in this 'ere territory, Caliph Hussein, but 'ere goes for a smoke, beggin' your pardon. There ain't nothin' like tobacco, says I, in its proper place, and it's a werry tight place we're in. Dang it, Mr. Magruder! Why didn't you up an' shoot that 'ere danged Austrian?"

The final words came forth with an almost explosive bitterness that startled Magruder. Solomon's face betrayed nothing. Glancing at Hussein, the American was amazed to see upon the Arab's features a brooding ferocity, and the look served to remind him that he was among men whose passions were swift and primal.

"I don't quite get you," he said, puzzled. "Why are we in a tight place? Logan seems to have handed us the city on a silver platter—"

The new caliph cut him short with a forceful gesture.

"This is no place to talk, brethren. Come into the shade, in privacy. My lieutenants will handle matters here and in the city for the present, and we have things of importance to discuss among ourselves."

Amazed at this sudden reversal from exultation to gloom, Magruder joined Solomon, following the tall figure of the caliph to one of the rooms formerly occupied by Yelniz. On the way thither a sudden thought struck Magruder.

"Lord, I clean forgot!" he said remorsefully. "Where's Miss

Worden, John? I suppose she got here all right with our friend yonder?"

Solomon puffed at his pipe before replying. He seemed very much disturbed.

"Mr. Magruder, sir, you ain't got no right to suppose nothing, so to speak, when that 'ere Logan is afoot. Dang 'im! Now, sir, you sit tight and listen, just like that. Them as asks questions gets less'n they asks, say I. We're in a werry bad fix, Mr. Magruder, we are that! Among the three of us, we've been an' bungled every-thing, dang it!"

More and more amazed, and not a little disquieted, Magruder accompanied the other two in silence to a large room guarded by the Nubians, where coffee and cakes awaited them. There Solo-mon settled down on a pile of rugs, bared his gray wisps of hair to the coolness of a creaking punkah, and stated that the first thing was to clear up what had taken place in the past.

"I've 'ad men a-watching that 'ere Logan in Cairo, and he went an' give 'em the slip," was his mournful comment. He then told how he had come to Suez by special train upon discover-ing the mix-up regarding Magruder's arrest, had found Hamid assassinated, and had immediately commandeered a destroyer to take him to Jedda. There, too, Logan had been a few hours ahead of him, and he had pressed on to Mecca, reaching there barely in time to meet Hussein's ambushed men and to join them in the attack on the fort.

There Hussein, in gloomy wrath, took up the tale in forceful Arbi.

"Allah blast the dogs! Half an hour before noon, Magruder *sidi,* I set forth with a few men and Miss Worden—most of my men had gone ahead, for I anticipated no danger. At the very entrance to my palace a band of Osmanli, led by this Austrian dog, fell upon us. That had been his first blow upon escaping, no doubt. May his house be uprooted by the jinn! A slave gave his life for mine and I escaped alone. My men were slain, and Miss Worden was either slain also or taken captive. As the men

I sent back from here report no sign of her body, she is doubt-less a prisoner."

The blow struck Magruder full force. He sat motionless, his teeth tight clenched, staring, wide-eyed, at the caliph. A grad-ual pallor crept across his bronzed cheeks as he realized to the full what it meant.

Clarice Worden, that slow flame of fire, that girl inimitable, was in the hands of the Austrian—or perhaps in the hands of the Turks! He knew the cynical Logan too well to think the man capable of aught save a cold selfishness.

Words were beyond him for a moment. Through his mind flashed the whole situation—Logan with three thousand veter-ans, drawing off to Medina like a crippled lion; barely enough Arabs here to hold Mecca. No hope of salvation! Magruder started to rise, but at the motion Solomon put forth a hand and stayed him.

"One minute, sir, beggin' your pardon! You ain't been and 'eard the worst yet, from the caliph's point o' view. Mebbe you know as 'ow the Moslem rajahs an' rulers of India, are werry rich men indeed, and werry pious?"

Magruder's gaze cut coldly into Solomon. "What has that to do with Miss Worden?"

"Well, it 'as more to do with 'er than you'd think, as the old gent said when 'is wife discharged the pretty 'ousemaid. Put a match to that 'ere pipe, Mr. Magruder, sir; it ain't 'alf burned down, and you're a-wastin' good tobacco. You 'ave a mortal lot to learn, sir."

The American obeyed the behest, compelled despite himself by the steady regard of Solomon. And so, from his two compan-ions, he learned a "mortal lot," indeed.

Solomon had known the father of Miss Worden very well, said father having been a consul in Alexandria in years past; thus he knew the girl and she him. Finding himself in urgent need of a messenger, and Miss Worden being in India on pleasure bent,

Solomon had cabled her. She had at once accepted the mission, which at the time seemed to involve no danger at all to herself.

This mission, it proved, was to convey to Solomon at Suez certain papers. These papers, in turn, were letters from the chief native rulers of the Indian states, certifying their moral and financial support to the projected Arab revolution and their religious allegiance to Caliph Hussein as the head of their faith.

Miss Worden had saved these letters from the *Ægean* disaster. Instead of giving them to Hussein, she had refused to give them to any one except Solomon himself; moreover, this suited Hussein exactly, since Solomon alone knew just how those letters were to be used. The annual moneys contributed to the upkeep of the holy shrines by the Indian princes were very large sums, indeed, and were very important in the caliph's scheme of things.

"Now, then," concluded Solomon, "that 'ere Logan 'as Miss Worden 'ard and fast, and if so be as 'e finds out about them 'ere letters, it'll 'it us werry 'ard indeed. 'E don't know about 'em yet—"

"And Miss Worden is not fool enough to tell him," cut in Magruder curtly. "Well, is that the situation? You don't know what to do?"

Solomon made no response, but the caliph nodded frowningly.

"Then," went on the American, smiling grimly, "let your new emir earn his title, Caliph Hussein! Those Turks are heading straight into the mountains, aren't they? Where will they halt tonight?"

"Probably at the wells of Al Ghadir," returned the Arab. "Beyond that is rough desert of sand and rock to Al Sufayna, with mountains beyond."

"Is there any other way of getting to this Sufayna, except the road by which Logan has drawn off his troops?"

Hussein gave him a keen glance. "Yes, for agile men. But there is no water."

"Good!" Magruder stood up and threw back his *abba*, tightening his belt beneath. "Now, will you let me prescribe the only obvious remedy, or not?"

"By Allah, if there is a remedy, name it!"

"*I* am it." And Magruder uttered a harsh laugh. His face was tensed and flinty; his gray eyes bit out at the others like frosty steel. "Give me two hundred of your best men, with rifles, and put them absolutely beneath my orders. Give each man a rifle, a hundred rounds of ammunition, five days' rations, three canteens of water, and nothing else. Give me sure guides. We'll strike direct for this Al Sufayna. What kind of ground beyond it?"

"Basalt and porphyry mountains," said Solomon calmly. "Werry 'ard to cross."

"All right." Magruder nodded. "We'll block the road and hold the Turkish column until you can reënforce us. With luck we ought to get the whole crowd in a trap and wipe them out. Logan will see that at once, and to save himself he'll give up Miss Worden safe."

"If she's safe when you get there," added the caliph gloomily.

"If she isn't, three thousand Turks will cover her grave," said Magruder, in cold rage. "Come, issue the orders and give me my men at once! We'll start now."

"And I'll go with you," said Solomon suddenly. Magruder eyed him.

"No, you won't. You're not built for mountain work, John. You stay here and—"

"Look 'ere," demanded the little man, "who's runnin' this 'ere bloody mess? If so be as I can't keep up, why, I'll drop out. It don't do no 'arm, says I, and it may do a sight o' good. I'm responsible for 'aving Miss Worden mixed up in this danged unfortchnit affair, and I'm a-going to do what I can for 'er!"

Solomon had his way. As Magruder observed, he usually did have his way.

Further, Solomon undoubtedly made it very easy for the American to control his Arabs. By reason of the caliph's little

jest about the jinn, Magruder found himself known among
the natives as Emir of the Jinn. That he was an unbeliever was
overlooked, but his presumed connection with the spirits of the
air was taken quite in earnest. The Arabs consequently rather
feared to address him, until Solomon smoothed out all diffi-
culties. Caliph Hussein also promised a straight road to paradise to those who fell beneath Osmanli bullets, and in half an
hour Magruder climbed into his saddle and set forth upon his
desperate quest.

They passed through the city, and, as the Arabs insisted on
halting for a brief prayer, Magruder had a brief glimpse, *en
passant*, of the famous Kaaba—the cubical house of worship,
known to Islam as the navel of the earth—which stands in the
center of the pillared Haram. Here there were more pigeons
than prayers, and Magruder was too taken up with thought of
what lay ahead to realize the forbidden sights that lay before
his eyes.

And now, with two hundred wild horsemen behind him, with
Solomon and the guides to right and left, he pressed on with
new energy, weariness falling from him. The soldiery had retired
too hastily to do much plundering in the city, which indeed
was almost deserted; one or two fires were being quelled by the
native wardens, and the city hall, post and telegraph offices were
in the hands of the caliph's men.

Passing through the Afghan quarter, Magruder headed out
over the ridges beyond; the city fell behind, and an hour later
the cavalcade was filing up the Fiumara, or torrent bed which
forms the road up to the Valley of Limes, which was no more
than a bulge in the canon. With the high hills towering now on
every hand, sunset found the guides striking off the road along
the winding flank of a granite mass, and at darkness they halted
to await the rise of the moon—a welcome halt to Magruder,
who was asleep at once.

Under precarious moonlight the march continued. It was a
march along precipices, over black, yawning valleys, up wadies
or cañons hewn out of the living rock, into the shaggy flanks

of sterile hills. Even the horses of the Arab mountaineers, used
to such trails, found it hard to keep this road; and once, toward
midnight, a refractory horse plunged away and took its rider into
the blackness below, a single shrill scream fading up upon the
night in farewell. Often it was necessary to dismount and lead
the beasts across rough, volcanic bubblings of rock.

Not until morn was a halt made for another hour of sleep.
And then in the gray dawn Magruder woke, and the guide took
him to a shoulder of rock and showed him from their hill crest
a gypsum-sprinkled plain that glittered under the first rays of
the sun like a mirror.

"That is the plain of Al Ghadir, O emir! By to-night we shall
reach Al Sufayna, which the dogs of Osmanli cannot possibly
gain before the following dawn. Thus shall we have rest and
refreshment before the fighting."

An hour later, the hills were gone and in place of them was
country which, as Solomon confided to Magruder, was "as near
the actual 'ell as anything I ever 'opes to see!" It was a wilder-
ness of flying sand, of rock, of clay; bald, pink granite, worn
into fantastic shapes; vast stretches of gravel, with no sign of
anything human. All was utter desolation, and as distasteful to
the Arabs as to the Americans. Wherever possible, the horses
were spurred into galloping flight, and by late afternoon the poor
beasts were drooping with thirst and weary unto death. Every
canteen was empty.

Magruder was in torment, for his horse was by no means the
elegantly broken and trained beast of civilization; besides the
lack of water, the rations of the force consisted largely of meal
and honey, nutritious but not altogether palatable, as cooked
by the Arabs; and even his iron body was beginning to break
under the strain of that forced march. How Solomon stood it
was a miracle, but the pudgy little man kept plodding along in
silence without a whimper.

Sunset brought them within sight of the mud village of Al
Sufayna, and, lest so large a body of Arabs attract comment,

twenty men were loaded with canteens and sent down through the barley and maize fields to renew the water supply. One of the guides drew Solomon and Magruder aside and pointed to a cloud of dust on the southeast horizon.

"Those dogs are marching fast, by Allah! They will reach the village ere midnight."

"Good!" Magruder beckoned one of the Arab leaders. "Take thirty men on the freshest horses, water them at the village, then ride out and harass those Turks. Remember their machine guns—give no battle, but hang on their flanks, do what harm you can and bring us word of them during the night."

With a fierce yell of exultant fury, the thirty rode down against the three thousand.

"If we 'ad a machine gun ourselves," said Solomon, when the canteens came back and the main force took up their road anew, skirting the village, "we'd come mortal near wipin' out them 'ere Turks, Mr. Magruder, sir. We 'ave an ideal spot ahead of us."

"I'll not bother wiping them out," returned Magruder dryly, "if they'll give up Miss Worden. If they've harmed her—by Heaven, I'll wipe 'em out to the last man!"

"Yes, sir; werry good, sir." And Solomon nodded gravely. "Only, if I was you, sir, there's one thing as I'd be werry slow to forget."

"What's that?"

"About that 'ere Logan being a clever man, sir. He is that! You watch out, just like that. I knows nothing and I says nothing, only you watch out."

"Quit croaking," said Magruder. "He's clever, but knowing this hill road is cleverer still. We'll nail his hide on the wall in short order."

They plodded on through the night and came at last to a small plain studded with great basalt blocks, through which they made a slow and painful road. Beyond this, as Magruder ascertained from the guides, was a good road rising steeply among the hills to the crest of a very rough ridge gained by a narrow defile. Accordingly he halted the weary riders where they were.

"Fifty of you ride on and secure the crest of that ridge," he ordered, and threw out guards in the rear, arranging for their relief. "We will hold this rough ground while we can and retire gradually on the crest in the rear. Their cavalry cannot sweep over us here, and it is fine ground for our purpose."

That night men and horses alike slept the sleep of the dead.

Magruder was not awakened until the sun was rising over the hills. The thirty scouts had just come in, water laden, weary unto death, and wildly jubilant. They had composedly massacred forty or fifty Turks who had fallen out from the columns, had harassed and sniped the columns themselves, and had not drawn off until Logan's regiments had entered Al Sufayna.

Better still, they had dragged with them two unhappy captives, both Turks who knew not a word of Arbi. Solomon fed the poor wretches and interrogated them in Osmanli. He found that during that terrible retreat upon Medina, Logan had lost over three hundred stragglers who had been coolly abandoned to their fate; and that a prisoner under a special guard was being carried by horse litter.

"They'll not leave the village until daybreak," commented the Arabs. "Two hours later they will reach this place, O emir!"

"Then let us breakfast, take the horses to the rear, and prepare to fight," said Magruder calmly. "Scatter out among these basalt blocks and remain in ambush. When I whistle thus"—and raising his fingers to his mouth, he blew a piercing note—"retire quickly to the horses and take another position a quarter mile to the rear."

"By Allah," exclaimed an admiring sheik, "this emir of ours knows how to fight!"

Magruder looked at Solomon and grinned unhandsomely. He was thinking of that prisoner in the horse litter, and the thought made his fingers itch for the trigger.

CHAPTER VIII

MEDINA

O N E   O F   the oddly beautiful cities of the East is Medina, or Al Medinah, and in the eyes of Moslems far more holy than Mecca. For at Medina lie buried the Prophet and his folk and the great names of Islam.

Seated in a plain, the old and new cities were well girt with forts. Under the afternoon sun stood out splendidly the minarets of the five mosques of the new city, and over to the eastern side, centered by the four great towers, was the shimmering green of the dome that covers the Prophet's resting place. But Medina, too, had felt the blast of war, and the leanness of the bazaars testified to the two-year dearth of pilgrim fattening.

Toward and through the Mecca gate was filing a torn and tattered procession. At its head rode a few over a hundred caval-rymen, convoying in their center a litter between two horses, a prisoner whose face was all but concealed in a bloody cloth, and the two commanders of the column, Yelniz Pasha and Logan Pasha. To meet them at the gate was Malik Bey who held the city for the sultan. But, as Malik Bey greeted his new Austrian master, his scowling features made sardonic comment upon the column.

It was a sorry column, in truth. Nine-tenths of the cavalry had disappeared. The infantry bore their two machine guns, and, marching in column of four, presented to view a scant six hundred men, mingled from two regiments. There was no baggage, except a file of camels loaded with water. There were no wounded—save those who could march.

"Seven hundred left of three thousand," commented Malik Bey, after Yelniz had introduced the savage-eyed Austrian, Logan Pasha. "Truly an auspicious beginning of your work, O Logan Pasha! Fortunately, indeed, I have six thousand more good men for you."

Logan's hand went out and gripped the Turk's throat.

"Speak otherwise to me, Malik Bey! Remember your place, or it shall be on the gallows! Now, take us to the governor's palace, and quickly!"

His pig eyes glittering with malice, the chastened Osmanli obeyed and from the groaning Yelniz extracted the story.

"O Malik, they awaited us this side of Al Sufayna—five thousand of the dogs, by my beard, armed with Maxims!" Yelniz groaned again and shifted his seat in the saddle. "You know that basalt field and long defile leading up from Al Sufayna? There it was they awaited us—caught the cavalry amid the broken basalt waste, annihilated them! We could not retreat; we dared not offer regular battle, for it would have been a long affair, with those dogs gaining reinforcements every hour. So Logan Pasha threw the column at them—ai, by my beard, a terrible thing!"

"Probably the least expected thing, also," observed Malik Bey, who was a soldier of true Osmanli breed. "This Austrian knows how to battle, at least. Go on!"

"We struck them like a thunderbolt," declaimed Yelniz, finding this comment very reassuring to his vanity. "We lost a hundred men to every foot of ground, but we smote them—ai, how we smote them! We broke through their lines, cut them off from their horses, slew a good four thousand of them, captured their wounded leader—a dog of an infidel, too—and met with no further hindrance. Those who escaped scattered into the hills and we marched on—what was left of us."

At the governor's palace, an immense structure in the new

city to the north, Logan dismissed his weary troops and turned to Malik Bey.

"In that horse litter is a woman who is my property. Give her a place to herself and slaves to attend her. Take this under your personal charge, for if she be so much as insulted by a word you shall be hanged. Take good care of that infidel leader; give him a surgeon and hold him under guard. Come, Yelniz Pasha—we have earned some rest."

Thus it came about that, when the call to the *eshe,* or evening prayer, droned out from the great minarets of Medina, Magruder sat on a cot in a narrow cell and suffered the ministrations of a deft regimental surgeon. He paid no attention to the assurances that the bullet which had raked his scalp had done small damage, and that, barring hanging or execution or fever, he would recover speedily. He felt only thankful when the door slammed and he was left alone again.

Not alone, however, for with him sat bitterness of spirit. Solomon had given him fair warning. Logan, by a devilish generalship, had done the maddest, least expected thing: had flung his whole column forward without even stopping for a parley; had sacrificed the most of his men in order to break through with a moiety—and had succeeded. The three hundred had done frightful work, but they could not stand the bayonet. Magruder groaned at thought of that last scene, before a bullet had toppled him over among the rocks.

Failed! The fugitives would bear back news of his failure, the news that all his vaunts had been fruitless—he had neither rescued Clarice Worden nor had he checked Logan's column. True, he had destroyed the column, but he was a prisoner, Logan was in Medina with eight or ten thousand men—and what of John Solomon? Whether Solomon had perished or had escaped with the few fugitives, Magruder knew not.

With such thoughts as these heavy on his soul, the American fell asleep and gained merciful respite until the morning following.

He was awakened by a phonograph grinding out records in Arbi and Osmanli—suras from the Koran, mingled with obviously homemade selections which would have caused a pothouse in Sodom to draw the blinds for shame. His window was too high for him to reach, but presently the sound of bugles and some orders in a well-remembered voice caused him to conjecture that Logan Pasha was putting the Medina garrison through their paces. He found food inside his cell door and forced himself to eat.

Logan Pasha was, indeed, enjoying himself this fine morning. He had found Medina, despite Malik Bey's six thousand men, ripe for revolt; the Medani have ever been an independent and fighting race. So Logan sent forth his cohorts, seized all the principal men of the city, levied a heavy tribute from the shop-keepers and merchants, took over all camels and horses, and threw his hostages into cells. All communication had been cut, the railway to Damascus was in Arab hands, and Medina stood alone. Logan Pasha was ruler, czar in his own right, and made the fact felt. From him was no appeal.

In such circumstances began the second phase of Jim Magruder's Arabian Nights. By treason and stratagem he had attained the spoil of Mecca at the cost of his liberty; he now lay in Medina, fortress girded, stoutly garrisoned, which had withstood years of siege and battle and which would be able to withstand the new caliph bravely—nay, even to conquer him! The Troy of Arabia was this city, girt on three sides by mountains, inexpungeable.

The sickening morning heat passed, and afternoon, with its cooling breezes, came. A sound at his cell door brought Magruder to his feet. The door opened and showed a file of soldiers and an officer.

"Come, dog of an infidel!" growled the officer. "The pasha desires thee!"

Magruder arose. His *abba* was in tatters, beneath which showed his khaki. He passed his hand over his unshaven features

in an unconscious gesture. The result of that gesture was startling, for the officer uttered a sharp exclamation and turned to
his men.

"Wait outside; I must examine this infidel for weapons."

The soldiers grounded rifles, staring with dull eyes at
Magruder. The officer came into the cell and as he leaned
forward in pretended search of the American, his voice came
in swift French to Magruder's ears:

"Your pardon! I did not know before that you wore the ring!
Tell me what I can do for you, and quickly! These dogs know
no French."

Was this some trap? Magruder suspected every one and
everything and repressed the thrill of amazed surprise that
seized upon him.

"Have you one of those rings, then?" he asked in French. "You,
an Osmanli!"

"Mais, oui! I dare not wear it openly. What can I do for you?
Logan Pasha—"

"Be careful! He knows the seal of Solomon," warned
Magruder, for in the eyes of the officer he read burning anxiety and knew the man was in earnest. The astounding fact that
this Osmanli was one of Solomon's men was explained the next
moment.

"I am no Osmanli, monsieur, but Hayeren—Armenian. Do
not breathe it, or these Turkish swine would murder me as they
have murdered my countrymen. Listen, now! I can do nothing
save lead you before Logan Pasha. To-day, however, I will reach
others in the city, and if you are alive by this night we may help
you. Keep a close tongue, and— Know you where Solomon is?"

"Most likely dead," said Magruder bitterly. "He was with me
at Al Sufayna."

The officer drew in his breath sharply. "Ai! Then have no fear.
By the true God, if Solomon is in Arabia, all goes well! Now
come, and pardon what I must do."

With a great show of roughness, Magruder was hustled forth and led away.

This astounding recognition buoyed him with brief hope, which soon fled, as imagination gave place to cold, hard fact. Willing the officer might be, but powerless he certainly was, here in the very palace of the governor. The best which could be hoped for, determined the American, was some palliation of the sufferings which probably lay before him, or else that Logan would give him a firing squad and a quick death. He knew better than to look for mercy from the Austrian.

Upon emerging into the sunlight, Magruder found that he had been confined in a cell of the barracks, just inside the outer wall of the new city. With the soldiers closed in around him, he was marched down the long street to the square before the inner gate. Here, at the gate itself, occurred an amusing and surprising incident.

In the shadow was lounging one of the many eunuchs who in Medina receive particular honor. He was a big, black fellow, flashily clad in a rainbow-hued gown, and was smoking cigarettes. His patch of shadow, cast by a tree, happened to be the only one by the gates; and out in the dust and sun sat an Arab, who was carefully and comprehensively cursing the eunuch by every saint in the Moslem calendar and begging him to vacate the shade for a better man. The cursing was an artistic matter; it covered several dialects, held great fertility of invention, and met with uproarious appreciation from the auditors, a crowd that blocked the street and contained several dignified Mutowifs or guides to the holy places. The beefy, black eunuch appeared lost in contemplative abstraction.

Perforce the soldiers stopped, and the officer began to clear a path. At this moment the Arab began in Turkish and the soldiers put on a wide grin. The officer himself was laughing when at length he got his men through the crowd to the Arab and ordered the latter to get out of the roadway.

"Is it not enough that this black son of a jinni must take all the shade, without your taking all the road?" demanded the Arab, without moving. He was a fat little man with the turban and garb of a sheik; his face was largely concealed, revealing only a wealth of whiskers that reached to his waist. "Since when have the Osmanli owned Medina?"

A murmur came from the throng, with sullen threats and mutters; the officer ceased to smile and peremptorily ordered the Arab away. One of the Mutowifin drew a long, curved dagger, and the throng began to close in; but at this instant came a clatter of hoofs and half a hundred cavalry surged through the gate with reckless disregard for the crowd, swept the street bare, passed on either hand of the soldiers and went on toward the barracks. The officer gave a curt order and his men marched on, with Magruder in their center. At the moment, the American paid no further regard to the scene.

Arriving at the governor's palace, Magruder was conducted inside and at once saw the efficiency of the new regime in evidence. The indolent *laissez-faire* of the Turk had vanished, and now sentries saluted smartly, aids dashed about in a businesslike manner, and everywhere the hand of precision was visible.

Passing a sentry, Magruder was conducted into a room where Logan, arrayed now in an Osmanli uniform which became him well, sat at a desk. In one corner were aids; behind the Austrian, Malik Bey and Yelniz Pasha sat perched like two forlorn birds on a divan. The guard was dismissed, a single soldier remaining at either side of the American.

Logan transfixed his captive with a coldly glittering eye. Malik Bey said something to one of the officers, who opened a door across the room, revealing a thick velvet hanging.

"Your name is James Magruder?" demanded the Austrian. Magruder smiled thinly.

"You ought to know me by this time, my dear missionary!" he replied, with as sprightly an air as he could summon up. "I must say I liked your clerical garb better than your present renegade's insignia. Somehow, Christians who become Turks never appealed to me."

With stony face, Logan appeared not to hear, but took a paper from a pile before him.

"I need hardly capitulate the charges against you, Mr. Magruder," he said shortly. "Your presence in Arabia will doubtless be reported to your government by the rebels, particularly in case of your unhappy demise at our hands. Therefore we must make the matter official, since your spineless government will be quite satisfied by a note or two on the matter. You are charged with having entered the service of the rebels, with having borne arms against the Osmanli troops, and you were captured in the act. I presume you will not deny these charges?"

Magruder glanced around.

"Is this a court-martial" he asked, thinking swiftly, while he sparred for time.

"I am the court-martial," was the cold response. "Your answer?"

"I'm afraid you're entirely at sea, your honor." And Magruder laughed at the amazement of those watching. "You're laboring under a misapprehension. If it please the court—"

"What do you mean?" snapped Logan. "You do not dare to deny?"

"Certainly!" Magruder waved a hand. "I have not entered the service of the rebels, for one thing. My presence on the field of battle was entirely due to other causes."

"What are they?"

"Will my answer be held in strict confidence?" said Magruder gravely. Logan, very plainly puzzled by his attitude, gave a crisp assent. The American went on, with increasing solemnity:

"Well, I will be frank with the court, because I cannot tell a lie. In the first place, I am working for a gentleman named Solomon—also an American."

Logan's eyes glinted with satisfaction.

"An unfortunate admission, if you intend to contest the charges, Mr. Magruder. You will state the nature of your work?"

"It is of a very delicate nature—or, rather, was," was the grave response. "You see, Mr. Solomon is a very enterprising Yankee, like all Yankees, and he is always ready to invest capital in new enterprises which promise large profits. It seems that he found such an enterprise here in Arabia and employed me to handle it for him."

"Quite correct," said Logan dryly. "And the nature of this enterprise?"

"As I said, it is extremely delicate. With the consent of the Sherif of Mecca, Mr. Solomon had secured various locations for billboards in and around the city of Mecca. The pilgrims and also the Arabs in these parts have from time immemorial been greatly plagued by fleas—a matter of history. My work, therefore, was to advertise and introduce in this part of the world an American invention in the shape of a flea powder which would—"

His auditors were quick to catch the implied metaphor, and from Yelniz Pasha broke a howl of wrath.

"Dog of an infidel!" sputtered the Osmanli, his eyes dancing with rage. "Do you thus compare the sons of Osman to ignoble insects? By Allah, your excellency give me this man and I will impale him on a stake at the gate!"

"Tie his hands above his head, also," added Malik Bey, cruel vindictiveness rampant in his Tartar's visage, "and wrap them well with pitch and straw. It would help him to die and would make a merry torch for these rebels to note. A good example!"

These words were no idle figures of speech. Magruder paled slightly under his bronze, but Logan turned to his two dignitaries with cold command:

"I would suggest, gentlemen, that you confine these gentle measures to Armenians and Arabs. Mr. Magruder is a brave man and shall be treated as such—if he will." Those last words sent a chill through Magruder as the Austrian again turned to him. "Now, sir, let us have no more levity. You are to have one chance, and one only, to escape the fate which you have richly merited. Yelniz Pasha is naturally eager to revenge the clever trickery which you practiced upon him, while I—"

"You got what was coming to you," broke in Magruder, his voice like steel. "I turned the tables on you neatly, and you were lucky not to get shot suddenly."

"I realize that fact," Logan smiled. "We have agreed, my dear Magruder, that you could, if you would, do us a service, in return for which you would obtain your liberty."

"And what is that service?" queried Magruder, as the other paused.

"To make whatever arrangement you like in the way of turning over to us the man John Solomon. In other words, deliver him to us—"

"Play Judas, eh?" sneered Magruder.

"No. Simply make a virtue of necessity. Times have altered, Mr. Magruder. What our fathers held unpardonable is to-day our natural action, for war has come to great extremes. We desire you to betray Solomon to us. On your part, this is an action of self-preservation and nothing else."

"Times have altered, yes," observed Magruder meditatively, "but still I don't observe any shrines being raised to Judas of Kerioth, Logan. However, your offer has certain phases which make it quite impossible. To obtain Solomon, I must go free, which involves your trusting my word in the matter. I don't imagine you'd do this."

"Certainly. You shall go free—within the city walls. Every day you shall report to one of my organization. At the end of a week Solomon must be delivered or—Yelniz Pasha may get his stake cut and sharpened. You can't get away, since we hold the city."

This was true enough. With the walls and gates well guarded, no one could enter or leave unseen—theoretically.

Magruder appeared to hesitate. He veiled his stormy eyes from the gaze of Logan and thought swiftly. He was between the devil and the deep sea. If he gave vent to his impulses, he would be turned over to Yelniz and impaled that same day; the Turk was eager for revenge. On the other hand, the Armenian officer had said that if he could live until night there might be a chance. Magruder raised his head. Chance or none, this was no moment for quibbling. He stood face to face with his destiny, with his self-respect, with his very faiths and convictions. Would he deny himself? No!

The passionate words that surged to his lips were not uttered, however. As he lifted his head to make hot answer, a stifled cry came from behind the hanging in the opposite doorway, and the sound of a struggle. Logan came to his feet swiftly.

"Take this man away!" he cried to the officers, indicating Magruder. "Bring him back here at nightfall—haste! Think well, Magruder; it will be yes or no."

The American was hustled off. At the door he turned and glanced over his shoulder. Into the room, from that curtained doorway, was advancing Clarice Worden!

At sight of the soldiers guarding her, at sight of the girl herself, Magruder drew back with a hoarse exclamation. But he was powerless in the hands that gripped him, and the bayonet pricking his ribs warned him in time. Bitterly he obeyed the behest and went out among his guards.

It did not occur to him that the fruitless effort of Clarice Worden to break in upon the scene might have changed the whole course of his future, for it was due to this that Logan had ordered him taken away. But had Magruder known why the girl had been permitted to overhear that interview, his bitterness would have been increased tenfold.

CHAPTER IX

MAGRUDER GOES FREE

AS MISS WORDEN was brought in before him, Logan rose from the desk and went toward her with extended hand.

"My dear Miss Worden," he exclaimed in a tone of deep concern. "I sincerely hope that you will pardon the somewhat brusque methods which I have adopted to insure your safety. We are placed in exceptional situations, and my whole attention has been devoted to the command of the men under me. Now that we are beyond further danger, pray allow it to be my pleasure to see to your comfort—"

The girl did not notice his hand, but her eyes met and clinched on his.

"I was with friends in Mecca, sir," she said gravely, "and was abducted forcibly. Your purpose in such action I do not know. I have no desire to deal with you in any way."

"But may I speak?" Smiling, Logan made a deprecatory gesture. "Perhaps, injustice to you, I should have told you some things earlier, but my excuse must be the perils of our march and the anxiety which weighed upon me. Now, let us see! The friends, of whom you just spoke, were represented by the Sherif of Mecca. The day before I left Suez upon my way here, the United States consul there received a letter from the sherif concerning you. This letter stated that you were safe and would be delivered to the British consul at Jedda upon the payment of ten thousand pounds sterling. How does that speak for your friends?"

She searched his face and found it serious, earnest.

"I do not believe that story," she answered, yet her clear words were tinged with hesitancy. "Sherif Hussein is a good man—"

"Certainly!" he assented quickly. "But those around him are not."

"You forget Mr. Solomon," was her curt return.

"An upright man—a very able man!" Logan assumed his expression of sanctimonious gravity. "But helpless in this crisis, Miss Worden. A man who has been swept away by the tide of human passions and finds it beyond his control. Solomon did his best to rescue you; he sent Mr. Magruder to assist you, not knowing that Magruder was already taking pay from the sherif's friends to act as a go-between in the matter of your ransom."

"I am tired of your lies." She made a gesture of contempt, facing him squarely. "You intended that I should overhear what passed in this room a few moments ago; if you thought to shake my faith in him, you failed. I am proud of Mr. Magruder! He is no more a go-between than—than I am!"

"Your belief does you credit," said Logan suavely. "I am in command here, Miss Worden, but my Osmanli confrères have agreed with me that as soon as the railroad is reopened you shall be sent to the United States consul at Damascus; until then, I am at your service to provide you with every comfort. Returning to Mr. Magruder: Since you disbelieve my statements, I presume you will also disbelieve in his acceptance of my offer?"

"Most emphatically!" She flung the words defiantly at him. "Even under your brutal treats—"

"Which, of course, were threats only." And Logan smiled. "What you Americans call a bluff. Pray proceed."

She continued, a little shaken by these words: "Even under such threats, Mr. Magruder will not betray Mr. Solomon to you! Were he capable of such treachery, such baseness, I might believe anything of him; but I answer for him as for myself."

"You know him well, then?"

"No. But he is an American gentleman. That is the answer."

Logan gazed at her a moment, then shook his head sadly.

"I am sorry, Miss Worden." His vibrant tones were low-pitched, gentle. "To-night you shall hear his answer to my offer. Until then, I beg that you will hold your opinion of me in abeyance. Believe me, I am doing what I think is best in your interest, and if I can prove to you that Magruder is a blackguard, out of his own mouth, I shall have accomplished a great deal."

"Yes—a miracle!" was her parting retort.

In his cell at the rear of the barracks, Jim Magruder passed a slow and hopeless day. Of his sole friend, the Armenian officer, he saw nothing at all. The was no lack of visitors of another stamp, however. During the afternoon hours it became a keen amusement among the Arnaut and Kurdish soldiers to sit outside Magruder's grated door and to converse anent the infidel inside, whom they dared not touch.

This was too good an opportunity for everyday cursing, so they discussed his probable fate. Magruder learned all about impalement, with its Turkish refinements; he also heard sweeping details of the Armenian massacres, in which had participated the last detachment of Arnauts to reach Medina before the Arabs cut the Damascus railroad.

Now, in the inscrutable plan of fate, this proved to be no mere incidental happening. Magruder was not a reckless, red-handed adventurer. He was a very average young man, and he had the average young man's instinct for looking out for number one in a tight place. Killing other men was not his usual pastime and did not appeal to him in the least. Love of fighting, as he might have expressed it, was not his long suit by a good deal! It so happened, however, that destiny had pitchforked him into a land of savagery; even here, given his own choice, he would never have dreamed of walking up and down the earth, seeking whom his guns might devour.

On this day, however, he learned something about the Turk-

ish mercenaries—for the Osmanlis are the ruling class only and
a very small one. These Arnauts and Kurds related with gusto
stories which were unbelievably true. They told these stories in
detail; stories of the Armenian and Syrian massacres, stories so
horrible that they were indelibly imprinted upon the American's
memory and haunted his imagination for months.

Magruder had never known that men could be so devoid of
humanity as were these mercenaries who squatted before his
cell door and told their deeds. To him, from that moment, they
became worse than wild beasts. Within his soul, from that day,
there upsurged the great, vital craving for justice, the craving
for retribution which is no personal thing but the urge of an
aeon of civilization. To shoot down these butchers became an
act freed from all the restraint of human nature—not murder,
but Nemesis.

So the day waned to its close, and finally Magruder was left
alone save for the guard at his door. As the call to the *eshe* prayer
was droning forth over the high city, a step in the corridor roused
the American. So they had come for him, then, and he must
face his threatened fate! But he was mistaken. In the doorway
appeared the figure of the Armenian officer, who said a low word
to the guard, unlocked the door, and entered.

"Careful!" The low word came in French, as before.
"Monsieur, all is arranged—"

"It's no use," broke in Magruder. "I had until this evening—"

"I know. Did I not hear what passed? Now, listen carefully:
You are to accept the offer of Logan Pasha; you must agree to
deliver Solomon to him within a week at most."

"What do you mean, man?" The American stared at his
visitor in blank wonder. "Who gave you such instructions
as this?" The idea of a trick flashed across his mind, but he
dismissed it instantly.

"The instructions were transmitted through me to you," came
the answer. "I have given them, and if you do not obey, your fate
be on your own head! Let me finish. You are to obtain an Arab

costume from Logan Pasha, and, upon leaving these barracks or wherever you may be, go direct to the Masjid al Nabawi—the Haram. At the main entrance, the Bab al Salam, a negro will await you. Show him your ring and trust the rest to Solomon's power."

Bab al Salam—the Gate of Safety! Not a bad omen, thought Magruder. Before he could make reply, the officer turned and left hastily.

What was to be done? Who had given these amazing orders? The American faced a forked road in this matter. Solomon's men here in Medina had ordered him to accept Logan's proposal— why? Merely to save his own life?

"They may have some scheme for getting me out of town safely," thought Magruder, desperately puzzled. "Yet that would involve passing my word to Logan—and I'm blamed if I'll accept his offer merely on a chance of saving my own skin! Besides, he no doubt intends to guard against my skipping out."

As though in very answer to his thoughts, he heard a voice lifted outside the building—the voice of an Arab, strolling past, apparently. A verse of an atrocious song reached Magruder's ears, in a wheezy voice that had no tune, but the words struck him like a whip:

"Suleiman the King loved Allah,
        And feared no man.
Were Suleiman a pilgrim
And standing before the Prophet's tomb,
        What man should he fear?"

Magruder gasped, not only at the aptness of the words, but at their sound. Surely that had been the voice of John Solomon—broken by that curious little wheeze, so different from the assumed whine of the Arbi words!

But no; after all, it could only be some odd resemblance, some figment of the imagination. John Solomon, if not dead, was a fugitive somewhere in the mountains, or getting back into Mecca and safety. At the wildest he could not have entered

Medina, for Logan's first move had been to institute strict search and examination of every one entering and leaving the city.

"No, I was deceived by some chance resemblance—but it sure gave me a start!" And Magruder, taking up the bowl of food set inside the door, began to eat. "However, I'll accept it as an omen. I may be a coward, but I'll obey orders and accept the proposition to save my neck. Just the same, I'll do no betraying! Damn the dirty dogs!"

With this resolution still upon him, an officer—not the Armenian, but another—arrived to take him before Logan Pasha.

On this occasion Magruder found the streets almost deserted. Above the Masjid al Nabawi, or Mosque of the Prophet, also known as the Haram or sanctuary, the glow of arc lights and the murmur of voices testified to the fact that Muhammad was one prophet not without honor in his own city.

Arriving at the governor's palace, Magruder was brought to the same room, which evidently served Logan as an office. Here he found much the same assembly as before, and his involuntary glance toward the other door showed the velvet curtain hanging. Magruder wondered vaguely if Miss Worden were in that other room now.

Logan wasted no time in preliminaries.

"Well?" he snapped curtly. "Do you accept or refuse my offer?"

"I—I accept," returned Magruder, not without a flush. The words came hard.

"So!" Logan nodded, his eyes narrowed suspiciously. "You agree to place John Solomon in our hands?"

"Within a week."

"Good!" Logan motioned the soldiers, who stepped back from Magruder. "Now, then, you shall have whatever help you desire from us. On the other hand, if you attempt to leave the city, you shall be executed at once. Twice a day, instead of once, you will present yourself to the officer stationed at the gate of the old city, through which you passed coming here. You will make these reports at the exact hours of morning and evening prayers. Is this clearly understood? Do you consent?"

"Yes."

"Then consider yourself at liberty." Logan's manner was not untinged with contempt. "What do you wish done for you?"

"Give me an Arab costume to cover this khaki"—and Magruder glanced at his Occidental garb—"for fear I might be taken for an Osmanli and knifed. That is all for the present. I am free to go, then?"

"Yes—for one week from to-night. If you try to hide from us, we will search every building in the city. Follow that officer and he will provide whatever you desire."

With vivid relief that his scene of shame was over, Magruder turned and followed the officer from the room.

Fifteen minutes later, completely equipped once more in Arab costume, the American stepped forth into the street, a nominally free man. He was now in the old city itself, and without hesitation followed the principal street toward the lights that denoted the great mosque which was his objective. Darkness had long since fallen on the land.

The thing done beyond recall, Magruder now was struck with shame at his own action, even though he had been ordered to do it. The humiliation of standing before his enemies as a self-confessed Judas had been bitter to him. Yet he did not conceal from himself the vast relief that had settled upon his mind. Perhaps he was a coward, indeed, he reflected, but the very thought of being handed over to the tender mercies of the Turks was a torment.

"If I don't get away and if there's no way of evading the issue," he determined in that moment, "I'll put a bullet through my own head before they get me."

There is no awe-inspiring approach to the holy of holies of Islam. Passing by the solidly built-up structures, almost before he knew it Magruder found himself at the chief gate of the mosque, a flight of broad steps that led upward to a high arch.

A single dark figure stepped out before him. In the blaze of

light that came from within the sacred enclosure, Magruder
made out a figure that seemed familiar. To his surprise, he found
that it was the same black enunch whom he had seen that noon
holding the shady spot by the gate in defiance of the cursing
Arab. Wondering if this could be the man who was to meet him,
Magruder held up his hand and showed the silver ring.

"It is well!" exclaimed the negro quickly. "Follow me and
imitate me carefully."

Magruder turned up the stairs. At the gate itself, the eunuch
removed his shoes, and Magruder did likewise, handing them
to a stolid gatekeeper. Then, moving forward, the negro knelt in
the obligatory prayer on entering a mosque; Magruder imitated
him closely, and a moment later they rose.

It was not without quick interest that the American glanced
around the famous place. The great, open enclosure was a blaze
of light. Modern arc lights spluttered side by side with magnificent hanging lamps; there were literally hundreds of lights
flaming on all hands.

Abandoning all further ceremony, the eunuch led the way
to a pillar and directed Magruder to seat himself, speak to no
one, and await the will of Allah; with which he moved away
and disappeared.

The scene was one of splendor, quite different from the simple
dignity of the Haram at Mecca. Long lines of delicately graven
marble columns edged the cloistered porticoes; here and there
sat learned men of the city's schools, expounding the Koran,
while others were reading, writing, chatting in low voices, or
meditating. The elaborate arch, marking the spot where the
Prophet prayed, was ablaze with candles and surrounded
with devotees. Farther inside the mosque was the tomb itself,
crowned by its high, green dome, and girded by an iron railing
where loafed the eunuch guardians, never absent. Beyond this,
again, was the garden planted by Fatimah, the Prophet's daugh-
ter—and so forth. Although Magruder knew that most of these

relics were spurious, none the less this was the historic place and over it hung an impressive atmosphere.

Suddenly the American observed that he was no longer alone beside the pillar. Another visitor was seating himself a yard away—so close that Magruder stirred uneasily. In the bright light he found that here was a most unexpected source of danger, for this Arab was no other than the same who had sat out in the road and cursed the eunuch that very day and who must have remarked the features of the infidel prisoner.

"Peace be upon thee!" remarked the newcomer affably, in the most elegant of archaic Arbi—a tongue difficult to learn. Magruder groaned inwardly and returned the greeting. The other tugged at his bushy whiskers and peered at him curiously.

"O brother, thy tongue has a strange twist. Why?"

Magruder cursed the curiosity of the fellow. Thinking to throw him off the scent and discourage further conversation, he replied with a few words of Persian he had picked up.

"Irani hastam. I am a Persian and speak Arbi badly."

"Oh, excellent!" exclaimed the other delightedly. "Come, now—" He continued with a flood of Persian that flung Magruder into blank dismay. How was he to answer the man? How to escape from this devilish impasse? Magruder glanced at the Arabs roundabout, as he wondered what would happen to him when the cry of "Infidel!" was raised against him, and began to perspire. The other paused for a reply and Magruder said nothing.

"Perhaps my Irani is not good to thy ears?" inquired the curious one, with asperity. "Or has Allah choked thy speech? By the Prophet, there is something queer about this!"

"Go away!" muttered Magruder. "Do not intrude upon me, brother, for I am mourning for my parents, who died yesterday."

The other did not respond for a moment. Magruder began to take heart, when suddenly the bushy whiskers seemed to emit a wheezy chuckle.

"For 'is parents, 'e says!" sounded a familiar voice. "And a werry good excuse it was, Mr. Magruder, sir! 'Ere's 'oping, sir, as 'ow I finds you well and 'earty! Dang it, sir, I just couldn't 'elp 'aving me bit o' fun, just like that—and werry glad I am to see you again, sir!"

CHAPTER X

MISS WORDEN SAYS SOMETHING

"JOHN SOLOMON! In the name of all that's holy—"

"Dang it, sir, '*ush!*" broke in the other hurriedly. "They're a-watching of you."

"Eh? Who's watching me?"

"That 'ere chap by the Makam. One o' Logan's men, 'e is."

Magruder glanced toward the Makam, the praying place of the Prophet. A little apart from the crowd about the small and elaborate arch stood a tall, cloaked Arab—the one designated by Solomon. But the American spent little thought on this spy.

"Great Scott!" he exclaimed, in a low voice, staring anew at the whiskered person beside him. "Are you really Solomon? It seems incredible! When did you get here, and how?"

Solomon chuckled wheezily but made no immediate answer. Having already determined in his own mind that Solomon could not, even if alive, get into Medina, Magruder's amazement was redoubled.

No wonder that this remarkable man was deemed something akin to supernatural by the Arabs! More than once already Magruder had tasted Solomon's quality and was to taste it again in more astounding fashion; but the smashing surprise of this appearance was dramatic in the extreme.

"We're in a werry tight place, Mr. Magruder, sir," said the pudgy little man softly. "This 'ere Logan, 'e let you free thinkin' as 'ow you'd get in touch with me men and 'e could grab me men, just like that."

"Oh!" ejaculated the American. "Then you know—"

"Yes, sir. It was me as give you orders to accept 'is offer."

"Then I don't see why you made me pass my word on a matter like that," returned Magruder. "You know that I'll not betray you."

"Yes, you will, sir, beggin' your pardon."

"Will what? Betray you? Are you crazy, or am I?"

"Not me, sir. I'm steppin' werry careful-like this minute. If them 'ere men of Logan's guessed as 'ow I was Solomon, instead o' bein' the Sheik Kadiri, as they think I am, I'd be in a danged bad fix. Recklessness is all werry well in its place, says I, but its place ain't where I am, just like that! Now, sir, you listen werry sharp!"

A Mutowif strolled past them, and Solomon broke off to recite a long prayer in the classical Arbi which is affected by elder men. Then, the danger past, Solomon leaned forward and issued explicit instructions:

"You sit 'ere for a matter o' ten minutes, sir. Then you get up and go back to the gate. If you meet an old friend o' yours, don't you dare let on as 'ow you knows 'im, but go straight out and turn to the right. I'll be waitin' for you."

Solomon wheezily drew himself erect, and, with a loud and angry muttering about the incivility of fools who refused to gossip with their elders, moved away and was lost among the cloistered arches.

Magruder sat motionless, capable only of blind obedience, stunned into submission. Why had Solomon and that black eunuch been making such a scene in the street that day, deliberately attracting to themselves open attention? This query he set aside for the moment. It was much more important that Solomon had given him his orders to accept Logan's offer; by the pudgy little man's own words, there lay some motive behind it, at present unfathomable.

A slow grin stole over the American's face. So, then, Logan had not set him at liberty for any ostensible work—Logan, too, seemed a man clever at fashioning the wills of men! The more he thought about it, the more Magruder was convinced that Solomon had been correct. Logan had expected that Magruder would lead his spies to others of Solomon's men, who would be efficiently wiped out. And how did Solomon expect to prevent this?

When the ten minutes were up, Magruder found the answer to this question.

Rising, he went to the gatekeeper and donned his shoes, noting the while that the tall Arab whom Solomon had pointed out was quietly following him. Then Magruder passed out the arch—and on the top step came to a pause, barely repressing a cry of swift amazement.

For there, standing looking at him with no sign of recognition, was Wali ibn Kasim! There in the flesh stood that adventurer of Hadramaut whom Magruder had last seen shot to death, as he thought! Remembering Solomon's injunction, Magruder passed on, his brain in a whirl, and turned to his right in the street without. The Hazrami followed and was lost in the shadows.

Sharply delineated by the lighted temple, the Arab spy came out into the archway and passed down the steps. He, too, came into the shadows; and then Magruder heard a little grunt of satisfaction, a blow, and a bubbling rattle of death. The next moment, Wali ibn Kasim was at his heels with a chuckle of grim mirth.

"By Allah, infidel! I am glad to see thee again."

"And I thee," returned Magruder. "I thought you were dead."

"So thought Logan Pasha, and I was close enough to it," was the answer. "Now go on, O friend of Suleiman, for there is yet another of these devils, and I must exorcise him."

Magruder obeyed, thinking, as he went, that this Hazrami was a man of parts.

From the shadowed street ahead came a low whisper, and his hand found that of Solomon. Magruder felt drawn into a doorway, heard a whisper of voices, and another door opened into a lighted room ahead. There he found himself alone with Solomon, a table set with food ready before him.

"Lud! Whiskers is all werry well in their place, but they spoil the effect, as the old gent said when 'e kissed—" The rest was lost in a mumble, as Solomon divested himself of false whiskers and robes and stood forth his old rosy-cheeked self. "Now, sir, sit you down and 'ave supper. Werry good supper it is, if I do say it. I suppose as 'ow you wants to know 'ow I got 'ere?"

"Very much, indeed." Magruder was not too curious to forget the food before him, and realized that he was famishing for decent cooking. "Logan has every gate watched—"

Solomon chuckled, drew forth his clay pipe, and began to fill it.

"Well, sir, I ain't no 'and at fighting, just like that. So while you was a-battling at Al Sufayna I slipped off wi' two of me men and got 'ere two days ahead o' you and 'im."

"Eh?—You slipped off that morning?" Magruder stared at the other keenly. "You slipped off and left us to do what we could?"

"Why not, sir?" The calm blue eyes twinkled at him. "Werry good job as I did so, says I. 'Cause why, Mr. Magruder, where would you be this werry blessed minute if I'd stayed to be shot up? Just tell me that!"

There was no answer to this logic; none whatever.

"But—er—did you foresee what was going to happen?" queried Magruder, remembering the little man's covert warning. "Did you—"

"No, sir, or I wouldn't ha' left them 'ere three 'undred men to be sacrificed," was the prompt response. "But I takes no chances, sir, just like that. There's two sides to luck, as the old gent said after 'e married 'is third. Well, sir, there's quite a bit been and 'appened since we was in Mecca."

"Yes? What?"

"The caliph 'as went an' proclaimed a 'oly war against the Osmanli, sir. You see, it's like this 'ere: We've captured Taif easy enough, but there's a law against any one on this 'ere sacred soil o' Medina, just like that."

"So?" Magruder glanced up. "What about your gentleman adventurer, Wali ibn Kasim, going after those spies of Logan's to-night?"

"I'm a-comin' to that, sir," was the calm answer. "The caliph is the 'ead of Islam, just like that. So 'e 'as said as 'ow it's a werry meritorious action to kill off any blessed Turk what's polluting the 'oly land with 'is presence."

"In other words, it's an open season on Osmanli, eh?"

"Just like that, sir." Solomon went on to set forth that with the exception of one or two heavily garrisoned cities, such as Sanaa, the entire coast strip of Arabia down to Aden was in the hands of the allied Arab tribes.

With the capture of Mecca, Caliph Hussein's position was for the moment firm. If, however, Logan could hang on to Medina until the Turks could sweep in from Syria and reopen the railroad, the situation would be serious, indeed. Via the railroad, men and supplies in unlimited numbers could be rushed through to Logan at Medina, and the Turks would retain the holy cities of Islam at any cost.

The one chance of the Arabs lay in capturing Medina speedily and so remove the base upon which the reconquest might be built. Solomon had taken upon his own shoulders this task.

"I don't see how you expect to do it," said Magruder bluntly. "The mountains are too far away to use such siege artillery as the caliph can command, and Logan is quite able to repulse any assaults."

"Right you are, sir." Solomon nodded his gray head sagely. "All the same, I 'opes that by the day arter to-morrow I'll 'ave Medina right an' tight in me 'and, just like that! There's forty thousand men in them 'ills, Mr. Magruder, within ten mile of 'ere—"

"Forty million wouldn't do you any good," cut in Magruder. "At least, until Logan has used up his ammunition. Your only chance will be to use stratagem."

"Well, now, if that ain't an idea!" Solomon's blue eyes twinkled. "Howsomever, Mr. Magruder, I 'ave me plans under way so to speak. Accidents is liable, o' course. You remember meetin' me and that 'ere eunuch in the street?"

Magruder nodded.

"We'd 'ave rescued you then and there, except for that danged cavalry that come down on us unexpectedlike! But all's for the best, I says, even if appearances be deceptive. 'Ere you are, just like that, and a werry good job. Now, sir, I expect as 'ow you'd like a bit o' rest in a real bed?"

"Why not throw in a bath and shave and a clean suit of clothes and a new pair of shoes?" Magruder laughed. "The dream would be a fine one."

"Well, we can 'ave all them 'ere things, sir, if you'll just come along o' me."

Wondering what the pudgy man meant, Magruder rose and followed Solomon through several rooms until suddenly a lighted chamber was disclosed and drew an exclamation from him. There was a portable English bathtub, filled and waiting, a real iron bed on which various articles of European clothing were laid out, and shaving materials.

"The shoes ain't 'ere," said Solomon apologetically, "but I'll 'ave 'em by morning."

"What kind of magician are you?" gasped the American. The other chuckled wheezily.

"Werry simple, sir. This is me own 'ouse, you see—I 'ave a bit o' real estate in warious places—and whenever I stops in Medina I likes a bit o' comfort. I'm gettin' on in years and a bit 'ard to please, as the old gent said when 'e fired the 'ousemaid. Now, sir, if you'll get a good night's sleep, it might be a good thing. We'll 'ave a mortal busy day to-morrow, just like that."

Magruder threw up his hands in helpless wonder.

"Thank you, John," he said simply. "I have to report twice a day—"

"I've 'eard about that, sir. We'll wake you in time, all shipshape an' Bristol fashion. Good night, sir."

"Good night," responded Magruder.

Bathed and shaved, he crept between the sheets and felt a new man. As he fell asleep, the thought of Clarice Worden occurred to him with disturbing force, but, he reflected, John Solomon had doubtless overlooked nothing. So, sighing a little, he relaxed in slumber and knew nothing more until the graying dawn was stealing in at his window.

He was awakened by Solomon in person, who looked as though he had been up all night, but whose cheery optimism seemed undiminished.

"Beggin' your pardon, sir, I'll be talking while you dress," said Solomon. An Arab bore in coffee and light cakes, then left them alone. "I 'ave your shoes 'ere, sir. There ain't much time, so we'll get down to business. First off, sir, you 'as to go to that 'ere gate and report. Well, you'll find Logan a-waiting there."

"Logan? How do you know?"

"Why, 'e's werry uneasy about some of 'is men as disappeared last night, sir. Clean vanished, they did—no bodies nor nothin'! You can say you spent the night in a bath'ouse. Then you must say as you'll turn that 'ere danged Solomon over to 'im to-night sure. Don't let on as I'm in the city, though! Be werry mysterious about it."

"You're not in earnest about this—"

"I just am, sir!" came the resolute answer. "Trust me, Mr. Magruder. Then you tell Logan as 'ow you 'as to see Miss Worden immediate, 'cause why, you wants 'er to write a letter what'll decoy Solomon. Then you see 'er and give 'er this 'ere note and bring back them letters from the princes of India what she's a-keeping."

Magruder took a tiny folded paper and thrust it into his pocket.

"But see here!" he exclaimed slowly. "Suppose I don't see her alone? And Logan will be sure to have me trailed—"

"Let'im," retorted Solomon. "About seein' 'er alone, why, you 'as to use your own judgment when so be the time comes. Judgment was give men to use, I says, and you 'ave an uncommon good lot of it, sir! When you leaves the palace, go straight to the Mosque of the Prophet, where you was last night, and I'll meet you there. All straight, sir?"

"I guess so." Magruder nodded, and Solomon helped him on with his Arab costume, saying that in a few hours more it would not longer be needed.

As the call to sunrise prayer was echoing, from the tall minarets, Magruder approached the gate of the old city. His mental condition was one of bewildered surmise; he understood everything, yet he understood nothing.

That Solomon had some scheme afoot for surprising the city went without saying; but how or when it could be done, was far from Magruder's knowledge. That it could be done at all seemed extremely improbable.

As he approached the gate, Magruder was halted by a sentry, and an instant later came Logan with two officers. So Solomon had been right about this! And the American saw that Logan Pasha was grim of mouth and stormy of eye.

"Where have you been?" demanded the Austrian. Magruder gave him a glance of surprise.

"Where? About the business in hand, naturally."

"And my men—what has become of them?"

"Oh, your men!" Magruder laughed as he saw the rage deepen in Logan's face. "They tried to follow me, which was not in the contract. I don't know where they are, but let's hope for the best. If they were good Moslems, we'll concede that they're in paradise. But now—I have results for you."

At this Logan repressed the anger roused by Magruder's first words. Evidently he was willing to sacrifice a few men if he could get hold of Solomon.

"The man we want is near here," went on Magruder calmly, "and there is a large force of Arabs in the hills—"

"I know that, fool!" grated Logan harshly. "Every road is barred!"

"No matter. If you will give me a free hand, I will guarantee to get Solomon here by to-night."

Logan started slightly and gave the American a keen glance.

"You are speaking the truth—yes. I think you are! What means will you use?"

"I must see Miss Worden and induce her to write a letter. I can find means of sending this to Solomon—"

Magruder paused as the Austrian smiled thinly.

"You'll not induce her to do much, my friend! However, you may try. Well?"

"I can guarantee, in any case, that Solomon will be in the city by nightfall. If this plan fails, I can try another."

"Miss Worden will not decoy him here."

"I would not ask her to," answered Magruder. "But the letter I must have. When can I see her?"

For a moment Logan studied him, then seemed to decide it would be best to say nothing more about the missing men. He nodded curtly.

"Come with me to the palace. You shall see her in half an hour."

No further words passed between them. Logan turned on his heel and Magruder followed, under vigilant watch by the officers. In ten minutes they entered the doorway of the governor's palace; Magruder was now certain of his ground with Logan, and felt confident that he could accomplish his mission with success if no new stumbling block arose.

In Logan's office he stretched out in a chair, filled his pipe, and eyed the Osmanli officers who passed around with a cold insolence that infuriated them. Magruder, in fact, began to feel rather proud of himself and his position. Overnight he had become an important man—and this importance rested upon Logan's estimate of him, for Logan had read truth in Magruder's words. The spy, who trusted none, now trusted his enemy.

Just as the term "Jap" infuriates the men of Nippon, so the insulting epithet of "Turk" is gall and wormwood to an Osmanli. Magruder, therefore, passed his time very pleasantly in telling the Osmanli officers what he thought of them, until Logan sent him a curt command to keep quiet and the officers cursed under their breaths.

In the midst of this, a black slave entered, salaamed to Logan, and the Austrian gave Magruder a gesture.

"Go with this slave. Miss Worden has been furnished writing materials. You will bring me her letter to read when you pass out."

So he was to see Clarice Worden in private—without having to give lies and pretexts to such an end! This was unexpected good fortune, a favorable augury of the outcome, thought Magruder.

Passing through that same curtained doorway in which he had seen the girl herself, at a bitter moment, the American found her awaiting him in the room beyond. Early as it was, she wore her dress of white serge and gave no evidences of hasty rising. Never had he seen her so beautiful, thought Magruder.

He halted suddenly, his hand outstretched in greeting, the smile fading upon his lips. She stood beside a writing desk, but in her eyes he read a storm of wrath, and in her flushed and angry features a message hard to interpret.

"How dare you—how dare you ask to see me, you traitor?" she demanded hotly. "How dare you show your face before me? After I was so sure of you—after I had declared that no American could be so treacherous! I am ashamed of you!"

"You've said something, all right!" exclaimed the astounded Magruder. "If you—"

"I do not wish to have anything to do with you!" she flashed. "Get out of here, or I shall have General Logan order you out!"

CHAPTER XI

SOLOMON IS DELIVERED

"WHAT DO you mean. Miss Worden?" exclaimed Magruder, in dismay.

"You need not bandy lies with me, sir!" she flung at him, biting off the words. "I heard the compact you made with Mr. Logan—General Logan. I should say—"

"Oh, you did!" Magruder saw the whole thing in a flash. His lips curved in a whimsical smile. "Say, Logan is one smart man, now!" He glanced swiftly around. To all appearance they were alone in the room—but he could not take chances.

"I do wish you'd write a letter for me," he went on, taking a step closer to her. In his left hand was the tiny folded note written by Solomon. "Probably you think I'm a good-for-nothing scoundrel, eh? I am, I admit it freely. All the same, you can get rid of me in a hurry if you'll write a short note."

"I'll have nothing to do with your villainy!" she cut in icily.

"Don't say that, please. Let me give you a chance to go back on your words. Think of the anguish this personal contact with me is causing you!" He was standing by the desk now, gazing across it into her wrathful eyes. His left hand opened and let the folded note fall to the desk top. "Won't you please sit down here and write that note? Logan isn't going to throw me out—not a bit of it! He got me this interview."

While he talked, he desperately drew her attention to the note. She hesitated, then her hand went out to it.

"What kind of a note do you want?" she asked. Her fingers spread open the folded paper.

"A letter to Solomon saying that you are well and must see him at once. A few lines only, Miss Worden!" He was playing now to her ears, and also, he guessed, to the ears of unseen listeners. It was a difficult job, but he persevered. She was looking down at the paper.

"Is that letter to be used in the betrayal of Solomon, you ask? I answer yes, it is—pardon my bluntness. I've agreed to hand Solomon over to Logan in order to gain my freedom; no mistake about that. But you told me once that—that if I ever asked a favor of you, you would grant it. Remember?"

He watched her with desperate eyes, staking all on that cast. She lifted her gaze from Solomon's note, her face flushing, and met his look squarely. He hastened on, hoping that she would understand, hoping that she would guess his unspoken thought, hoping that she would realize that he was lying for those hidden ears. What was written in that note he did not know, but it had brought the crimson to her face.

"Don't you remember that day I met you at Sherif Hussein's house in Mecca and you were good enough to make that promise?" She had done nothing of the sort, of course, but Magruder gained new hope from the steady, golden-brown eyes of her. "Well, I claim it now—to save my life, Miss Worden! You may think me a miserable coward, but I'm really frightfully anxious to get out of this cursed country. I was a fool ever to mix up in this affair. You won't refuse—you won't go back on your word when it means life to me, will you? What is Solomon to us? Come, Miss Worden, be sensible!"

A sudden, smiling glory flashed into her eyes and out again, and he repressed a sigh of relief. He had won the cast! Rather, Solomon's message had won it for him.

"When I made that promise, sir," she returned in cutting accents, but the words told him a different story, "I did not anticipate such a situation as this. However, I shall keep my word with you; the betrayal of Solomon is on your head alone."

With a cold gesture, she sat down at the desk, on which stood pens, ink, and paper. A swift movement of her hand—so swift that Magruder barely caught it—slid a thin, folded packet beneath the paper on which she was about to write.

Magruder watched her with inward exultation tearing at his heart. He saw that Logan had endeavored to detach the girl from all trust in him and was playing a crafty game with her; it merely added another mark upon his mental register. When, if ever, he came to a reckoning with Logan Pasha, he was going to make himself felt, and the present situation gave him hope that the reckoning was not far away.

Whatever Miss Worden may have guessed, she played the game as indicated by Magruder. With no trace of any emotion in her features, she wrote a few lines, then abruptly rose and stepped back, motioning toward the desk.

"There is what you have requested," she said stonily. "Take it and go!"

Magruder leaned forward and glanced at her note. It was brief and exactly as he had ordered. He folded it, with a nod of satisfaction, and deftly slipped into the wide sleeve of his *abba* the thin packet that lay underneath.

"Thank you!" he exclaimed lightly. "When next we meet, Miss Worden, I trust you will have so far forgiven me that—"

"I beg you, leave me!" she broke in, crumpling between her fingers the tiny ball of paper that had been Solomon's message.

Magruder bowed silently and turned to the door.

In the office beyond, he found Logan as before; the Austrian eyed him with a covert smile, as though admiring the way in which Magruder had attained his supposed end. Logan took the girl's note, glanced at it, and returned it with a curt nod.

"Very well. What are the details regarding Solomon? When and where?"

"I don't know yet," answered the American thoughtfully. "I

may not know before afternoon. Where can I get in touch with one of your men in private?"

"H'm! You know the bookshop of Hamza, in the street that leads to the mosque? You can easily find it. I will have it watched. Go in. One of my men will follow after you and speak with you. Let me know by what gate Solomon will enter the city—that's all."

"He may be already in the city, for all I know," returned Magruder, at which Logan looked somewhat startled. "May I depend on you to make whatever arrangements I request? We cannot make the trap obvious, and I do not care to fall down on such a job through any bungling of yours."

"There will be none on my part," was the response. "Look to yourself, Magruder!"

"I should worry!" chuckled the American, turning away.

To his infinite relief, Magruder left the place without hindrance. Once in the street, he slipped the packet from his sleeve and placed it in an inner pocket of his tunic. It was presumably written on Indian paper, for it was very thin yet well wrapped.

Taking his way to the Mosque of the Haram, he passed the gatekeeper, this time without a guide, made the customary genu-flections, and took his way to the same pillar beside which he had sat the previous night. The scene by day was much the same in the attendant crowds, but, robbed of the illumination of the lamps, the place looked shabby. Gone was its half-shadowed mystery, and in the bare light of day the place appeared exactly what it was—neither so ancient nor so glorious as its history. Magruder mentally decided that the Grand Central Station was ten times as magnificent.

Suddenly the figure of the disguised Solomon appeared and seated itself beside the American as before.

"Well, sir, what luck?"

"Fine!" replied Magruder. "Say, what was in that note of yours?"

Solomon chuckled in his wheezy manner.

"Why, sir, it was just a brief encomium on your wirtues, so to speak, with an order to deliver them 'ere letters.'Ave you got 'em?"

"Yes." Magruder's hand went toward his pocket, but was checked by the other's voice:

"Not 'ere, sir! There's too many eyes a-watching, as the old gent said when 'e met the pretty 'ousemaid in the garden. You set still a minute. I 'ave to time me connections close, 'cause why, there's a mortal lot o' things to be done yet."

Magruder relapsed into silence, staring at the crowd and watching the tattered green curtain around the tomb of the Prophet inside the railing. Night and day that tomb was guarded, for the mosque was never empty; and Magruder wondered what the scene must be like in the three months of pilgrimage, when hundreds of thousands of Moslems crowded the city.

"Is that really the tomb of Mohammed?" he said, after a space. "It seems hard to realize that behind that curtain lie the Prophet and the two first caliphs of Islam."

Solomon chuckled again.

"No one ain't never seen be'ind that 'ere curtain, sir, but I'd be werry sorry, indeed, to gamble that the body o' the Prophet is there! Now, if I was you, sir, I'd get up and go out and meet Wali ibn Kasim, who's waitin' outside the gate. Trust 'im, and I'll meet you in a matter o' twenty minutes or so."

Knowing Solomon well enough to obey orders implicitly, Magruder rose and departed from the Haram. As he went down the wide steps outside the gate, he saw Wali waiting. The Hazrami made him a sign to follow and strode away down the main street, turning suddenly into a doorway. Magruder followed, and the door was shut and barred.

"Come quickly, O Emir of the Jinn!" exclaimed Wali, with a grim laugh.

Magruder accompanied him through the house, which seemed deserted into a garden in the rear, through a gate in the garden wall that led into a narrow alley, and down this to another gate into a second garden.

"If any followed, Allah help them!" murmured Wali piously. "Now we are in the house of Suleiman and need fear nothing."

Crossing the garden and entering the house, Magruder came to rest in a room adorned with rugs and weapons, each one a priceless treasure; and not a few of these jewels of art were inscribed as gifts to Solomon from various princes of the earth. Wali departed, and, lighting his pipe, the American strolled about the room examining its marvel. He was still engaged in this task when Solomon himself entered with a sigh of relief.

"Now, if you please, sir, them 'ere letters!"

Taking the packet, Solomon carefully ripped open the oiled silk in which was incased and disclosed a sheaf of thin letters. After examining these in silence, he clapped his hands and there entered a man who greeted Magruder with a smile of recognition. It was the son of Caliph Hussein, the same who had engaged him in Cairo!

"Take these to your father, with word that the city is to be taken to-night," said Solomon. "He will follow all arrangements as previously made by me. The Emirs of Hail and Riadh will attend to the stone railroad station and the new city; your father's men will enter to the inner city as arranged."

Magruder wondered how this had been arranged, and then bethought himself of the Armenian officer. So that was it! With a secret friend in charge of a gate, the matter was simplified. The caliph's son bowed and took the papers.

"The Medani hostages?" he said quietly. "Their safety must be put above all."

"I have arranged for that with my own men in the town and with the townfolk," nodded Solomon. "They are to be liberated at the first shot. That is all. Allah give thee peace!"

"And thee," responded the Arab, and was gone.

For a space Solomon sat in silence, his wide, blue eyes fixed upon the wall in abstracted gaze. Then he fumbled for his clay pipe and began to fill it mechanically.

"I ain't no 'and for fighting," he said slowly, as he had once before said the same words. "It's out o' me line, so to speak, to be 'andling armies and a-takin' cities like this 'ere, and I'm a-gettin' on in years, Mr. Magruder, sir. When I think o' what's a-going to 'appen tonight and the fightin' there's a-goin' to be, it fair makes me shiver, it does that!"

He threw back his shoulders, as if throwing off a weight, and turned to Magruder.

"Now, sir, I ain't a-going to tell no one me plans, but I'll want a promise from you. To-night I wants you to stick werry close to Miss Worden an' be responsible for her."

"I'll do it, most certainly," responded Magruder.

Solomon produced two loaded automatics and silently handed them over. Then he drew forth a paper and opened it.

"This 'ere is a plan o' the governor's audience 'all, sir. Look at this door." And he pointed to an exit marked to the right of the dais. "It leads out through these 'ere rooms into the palace gardens. You're to take Miss Worden out there, some'ow, and you'll find Wali ibn Kasim waitin' for you. Stay there till I comes; that's all."

Magruder fixed the plan in his head and nodded.

"Good! I'll do it. When shall I take her out through those rooms?"

"First chance you gets arter the rumpus starts," was the laconic answer. "Now you listen werry sharp, sir, 'cause why, we can't 'ave no mistakes made. This 'ere is what you're to tell that danged Logan."

Solomon lowered his voice. For ten minutes Magruder listened, startled and amazed by what he heard. He ventured a protest, but it was cut short with some asperity, so he said no more. Very placid and confident, Solomon spoke his mind plainly, leaving no chance for error, and if there were any excitement stirring within him, it did not show in the blank, pudgy features or in the calm blue eyes. The man, thought Magruder, was a human marvel!

"You do just like I've said, sir," concluded Solomon, with a sigh of relief, puffing at his old pipe the while, "and we'll 'ave no more talk on it till you gets back 'ere safe and sound. But mind, there ain't going to be no child's play to-night! The destiny of an empire, as the storybooks say, is 'anging on this night's work, sir. And werry ticklish business it's a-goin' to be, as the old gent said when 'e married 'is third. Now we'll 'ave a bite to eat, if so be as you'll join me."

It was toward noon when Magruder left the house, guided by Wali along an intricate exit similar to that by which they had entered. Entering the bookshop of Hamza alone, the American was almost at once joined by an Osmanli disguised in Arab costume. To him Magruder stated that he must see Logan Pasha immediately, and the two passed forth to the palace.

So it happened that at noon Magruder stood once more in Logan's office. To his curt demand that he see the Austrian in private, Logan responded by an order that cleared the room of all save Malik Bey and Yelniz Pasha.

"Now, Logan, I've some news for you," said Magruder quickly. He was playing the part of an ambassador, and could stick at nothing; for the matter of that, Solomon had stuck at nothing in giving orders, knowing that Medina was completely cut off from the outside world. "This Arab rebellion is going to smash, and I'm glad I cleared out in time."

"What!" The two Osmanlis broke into exclamations of surprise, but Logan regarded the American steadily from narrowed eyes. Magruder nodded confidently.

"Yes. In the first place, the Germans and Turks in Syria have managed to reach the Suez Canal. They held it long enough to blow up a mine, and block it temporarily. That has cut off the promised English and French aid to the rebellion. In the second place, the Arabs had cut the Damascus railroad, as you know, this side of Tebuk. Now it appears that the Turks have flung down a sizable army from Ma'an, have completely defeated the Arabs, and are marching toward Medina. All in all, the rebellion is pretty near done up. I've managed to communicate with Solomon, and here's the answer I received."

He paused, holding his hearers in suspense. Logan's steely eyes were glittering with delight at this news; he evidently doubted nothing.

"Solomon says that the game's up for him," went on Magruder. "If you'll promise him safety and protection out of Arabia, he'll show up to-night and make terms. Without him, as you know, the revolt will go to pieces like a busted balloon. He's in the city, by the way; slipped in the other night in disguise."

The two Osmanlis uttered hearty thanks to Allah for this news. Logan frowned.

"So he's in the city?" was the Austrian's comment. "Then we might hunt him down—"

"And he'd fight to the last, in such event," broke in Magruder. "See here, Logan, I hate you like the devil hates holy water, but this is absolutely the message I was told to give you—and if you win out, I save my own skin. Solomon will come here to the palace tonight, place himself in your hands, and will deliver over to you the chiefs of the revolt with their leading men. Those were his exact words. From you he wants safe-conduct on your word of honor. Now, does he get it or not?"

"It's best to take no chances," said Logan slowly, unconsciously quoting his master opponent. "Yes, we'd better accept his offer and let him go. We can take vengeance on the Arabs whom he'll deliver to us, and when we finish with these tribes they'll not rebel again for fifty years! Eh, gentlemen?"

Yelniz Pasha gave guttural assent, as did Malik.

"Very well," said Logan to Magruder. "Tell him I accept. When will he come here?"

"He said about ten o'clock this evening," rejoined the American. "The Arabs in the hills are planning an attack on the north side of the city for to-night, which he sends you as news, earnest of his intentions."

"Those who attack will not go home again." And Logan laughed grimly. "Thank him for me."

Magruder nodded. "He also said that if you would receive him in the audience hall it would facilitate matters. He will bring with him a dozen Arabs, all leaders of the revolt, and these will remain in your hands if you can seize them. Is this agreeable?"

It was highly agreeable, and Magruder went away laughing to himself. He did not return direct to Solomon's house, but, meeting Wali ibn Kasim, was conducted through other dwellings to the flat roofs, by means of which they reached their goal unfollowed and unhindered.

Once more in Solomon's gem-adorned room, a room more splendid than that of any emperor, Magruder reported the success of his mission and then, by invitation, stretched out upon a divan to watch proceedings.

What went on the American could not understand, but he saw enough to cause him renewed amazement at the talents of the pudgy little man. There appeared a succession of visitors, Abyssinians, Somali, Arabs of a dozen tribes, Persians, Afghans, Javanese, and others innumerable. All the tangled races of the Eastern worlds seemed represented in that room, and to each man Solomon spoke in his own tongue, hearing reports and issuing orders. From the little he could gather, Magruder conjectured that each of these lieutenants was charged with some special duty, and he wondered anew at Solomon's infinite capacity for detail.

The afternoon was spent, and the lights were lit before the last visitor went, and Solomon, with a wheezy sigh of relief, stowed away a little red notebook in which he had been writing.

"Now, sir, we're all fixed shipshape. If so be as you 'as no objections, we'll 'ave a werry fine supper. There's nothin' like good wittles to put 'eart into a man, as the old gent said when 'e kissed the cook. Then we'll go take a little walk and end up at the palace, just like that!"

Solomon proved as good as his word, and indeed his supper looked very much like rank enchantment. He clapped his hands and curtains at the end of the room fell apart, disclosing another room beyond, set for dinner in Occidental fashion and with half a dozen other guests awaiting them.

As if in a dream, Magruder moved forward. He found the son of Hussein who had met him and Logan at Jedda, and who now apologized courteously for his mistake on that occasion; he met also the third son of the caliph, a tall, bearded man educated at Oxford; he found Wali ibn Kasim, who could be a thorough gentleman at will; and, with these, three others whose very names struck him dumb. For here were men famous in the East, yet more famous for that few men had ever seen them—the Emirs of Hail and Riadh, and the latter's son, rulers of interior Arabia, emirs of the breed of Saracen!

That dinner, as Solomon had prophesied, was fit for kings. At its close, the Emir of Hail gave an order to one of the attendants, and into the room filed twelve men, of huge size for Arabs, wearing the large burnoose of the desert. These the two emirs addressed in a dialect unknown to Magruder.

When, two hours later, the American passed out to the street alone with Solomon, he had scarcely spoken. Then the pudgy little man vouchsafed to explain that by connivance of the Armenian officer the emirs had entered the city in disguise, with some of their men. The twelve, he stated in morose gloom, were men who had offered themselves as victims.

"Victims?" repeated Magruder "What for?"

"They're to go with us into that 'ere palace," said Solomon slowly. "They 'ave work to do, sir—mortal 'ard work it is—and the chances is they won't come out alive. But them 'ere men are willin' to die, just like that. Dang it, sir, I'll never take on a job like this 'ere one again! It ain't neat. It ain't ship shape. This 'ere setting up of kingdoms and empires is all werry well for them as likes it, I says, but give me a job where there's some respect for 'uman life, just like that."

"But, see here!" exclaimed the American. "How about us? We're going to the palace, too!"

"Well, sir"—and Solomon chuckled wheezily—"this 'ere is one time where I 'as to take me chances."

CHAPTER XII

THE TAKING OF MEDINA

ROMANCE IS one thing and history is quite another. Somewhere in between lie the notebook diaries of John Solomon, and whether or not history remembers his name or recites his deeds as they are recorded in his notebooks—what matter?

As romance would have it, Medina was taken on a moonlight night, with flashings of swords and banging of cannon. But, as Solomon records, there was a miserable drizzle of rain which lasted through the early evening and left everything wet and cold. As the Medani count rain, when out of season, as good luck, no harm was done.

Promptly at ten that night, Magruder and Solomon approached the governor's palace, the twelve devoted ones in their train. They had seen the Osmanli legions marching out to the north side of the city, and even now there was an irregular popping of guns denoting an attack in some force on that side of town.

Magruder, halted by the sentries, assumed the lead when an officer appeared. With no loss of time, the fourteen were led inside the palace, straight to the hall of audience. Here, amid a blaze of lights, was a distinguished company to receive them. Logan sat upon a raised dais at the far end, Yelniz Pasha and Malik Bey a little behind him. Around the walls were ranged officers, and, seated apart near the door to the right, was Clarice Worden. That Logan had brought her there to witness the final treachery, as he supposed, of Magruder and Solomon, the American did not learn until later.

Logan rose to receive them, his virile features grim and stony.

"I have fulfilled our agreement," said Magruder, advancing. "Logan Pasha, here is Mr. Solomon."

He stepped aside, and, unnoticed, made his way to Miss Worden. Seizing the chance afforded him by the general interest in Solomon, he leaned over and spoke in a low whisper:

"Be ready! When I speak the word, jump up and get through this door. Understand?"

She nodded slightly, and Magruder straightened up.

Logan had prepared the trap well. Solomon flung off his hood and revealed his mild features, amid a little growl from the Osmanlis; at the same moment, the doors were closed and a score of the officers who ranged the hall quietly moved around the dozen Arabs. These stood motionless, apparently overcome by surprise.

"Well, Solomon," said Logan in English, a thin smile of cruelty on his lips, "you seem to have bungled the revolt. You Britishers are poor conspirators. So you're ready to throw up the game, eh?"

"Beggin' your pardon, I ain't," said Solomon emphatically.

His blue eyes held the steely gaze of Logan in silence for a full half minute.

"What do you mean?" snapped the Austrian.

"First off, sir, let's 'ave our accounts settled up shipshape." Solomon reached in his pocket, at which Logan's hand flipped to his revolver—but the little man produced only his red notebook, wet his thumb, and turned over the pages. Finally he nodded and held out the book to the Austrian.

"If you'll be so kind as to look over this 'ere account, sir—Logan Pasha, in account wi' John Solomon."

Smiling now at the apparent childishness of this byplay, Logan took the notebook and held it to the light. As he read what was written there, his smile faded and his keen face drew into swift tension. Then sudden passion surged into his eyes and he flung down the little book with a curse.

"What does this mean?" His voice rang out like a clarion. "Are you trifling with me?"

"It means, sir"—and Solomon's head flung up—"it means as 'ow you've lost Medina! Listen!" He paused, and the silence was broken by rifle cracks. "That's Caliph Hussein and the men from Hail and Riadh—"

"Come!" Magruder reached down and seized the wrist of Miss Worden. As she rose, he half threw her behind him toward the door.

In that instant of time, terrible things happened. Magruder paused in the doorway, fascinated, incredulous. He saw the dozen devoted Arabs whip out automatics in each hand, he saw the weapon of Logan leap forth and spit fire and Solomon's figure fell. Then the dozen Arabs deliberately opened fire on the Turks crowded around them.

With horror clutching at him, Magruder turned and slammed the door on that hall of doom. He realized now what those Arabs were doing, why they were dying. Around them were the chief officers of the garrison—who were being destroyed to leave the Turks leaderless!

Magruder collided with a figure, caught the voice of Miss Worden, and his hand gripped hers in the darkness. The touch steadied him. Remembering the plan of the place, he drew her ahead down a passageway, opened a door, and they entered a lighted corridor.

"What is it?" cried out the girl, pausing. "What—"

"Battle!" exclaimed Magruder. "Come with me, and quickly! I'll see to your safety."

Two Turkish officers came running into the corridor ahead, shouting as they came. The American lifted his automatic and fired. One of the figures plunged forward; the other darted into a doorway and vanished.

"Hurry!"

Shots rang through the building amid the shouting of men and trampling feet. Magruder led the girl onward, in desperate haste, and a moment later uttered a cry of joy at reaching a door that opened on the palace gardens. In the light stood Wali ibn Kasim, waiting.

"Good hunting, O infidel!" The Hazrami laughed wildly. "This way!"

They followed him blindly out into the garden. Over the city was pandemonium let loose. A storm of shots was punctuated by the deeper boom of guns, and two or three machine guns were rending through the far shouts of battling men. In that night the gathered tribes were bursting in upon the holy city: men of Hail and Riadh, men of Gahtan and Zahran, the Koreish and the Rkubeh and the Beni Harb.

"Listen!" Magruder halted as Wali ibn Kasim seized his arm. They had come to a long, low summerhouse of stone amid the gardens. "A thousand men are before the palace, seeking Turkish blood. There is but one way for Logan Pasha to fly, and that is by way of this summerhouse, which connects with one of the forts by an underground passage. Now, set the woman inside, where the walls will protect her from bullets, and let us wait here."

Magruder's chief fear was for Clarice Worden, whose hand trembled on his arm. His fingers closed upon hers for a moment and he led her to the doorway.

"Inside with you, young lady!" He attempted a light tone without great success. "I think you'll be in no danger."

"But you!" she cried hastily. Magruder laughed.

"Oh, we're all right! You get in there and shut the door. Please, dear girl!" His voice deepened into earnestness. "Don't you see that if you're safe our loads are lightened? Don't hesitate, for every moment is precious! And if I don't see you again, Clarice— just remember that I—I am very proud to have known you."

He dared not say what was in his heart, and gently urged her inside. The door slammed, and a lock clicked home. Magruder turned to find Wali extending a cigarette.

"We have five minutes, O infidel! If we die, let us die with good tobacco in our throats."

"Why this talk of death?" queried Magruder, taking the cigarette.

"Well, why not?" returned the Hazrami coolly, and struck a match. "Presently Logan will come here, or such of his men as remain alive. It is their only way of escape."

"And Solomon sent us here!" cried Magruder, incredulous. "He sent Miss Worden here, knowing this?"

"Of course!" Wali laughed and exhaled a thin cloud of smoke. "We be men, thou and I, O infidel! This woman of yours is inside and the door locked. It is our task to keep them from breaking down the door until Solomon comes."

Sudden recollection flooded upon Magruder's brain.

"Solomon is dead!" He remembered that last scene in the hall. "Solomon is dead, O Hazrami, for I saw Logan shoot him down!"

"When bullets harm Suleiman," was the confident answer, "then shall the world end. Nay, have faith! Is this not good tobacco, now?"

Magruder swore under his breath, as he fully realized their position.

Yet how to better it he knew not. There was nowhere to go; the whole city was in turmoil. Solomon was dead, but the chances were that Logan would not escape from that death-ridden hall of audience. And, after all, Clarice Worden was safe enough in that stone summerhouse, unless the door were battered down. The only obvious danger was to the two who stood outside.

"Why not get inside there?" Magruder motioned toward the door behind them.

"Because Suleiman commanded to stay outside," returned Wali coolly. "Listen! You hear that firing to the north? The troops on that side have been taken in the rear from the city and are between two fires! You see that glow against the sky?

The wooden barracks are burning. By Allah, it is not to my taste to bide here idle!"

Magruder was thinking desperately. After all, Solomon had ordered wisely. Were he and Wali to get inside the summer-house, thought Magruder, the danger to Miss Worden would be increased tenfold. Suddenly Wali flung away his cigarette.

"Ah! Now, O Emir of the Jinn, we shall have the rats running to us! See the mob has broken into the palace! Ai, there is good hunting ahead of them!"

The dark face of the high brick building began to gleam with lights and to resound with exultant yells. Straggling shots echoed forth, and on a wooden balcony that overhung the garden a fierce struggle was going on that ended only when the ancient balcony gave way and precipitated the battlers to death. Magruder suddenly wakened to the fact that if he wanted to see Broadway again he must not stand dawdling here until attack came.

"Get into that shrubbery!" He caught the Hazrami's arm and pointed to the bushes that inclosed the path to the door of the little stone house. "I'll hide on this side. Do not fire until I do, Wali—have a care to that!"

"I am no assassin," was the proud rejoinder.

"And I am no suicide," said Magruder grimly. At that Wali ibn Kasim laughed softly.

"O emir, it is pleasure to know such a man as thou art! After all, there is little profit in dying—and I remember now that Suleiman gave command to do this same thing."

"You came near remembering too late," muttered the American. "Anyway, Suleiman is dead."

To this a laugh of mocking incredulity came from the bushes whither the Hazrami had gone, and Magruder took up his own position to the left of the door. Suddenly from the tumult-filled palace came a voice lifting over the clamor—a voice that rang terribly on the night—and Magruder knew that Logan Pasha was not yet dead.

If Logan reached that underground passage and got through to one of the forts, there was no telling what his audacity might not accomplish. He would not scruple to turn a field gun on the tomb of the Prophet—an act which would be prevented at all costs, even to giving up the city by the Arabs.

"Why did Suleiman place us here alone, without help?" growled Magruder.

The concealed Hazrami chuckled. "O emir, other men could not have reached this place alive. I managed it because I am not as other men— Ai, here come the rats!"

Two Turk officers came leaping down the paths, smoking revolvers in hand. They dashed to the door, and one, of the cavalry, drew his scimitar, with an oath, when the door refused to open. Magruder, who shared Wali's scruple about shooting from ambush, lifted his voice:

"Drop your weapons, and your lives shall be spared!"

A shot answered him, followed by a howl of rage as the two officers sprang for his place of shelter. Magruder fired and the first fell headlong. Then from across the path leaped the Hazrami and grappled with the cavalryman.

"Ho, dog of a Turk!" And the adventurer laughed wildly. "Come, give me a little fun before you die!"

Thus speaking, Wali wrested away the Turk's revolver, drew out a shimmering knife, and attacked—knife against scimitar! It was a mad thing to attempt, but the Hazrami was master of a supreme craft. Slipping from the savage whirls of the curved blade, he seemed to fling himself forward bodily, brought the Osmanli to earth—and rose with the scimitar in hand.

"This is a good weapon," he laughed, panting a little. "Take it, O emir!"

He flung it toward Magruder and slipped away into his hiding place.

Now the garden was filled with voices and the shouts of men. Lights from the palace windows pierced the darkness, giving a dim radiance upon the pathways—and then with savage abruptness the storm burst. Magruder glimpsed a body of men running desperately toward him, and in the lead was the Austrian. The American raised his automatic grimly; there would be no further offers of quarter!

As Magruder pressed the trigger, however, Logan slipped in the wet grass and fell headlong with a muffled curse. Another man fell to the shot, then Wali's weapon spoke out. For an instant the party paused—for an instant only. A shrill yell of savagery went up, and a dozen revolvers sent lead ripping into the bushes.

The scene became an inferno. The Osmanlis rushed forward. Magruder's first weapon was empty, and he emptied his second likewise, trying hard to distinguish Logan in the gloom. Still the Turks came on, the four or five who were left, and suddenly the figure of the Hazrami shot out into the midst of them, knife in hand.

Catching up the scimitar, Magruder leaped into the path, scarce conscious that a bullet had ripped across his scalp. Men swirled around him and he struck out savagely; the keen scimitar went home and was wrenched away from him. Barehanded he launched into the mêlée, berserk madness upon him, his fists driving out with terrific blows. Bodies reeled into him, and he was flung staggering into a tall figure. Clutching out, Magruder's fingers gripped a wrist—and he looked into the snarling face of Logan Pasha!

The two men recognized each other at once. From each broke a low, wordless cry of hatred, but Magruder's hand had closed on the Austrian's revolver wrist. Breast to breast they stood. Magruder got in one short-arm jab, and then was locked in a desperate embrace.

"Here!" Logan's voice lifted vibrantly to some one behind Magruder. "In the back! Get him in the back! I have him!"

Desperate, the American forced his opponent backward by sheer strength and tried to wrench himself around. The movement partially saved him, but he felt a keen blade gash into his body, and a cry of anguish was torn from him. On the instant, Wali shouted, and the Turk who had struck went down with death in his throat.

Magruder felt his strength ebbing. He strove to bend Logan back, but the Austrian stood like a rock. Gradually Magruder felt his hand giving way, felt the revolver coming down—and, with anguish tearing at his body, he could not resist.

"Behind you, O emir!" rose the panting voice of the Hazrami. "Another—"

With an awful horror of the steel that hacked from behind, Magruder summoned up all his failing strength. He flung himself sideways, and, surprised by the effort, Logan gave ground, lost balance. Magruder whirled him—and felt a knife go home in the other's body.

"Mein Gott!"

One awful, spasmodic cry was wrenched from the Austrian as Logan received the blow that had been intended for Magruder. The American's power gave way; he staggered back and clutched at the door for support, staring down at Logan. Even in death, the great will of the Austrian still prevailed, for, with a final convulsive effort, he whipped up his revolver and pressed the trigger. The bullet smashed into the door an inch above Magruder's head, and Logan sank into a crumpled heap, dead.

Vaguely the American was conscious of a flood of men surging around—men who gave exultant shouts for the caliph—and then electric torches flashed forth and in the radiance appeared the figure of John Solomon. Magruder laughed terribly, tried to step forward, felt his knees give way—and fell headlong above the body of Logan.

CHAPTER XIII

FINIS!

IN MEDINA fashion, the rear of Solomon's house was adorned with a large, latticed balcony, which in turn overlooked a garden. In this balcony, upon a day a week after the taking of Medina, sat two men—John Solomon and Hussein, Caliph of Arabia.

"You can do nothing for me," said Solomon, a trace of sadness in his blue eyes, as he sipped at his coffee and puffed his old clay pipe. "I'm going away from this part of the world, Hussein. I cannot stand this fighting and bloodshed. I am going away into the islands of the Eastern seas and open a shop like I used to have at Port Said." He sighed, and finished in English: "This 'ere bloodshed don't suit me, none whatever. I'm a-going to be plain John Solomon, ship chandler, and spend me last days in quiet."

The caliph's grave eyes twinkled as he surveyed his friend.

"O Suleiman," he replied, holding the conversation to Arbi, "man proposes, but Allah disposes. Tell me, I pray you, what my gratitude may do for you. If you lack jewels, I have them; women, I can give them; power, I can bestow it—"

"I'll tell you what you can do with them 'ere jewels," said Solomon suddenly, then repeated the words in Arbi: "Look down at the garden, Hussein!"

The caliph turned.

Below, in the brilliant sunlight that warmed the cold Medina air, were two people. Lying on a cot beside the fountain was Jim Magruder, thin and pale, but gazing up at Clarice Worden with eyes that spelled happiness. She had been sitting beside him, book in hand, but her eyes, too, were fastened on his and the book was forgotten. Solomon chuckled wheezily.

"Your Emir of the Jinn, Hussein, has done more than he bargained for when we got him. Suppose, then, that you turn over to him a few of those precious gifts which I do not need!"

"I had intended to ask you how I could fittingly reward him," and the caliph frowned. "But, Suleiman, such a man as this will not take gold and jewels as reward. I have looked into his eyes this morning, and there is something there puzzling to me— something that tells me wealth means nothing to him."

"And quite right," assented Solomon. "But it's just the same here in Arabia as in the United States or anywhere else, Hussein. A young couple starting out in life will need money. I'd suggest that you make up a present worthy of you, and I'll see that it reaches Miss Worden before the wedding."

"The wedding!" The caliph stared at Solomon, then glanced down at the garden. His face cleared, then frowned again. "Who—those two down there? Impossible, man!"

"Why so?" queried Solomon.

"They hardly know each other. Surely these Americans do not marry on an acquaintance of a few meetings?"

"Well, some on 'em do, but not them 'ere two." Solomon reverted to English and gently tapped his pipe as he gazed down at the garden. "Howsomever, sir, it's a-coming, just like that. If I was a bettin' man, now, Hussein, I'd lay you odds o' ten to one that them two will be married before they reaches Alexandria on the way 'ome."

Hussein stroked his grizzled beard, then laughed.

"Infinite is the wisdom of Suleiman!" he declared, rising. "I'll attend to that gift, my brother, at once."

Solomon did not seem to hear. He flung open the lattice.

"Well, sir and miss, 'ow's that 'ere wound coming?"

"Fine, John, fine!" Magruder's voice lifted heartily. "Come

on down and join us; you ought to be an invalid, too, with that bullet scrape over the ribs!"

Solomon tenderly prodded himself in the ribs, then chuckled.

"Why, sir, I'd plumb forgot that 'ere scratch! Thank you werry much for the inwitation, sir and miss, but I won't come down. Sometimes loneliness is a werry blessed thing."

He gently closed the lattice. From below, the clear laughter of Clarice Worden rang out, followed by the voice of Magruder in low tones. Solomon sighed a little, then took a red notebook from his pocket.

"I clear forgot to enter up that 'ere Logan's death!" he muttered. "Well, I may be gettin' on in years, but I knows a thing or two when I sees it. A werry fine pair they is, and no mistake; and I'm blessed if I ain't a-goin' to be at the weddin' meself."

JOHN SOLOMON, RETIRED

CHAPTER I

SHIP'S STORES

"**I**'VE 'ANKERED all me life to see the South Seas, sir," said the ship chandler, "and 'ere I be, just like that, a-sittin' in Java and a-watching life. It's werry fine, Mr. Carter, to 'ave a good philosophy o' life, as the old gent said when 'e kissed the 'ousemaid."

Carter laughed. He had come to this ship chandler's shop near the wharves to buy a new kedge for his skiff, and he had remained to delight in the odd conversation of the chandler, a complacent little cockney by the name of Solomon.

These things happened in Surabaya, the great seaport city at the east tip of Java, where men of all lands come together and there is no new thing under the sun. Carter was selling typewriters and shoes for New England firms.

"Sure," he returned. "Just what is your philosophy of life, Mr. Solomon?"

"Not to 'ave none," was the prompt retort, accompanied by a wheezy chuckle. "I 'ave me shop to keep from rusting out, so to speak, and 'ere I sits in me declining years: content to be where no one knows me nor I them, and where I can smoke me pipe in peace. 'Ere, Mr, Carter, 've another o' them 'ere cigarettes; sent to me from Egypt, they was. Me boy will 'ave some coffee ready in a minute."

Carter, who had picked up some bundles, set them down again and accepted the invitation. They were sitting on a broad veranda adjoining Solomon's little shop; it was the hour when all sensible Dutchmen were enjoying a siesta, and the presence of an electric fan was most agreeable, to say nothing of the suggested clink of iced coffee.

The shop was dingy and unpretentious. Above the door hung a sign reading, "John Solomon, Ship's Stores," repeated in Dutch, Malay, and Chinese. The owner was a pudgy little man, plainly but neatly dressed, with a moonlike face and mild blue eyes. He wore an old tarboosh cocked jauntily over one ear, with a wisp of gray hair showing around the edge, and smoked an old clay pipe with tobacco whittled from a black plug.

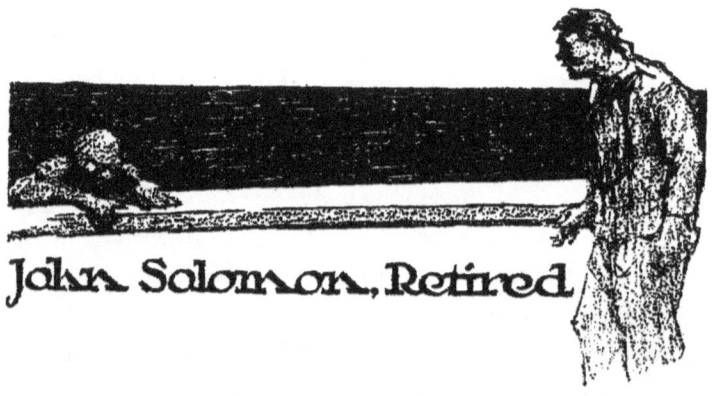

John Solomon, Retired

Solomon's words about being quite unknown struck Carter as false, in a sense. He had noticed how stately Arabs, in passing, had saluted the pudgy figure on the porch as they would never salute the Dutch rulers; and once or twice he had seen Chinese traders make a sign, as they hurried along, to which Solomon had responded with a wave of his pipe.

"Beggin' your pardon, sir," spoke up Solomon, eying one of Carter's bundles which had become torn at an end, "ain't that a doll in there? I didn't know as you was married."

"Probably not, considering that we've never met before," said Carter dryly. "Yes, it's a fine Dutch doll, which I'm going to send home to a niece of mine back in Boston. Married? Heavens, no!

I've nothing to marry on, except the ability to talk Hollandsch which landed my present job; and I've no girl to marry, anyhow."

Solomon rose stiffly, explaining that he had one artificial leg which somewhat hindered his freedom of movement.

"If so be as you're interested in children, Mr. Carter," he went on, "you might like to 'ave a look at summat as I've in one o' the back rooms, while we're a-waitin' for that 'ere coffee."

"What is it—a baby?" chaffed Carter, as he rose.

"No, sir," was the serious answer. "But I 'ave a godson back in New York—John Solomon Grattan, 'is name is.* I've been gettin' a bit of a box ready to send 'im on 'is birthday, sir, and, seein' as 'ow I got a little too much stuff together to fill the box, it struck me as you could use it for that 'ere nevvy or niece o' yours, if I might make so bold, Mr. Carter."

Not sure whether Solomon were about to sell off some children's toys, or whether he were merely humoring an old man's whim, Carter followed the ship chandler through the shop into a bare little room directly behind. A curtain divided this from the other rooms beyond, where Solomon probably had his living quarters. Standing on the bare floor was a small chest, brassbound, with a few half-wrapped objects on a pile of paper beside it.

Solomon opened the chest and complacently began to show forth its contents. For five minutes Ralph Carter was literally stricken dumb. He feared to offend this strangely likable little man by asking questions, yet those pudgy fingers brought to light such things as Carter had never dreamed of sending home—things he could never have found, and could not have bought if he had found them!

Though it might seem a sin that a child should play with such things, what things these were to delight the heart of a child! Here was a doll, cunningly carved and jointed from new ivory by Chinese artificers, dressed in old court costume, with such embroidery as never doll's clothes knew before, complete to jade

---

* *See story entitled "John Solomon, Argonaut."—H.B.-J.*

bracelet and hairpins. Here was a toy train of cars of lacquered wood and steel inlaid with Trengganu goldwork—the toy of a sultan's child!

Here was a sarong of the sheerest Perak silk, woven with Malay children dancing through its folds; here a teak elephant with ivory tusks and ruby eyes, a rajah's howdah on its back; here a buzzing toy massed with bird-of-paradise feathers; here a popgun that might have been made for some dato's son, so thickly was it inlaid with ivory and pearl and shark skin—playthings for which princes might have sighed in vain!

"Now, sir," began Solomon, "you take that 'ere Chinese doll and the train o' cars for your niece, 'cause why, that'll give me room to pack all these 'ere things in the box. If—"

"But—good gracious, man!" exclaimed Carter, struggling to express himself. "I can't afford to buy such things!"

"I knows that werry well, sir," and the blue eyes of Solomon twinkled at him. "You take 'em as a little present from me to 'er, just like that; and no 'arm done, neither, as the old gent said when 'e buried 'is third."

"Why, I—I don't know just what to say, Mr. Solomon," stammered the American. "Such gifts as those are fit for princes!"

"I ain't exactly a poor man," and Solomon chuckled. "It warms me 'eart to be givin' when so be as I 'as a chance, Mr. Carter. Now—"

At that instant a bronze gong in the shop rang sharply. Solomon called out in a tongue unknown to Carter, and into the room from the shop came a Chinaman who carried a small parcel wrapped in silk. His oblique eyes flitted to Carter, and he stood silent.

"This 'ere gent is a friend o' mine," said Solomon calmly. "Speak out!"

"My masteh," said the Celestial, "asks you to aid him foh the sake of fliendship."

Solomon looked very much perturbed.

"You tell Mr. Wing Fu," he answered with some hesitancy,

"as 'ow I said I wasn't goin' to 'elp nobody, just like that. I'm 'ere, and 'ere I'm a-goin' to stay."

The yellow man's face did not change. He went on, as though reciting a lesson:

"My masteh asks you to aid him foh the sake of blothe'hood."

"Brotherhood!" Solomon started. "Look 'ere! You go back and say as 'ow I'm an old man and 'e ain't got no right to be askin' such things o' me, that's all!"

"My masteh," went on the Chinaman, "he say to show you this."

With a swift movement he unrolled the silken parcel, and disclosed a cord that seemed to be of silver, yet was flexible. At each end was a great knot.

Carter glanced at Solomon and saw that the pudgy face of the man was losing its ruddy color, and his blue eyes were fastened upon the silver cord. The Chinaman caught hold of one of the knots, worked at it with long yellow fingers, and just as it was about to fall apart a cry broke from Solomon:

"Stop it! I'll 'elp him—dang it!"

His features as inscrutable as though carven in yellow jade, the Celestial tightened the cord again, wrapped it up, and slipped out of the room. His wonder at the playthings forgotten in his greater wonder at this strange scene, Carter turned to Solomon and found the little man wiping his brow.

"Dang it!" said Solomon, with a wheezy sigh, and stared at the American.

"Exactly," smiled Carter, yet with puzzlement in his gray eyes. "Do you mind if I ask what that cord was?"

"No, I don't." And Solomon picked up the two packages he had given Carter. "Come out on the porch, where it ain't so 'ot, if you please, sir."

A moment later they sat opposite each other at a table laden with silver flagons of iced coffee and a plate of delicate Arab cakes. Carter was no longer to be surprised by unexpected richness.

"This 'ere," said Solomon, slowly and reflectively, "is in the East—and werry far in the East, Mr. Carter. A matter o' ten minutes ago I was just a-thinkin' 'ow 'appy I was to 'ave me mind free o' care, just like that. And now I 'as to 'elp out an old friend, and a werry ticklish job it is, sir."

"I don't doubt it," said Carter cheerily. "The Chinese are usually first-chop fellows, but I'd hate to get mixed up in their feuds. About that silver cord—"

"Oh, that!" Solomon nodded, then went on, with slow hesitation: "Why, sir, that's the emblem of a Chinese secret society, so to speak. Up in China, sir, you 'ave Russia in the north, but you 'ave Asia in the east, west, and south, just like that, and a werry secret thing Asia is. Mr. Carter. I—I—I—well, I'll be—I'll be danged!"

Solomon blindly set down his pipe and leaned back with a deep breath of amazement. His eyes had fallen upon the doorway, and remained fixed there like two blue saucers. Carter turned, and saw nothing at all except a slip of paper that had apparently fallen inside the doorway.

"What's the matter?" demanded the American sharply.

Solomon did not reply, but clapped his hands, and again hastily there came to the doorway an Arab dressed in spotless white. Solomon addressed him in a very agitated fashion, and the Arab called a second like himself. They both seemed to be denying vehemently any knowledge of the paper, which the first Arab picked up and handed to Solomon. He dismissed them and laid the paper before Carter, with a flare of anger in his usually placid eyes.

"Look at that!" he fairly growled. Then his face was once more emotionless, and he picked up his pipe and filled it anew.

Looking down at the paper, Carter frowned, perplexed by all this bother over a scrawled, or rather brushed, Chinese drawing. It was a very sketchy representation of a foot with outstretched claws, and nothing more.

"H'm! Did our recent visitor drop this?" queried Carter.

"Nothing very exciting in it! What's the meaning of it, Solomon? A cat's paw?"

"No, sir. A lion's paw, or a tiger's paw, as the Chinese call it. Another emblem o' that 'ere secret society. Well, sir, now I *am* in for it, and no mistake, as the old gent said when 'e married 'is third!"

Carter stirred uneasily. This host of his was a very peculiar chap, beyond a doubt!

"Then our visitor with the silver cord dropped this paper?"

"No, sir. 'E come to me from Mr. Wing Fu, who 'as a big shop just over the Red Bridge. This 'ere tiger's paw was put 'ere by some one else—just who I can't say. But it was sent by another man as 'as gone out o' that 'ere secret society and set up in business on 'is own, so to speak; a werry intelligent man 'e is, too. You might 'ave 'eard of 'im, sir—a Dutch hall-caste 'e is, wi' Chinese blood in 'im, by name o' Herman Stoppel."

"I sold him a typewriter last month," said Carter dryly.

He knew very well who Herman Stoppel was. A half-caste in blood, but a Dutch exterior, Stoppel was a wealthy trader whom honest men avoided, and whose trading schooners bore devilish names and shady reputations throughout the thirteen ports.

It seemed more than a trifle odd to Carter that John Solomon talked so freely about that secret society. He had already conjectured that there was a good deal more to Solomon than appeared on the surface, and he wondered if the man had some ulterior motive in thus explaining circumstances which ordinarily would be passed over without explanation. In the China Seas, men do not talk of secret societies, for in many words there is folly.

"I've seen quite a bit o' you, Mr. Carter," observed Solomon. "Without your knowing it, that is. In other words, sir, I've 'ad you inwestigated."

Carter met the blank blue eyes with a puzzled stare. He could not have been more astonished had Solomon suddenly drawn a revolver on him, but he said nothing.

"Yes, sir," went on the other, after a brief pause. "I'm partial to Americans, for reasons of me own, just like that. Would you 'ave any objections to takin' up a line o' work with an honest Chinaman—that 'ere same Mr. Wing Fu? If it was made worth your white?"

"I'm afraid I would have," and Carter laughed shortly. "None of this secret-society business in mine, Solomon. No tong fighting, thanks!"

"There ain't goin' to be none, sir. Now, Mr. Carter, if so be as you 'ad a chance to earn good money and come back to your present business later on, with a five per-cent interest in a mortal pot as is goin' to be fought for werry soon indeed—would you take it? More by token, if you could do an American girl a werry good turn by doin' of it?"

"Come down to figures," said Carter quietly. "What salary, and what's the pot?"

"Five 'undred gold dollars a month salary. A five-percent interest in a two-million-dollar pot, just like that! Only, with an element o' danger attached—don't forget that, sir!"

Carter sipped his iced coffee. His eyes were cool and reflective, but behind them burned a consuming fire. A hundred-thousand-dollar stake was worth "an element of danger!"

Ralph Carter was no stranger to peril, in a certain sense. He had been in these seas for two years, and with the usual white man's dream of wealth; had hunted rubies in Burma, and gold in the Malay States, with the usual result. He had a tiger robe, a working knowledge of Low Malay and Dutch, a good deal of experience, and the realization that unless one could get "on the inside" there was no sudden wealth to be had for the asking.

Here, it might seem, was his chance to get on the inside. But, he asked himself, *was* it such a chance? He knew nothing of this man Solomon.

"I've no stomach for Chinese feuds," he returned slowly. "From your hints, I gather that Herman Stoppel has sidestepped his chink brethren and would like to cut their throats, or they would like to cut his."

"Beggin' your pardon, sir, it ain't nothing of the kind," said Solomon. "I'll take me davy on it, sir! 'Ere it is, all shipshape and proper: This American girl, name o' Bergen, 'ad a werry ill brother who bought a plantation on one o' the Spice Islands—the Moluccas, and she come out to 'elp 'im run it. 'E up and died, just like that.

"Well, this 'ere Mr. Stoppel, 'e cut in makin' love to 'er, and 'elped 'is friends to steal 'alf the plantation, pretendin' all the time as 'ow 'e was a good friend to 'er, which same she still thinks. Stoppel is a goin' there this week in 'is schooner *Zamiel*, takin' a friend o' his to manage things for 'er. Mr. Wing Fu, 'e wants some one to cut in a 'ead o' Stoppel—some one as is honest and can fight Stoppel—"

Carter held up a protesting hand.

"Your tongue's running away with the story, Solomon. A plantation isn't worth two million dollars. Stoppel is a dirty bound, by all accounts, but if she wants to marry him, that's her lookout. Now, then, what *is* worth two million dollars? And where do Wing Fu and his tong come in? You've missed connections."

" 'Is tong, as you call it, sir, don't come in," said Solomon wearily. "Stoppel 'as been and got 'imself in bad with the Chinese, but they ain't after 'im, as you might say. It's 'im that's warning them off 'is trail."

"I see," and Carter nodded. "Well, what connection is there, then?"

Solomon leaned forward earnestly.

"None, sir, between Mr. Wing Fu and Stoppel; it's the other way round, as the old gent said when 'e 'ad mixed 'is drinks and was a-tryin' to get 'ome. Miss Bergen's brother, 'e 'ad known Wing Fu at college—"

"At college!" exclaimed Carter amazedly. Solomon sighed resignedly.

"Yes, sir, this 'ere Mr. Wing Fu ain't an old man, so to speak. Mr. Bergen 'ad known 'im at some college in the States, and out 'ere threw quite a bit o' trade in 'is way. So Mr. Wing Fu, findin' out about this 'ere Stoppel's plans, is startin' in to fight 'im on account o' the friendship 'e 'ad with Miss Bergen's brother. Chinese is that way, sir—werry good friends to 'ave in a pinch."

Carter nodded, having heard the same thing expounded previously by others.

"What is it that's worth two million dollars?" he asked abruptly.

"Blessed if I know," was the surprising answer. Solomon frowned slightly as he spoke. "Mr. Wing Fu, 'e don't know, neither. Miss Bergen, she don't know. But Stoppel, 'e knows, right enough! It's something on the Bergen plantation—"

"Look here, are you in with a pack of lunatics?" broke out Carter, half angrily. "You've talked about a two-million-dollar pot—well, who's paying my salary, then? Don't tell me a bunch of Chinese are going after something in blind hopes of getting a fortune!"

Solomon puffed placidly at his pipe for a moment.

"It's 'ard, mortal 'ard, to explain," he made slow answer. "Stoppel, 'e's a-trying 'is blooming best to oust Miss Bergen and grab 'er plantation; 'e is a-going into it 'eart and soul, just like that! Mr. Wing Fu 'as gathered enough to know that Stoppel expects to clear two million on the thing—that's all we knows, sir! Wing Fu is a-fighting Stoppel for the sake o' Miss Bergen, and I'm a-going to 'elp in a friendly sort o' way. Now, sir, that's every danged bit I can tell you, and if so be as you don't like it, why—why, I'll be danged disappointed in you, sir! Will you take the job, or not?"

"What job?" queried Carter bluntly.

"Obeyin' orders, for the present."

"Yes," said Carter. "I'll take it."

CHAPTER II

STOPPEL CHOOSES WAR

LIKE GRAVITATES to like throughout the world. As a case in point, Herman Stoppel's fine fore-and-after schooner *Zamiel* possessed a crew wholly of Dutch and Chinese half-castes, like her owner.

Despite her unholy name, she had been making money fast for Stoppel since the war had boosted freights from Singapore and Sydney and all other ports. So it was rather odd to find her laid up at Stoppel's Surabaya wharf, down the river on the bay, lazily doing nothing.

Herman Stoppel was doing something, however—he was waiting, and with an ill grace. Each time he stopped in at the cable office and received a shake of the head, he went forth cursing; his large-built, powerful, white-clad figure exuded repressed vitality, and his dark eyes with the Mephisthelean uptwist of the brows that hinted at his Mongol blood were surcharged with raging impatience.

Then suddenly a cablegram came for him. While he was reading it with savage satisfaction, Mr. Wing Fu was reading a copy of the same message. Then Mr. Wing Fu took his silk hat and stick, went across the Red Bridge, engaged a boatman, and was wafted down the River of Gold. As he went, he pondered over that message, reading it anew, with a frown:

HERMAN STOPPEL, *Surabaya.*
If as described, stuff should bring over two million. American demand very heavy at present.

The signature was an initial, no more; the message had been sent from San Francisco. Mr. Wing Fu thoughtfully examined the banks of the muddy canal and spoke in classical Chinese, which his Javanese boatman could not understand:

"What is it for which the demand is heavy? No one seems to know except Stoppel. By the venerable ancestors of my parents, I am puzzled! I must in honor protect Miss Bergen from this thief; yet I know not what he purposes to steal! Nor does she! Stoppel knows, and he alone. Well, I shall reason with him for the last time."

When he stepped out upon the Stoppel wharf near the *Zamiel,* a Straits Chinaman who was working on a broken plank glanced up and nodded. Mr. Wing Fu buttoned his frock coat, left open the top button for better access to his armpit holster, and advanced to where Stoppel awaited him at the schooner's gangway. His yellow features were very earnest, very poised, and his thumb rested on the spring which would release his dagger cane's blade with a light pressure. Mr. Wing Fu was among enemies, and knew it. Also, his friends knew it.

"Hao nina!" said Stoppel amicably, feeling that he could well afford to be amicable. "Will you come down to my cabin?"

"Thank you," smiled Mr. Wing Fu. The Orientals know how to smile meaning into words. "My constitution is so delicate that I must remain in the open air."

"I am all sympathy," returned Stoppel blandly. "My own health is so poor that I must go voyaging to the islands to convalesce."

"Oh! Accept my regrets," said Mr. Wing Fu very earnestly. "I had heard that you were on the point of making a great deal of money—two million American dollars. I am glad that you have given up this idea, for the sake of your health."

Stoppel's burly features reddened slightly. His Mongol blood was uppermost just now, however, and he made no comment on his visitor's surprising knowledge.

"Will you smoke?" Stoppel extended a cigarette case, and Mr.

Wing Fu accepted. "I hear that the cockney ship chandler," he went on, "has received a celebrated Chinese painting."

"Yes." Mr. Wing Fu puffed reflectively. "The picture of a tiger's paw."

"I hope," said Stoppel, with Dutch bluntness, "that he will consider it valuable."

"That would depend upon the source," returned Mr. Wing Fu idly. "Foolish people have played with the tiger's paw to their great detriment. The tiger's claws have a terribly strong grip, my friend. I have known them to rip open a man's belly."

A fleeting grin twisted Stoppel's handsome, powerful lips into cold cruelty.

"Bullets will slay tigers," he answered. Mr. Wing Fu nodded.

"You are determined upon this voyage then?"

"Yes," said Stoppel, almost defiantly. His eyes were a trifle uneasy, as though he were inwardly more than a little afraid of this gentlemanly, quiet yellow man.

"I wish you great benefits to your health," and Mr. Wing Fu smiled again. "The islands are not healthy to all people, however."

"Proper precautions may be taken," said Stoppel, just as sweetly.

"Of course," responded Mr. Wing Fu. "Of course. Do you return in ballast, or with a cargo?"

Stoppel's eyes gleamed. He knew the reason for this visit at last.

"With a cargo," he said, grinning widely. "A cargo of emerald and ruby—and other things, my friend!"

Mr. Wing Fu made a little gesture as though dismissing the subject, and tossed his cigarette butt over the rail.

"May you find all that you seek, and more," he winged the Parthian shaft neatly. "And if you have any commissions that my firm could execute, in the event of your health not finding any benefit, we shall be very happy to be at your service."

Stoppel expressed his thanks, and Mr. Wing Fu took his

leave. He took it very circumspectly, with a watchful eye upon the half-castes of the *Zamiel's* crew, but he regained his waiting *tambangan* without incident.

Ultra-Oriental had been that conversation, each phrase pregnant with unsaid meanings, and each man had been perfectly understood by the other. Stoppel, for example, knew that Mr. Wing Fu was ignorant of his aim and purpose, and knew also that he had been duly warned. Mr. Wing Fu knew that he was defied to do his utmost. That talk of a cargo of emerald and ruby was utter jesting, of course.

The boat's three-cornered sail was run up, and Mr. Wing Fu was wafted up the Kali Mas to the Red Bridge. He paid his boatman at the landing here, dodged a coolie truck and a racing motor, and escaped into the peace of the Chinese quarter, with a sigh of relief. In another five minutes he passed through his own office and joined Solomon and Ralph Carter in the privacy of the back room.

"Failed," he said in excellent English, dropping into a chair and taking a cigarette from a taboret. "He goes in ballast—and defies us."

Solomon methodically whittled tobacco into his pipe. Carter kept silent, as he had learned to do in the past two days, since his acceptance of this fellowship.

"Put a knife in 'im," suggested Solomon after a moment. Mr. Wing Fu smiled faintly.

"Murder, my dear Mr. Solomon, is an easily used weapon. Suppose you try it."

"Who, me? I ain't in that line o' work, sir."

"Neither am I." Mr. Wing Fu and John Solomon smiled as men who understand each other.

"Werry right you are," observed Solomon. "An easy weapon it is, just like that; a reg'lar two-edged sword, that's what I calls it! Cuts back, it does, well as for'ard. Well, we ain't murderers, Mr. Carter! You needn't to be lookin' so grave-eyed about it, as the old gent said when 'e up and kissed the 'ousemaid."

Carter laughed shortly.

"I'm not worried about you chaps. What's to be done?"

"Stoppel sails to-night," said Mr. Wing Fu promptly. "He must be stopped."

Solomon lighted his pipe, and through the gray smoke his blue eyes twinkled.

"I'll stop 'im," he volunteered. "A couple o' them 'ere Arab friends o' mine can bore a 'ole through the *Zamiel's* planks after dark, and 'ave three feet o' water in 'er afore 'e knows it. What then?"

Mr. Wing Fu leaned forward and spoke earnestly for two minutes. Solomon nodded, and Carter, after a surprised glance, rose.

"Then I'd better pack," he said quietly. "No time to lose, eh?"

Mr. Wing Fu touched a gong, and one of his countrymen appeared at the door, to whom he addressed a few words in Chinese. Then he turned to Carter, rose, and shook hands.

"Good luck!" he said smilingly. "Mr. Solomon will meet you at the Kleine Boom in an hour, with tickets and necessary funds. You've just time to make the steamer."

"And after I get to Banda Lontar?" queried Carter. "Stoppel bought a typewriter from me three weeks ago, and will know—"

"He probably knows now that you are with us," was the Celestial's dry comment. "However, no matter about that. The first thing is to apprise Miss Bergen of the situation; the second, to guard her interests; the third, to discover what Stoppel is after, and to frustrate him."

"I will be alone?" asked the American.

"Hardly, my friend! I have an agent at Banda Neira—"

"I'm a-goin' to the islands meself," broke in Solomon, to the surprise of Mr. Wing Fu.

"To-day?" exclaimed Carter. "With me?"

"No, sir." Solomon chuckled wheezily at the astonished glances bent upon him. "No, in a couple o' days."

"But there is no steamer until next week, after to-day's!" remonstrated the Chinese.

"I knows that, sir," was Solomon's unruffled answer. "This 'ere game is werry interesting, as the old gent said when 'e married 'is third. So I'm a-going along o' Mr. Stoppel, just like that."

"You're going—with Stoppel!" repeated Carter blankly. "Why, he knows that you're in with Mr. Wing Fu, here—he knows you for an enemy—"

"And werry contemptuous o' me 'e is," was the sage response. "You wait and see! I knows 'im. It'll fair tickle 'im to death to 'ave me on 'is bloody ship. Now you take that 'ere mylord o' mine what's at the door, Mr. Carter. I'll meet you at the custom 'ouse."

Rather bewildered, Carter took his leave. In the street he found Solomon's victoria, locally termed a "mylord," and sank into the cushions while the driver bowled him along to his lodgings in the residence quarter. The half hour's drive gave him time to get mentally squared off, and he began to realize that Solomon's plan was not so wildly incredible.

Stoppel knew the little cockney for an enemy, and despised him; and for this reason would be glad to take Solomon to the Moluccas in order, as he might think, to keep Solomon under his eye and hand. The Eurasian was the type of man who likes to have his enemy in sight and within scheming distance.

Besides, if Solomon said that he would go to the Bandas with Stoppel, he would do it by some hook or crook—even if he had to stow himself away aboard the *Zamiel*. In the past two days Carter had come to know John Solomon fairly well, had found him a man of amazingly unsuspected abilities, and had come to respect his piercingly accurate judgment of men and things.

So arguing with himself, Ralph Carter gained his lodgings, packed a suit case, and took his mylord back to the Kleine Boom. After all, he considered, Stoppel's bark might be worse than his bite, nor was he apt to murder Solomon in cold blood!

At the customhouse landing he found Solomon awaiting him with a *tambangan* ready. They at once got into the boat, and on the way out to the anchorage, where the squat but comfortable little steamer of the Koninklijke Paketvaart Maatschappij lay with steam up, Solomon handed Carter his tickets and a hundred dollars, gold.

"She goes direct to Banda Neira via Macassar," he said. "And I wishes you a werry 'appy trip, sir."

"Same to you," and Carter chuckled.

"You want to watch werry sharp," cautioned Solomon gravely. "You'll 'ave two weeks' time afore we gets to Banda, and one or two o' Stoppel's friends may run into you."

"And you'll cable Miss Bergen that I'm coming?"

"Yes, sir." Solomon wriggled uneasily. "But 'ave a care with 'er, sir. You see, she ain't werry certain about Stoppel in 'er own mind, and you'll 'ave to 'andle 'er gentlelike. Women is werry uncertain quantities, as the old gent said when 'e buried 'is third! There's a letter o' recommendation from Mr. Wing Fu in them 'ere papers—"

"See here!" demanded the American hotly. "Who does she think I am?"

"Women is apt to think 'most anything, sir. I expect she'll take you for a gent as wants to buy 'er spice groves, from Mr. Wing Fu's letter."

"And its up to me to play that part?"

"Until so be as you thinks it safe to tell 'er the truth, Mr. Carter. And don't forget to praise 'er old furniture, sir—that's one of 'er 'obbies. But 'ere we are—"

Carter mounted the ladder and waved farewell to Solomon, feeling very much confused. Solomon had craftily kept from him until the last moment the exact part he would have to play with Miss Bergen; evidently the little cockney had no great opinion of young women.

"Nix—she must be an old maid!" thought Carter, as he went to his stateroom. "What's this talk about old furniture? Seems like a queer hobby to ride in this part of the world! Well, I'm on a queer job myself, and that's a fact!"

He tipped the steward, entered his stateroom, and slammed
the door. As he did so, a scrap of folded paper on the floor caught
his eye, and he picked it up and opened it. Before him appeared
a sketched tiger's paw—the duplicate of that which Solomon
had found!

"Well—I'll be—be blessed!" ejaculated Carter. "It's not an
hour since Solomon got my reservation—yet the thing is here
waiting for me! All right, Mr. Herman Stoppel. You may think
you have my number, and I'll admit you're a very slick individ-
ual—but you watch out! Something mighty unpleasant is apt
to happen to you one of these days, if you play any more of your
little tricks around me!"

CHAPTER III

THE BANDAS

LIKE EVERY one else aboard, Ralph Carter stood on the deck of the packet boat as she steamed into the Sun Gate, and gave himself up to enjoyment of the wonderful scene.

No further evidence of Stoppel's men had come to him after that first warning when he had come aboard. If any were on the ship, he had not encountered them.

The Bandas are three islands divided by narrow channels: Gunong Api, the volcano, Banda Neira, the town, and Banda Lontar, the plantation. As the ship headed in between, it seemed to Carter that she was entering a blind cleft amid the towering rocks; but presently the cleft opened out, the vivid blue of the water and green of the hillsides was broken by a strip of white beach, and high into the sky towered the great striped volcano with its eternal vapor.

Then the ship was through, and with exquisite delight Carter saw before him the heart of the Spice Islands. He had plenty of time to enjoy it, since the steamer warped for half an hour against the strong currents of the Sun Gate, beating up slowly to the wharf. Against the green hills stood out the white, red-tiled town, the ancient fortifications rising behind, and throughout the hills were dotted white plantation houses. On the other side, across the channel or Oostergat, appeared Banda Lontar, a solid mass of foliage, with its nutmeg and sheltering kanari trees.

"Talk about vivid coloring!" breathed Carter admiringly. "If

New York could ever see this place, it'd have a string of tourists all winter! I'm glad I came."

Almost too soon, it seemed, the boat rode up to the wharf, where the Resident and residents of Banda Neira awaited her coming. And there Carter found himself awaited also, for as he stepped ashore a polite Dutch officer touched his shoulder and informed him that the Resident wished to speak with him.

The Resident examined his papers, then introduced him to a young lady by the name of Mejuffrouw or Miss Willhelmina Bergen. And after that, Carter quite forgot what happened until he found himself walking up an adjacent wharf beside Miss Bergen, while she conned Mr. Wing Fu's letter, and a native boy marched before with Carter's grip to the ferryboat.

It was because of the former Dutch extraction of the Bergens, and because this girl's father had been an American consul in Holland, that her brother had been enabled to acquire a plantation in the Spice Isles—no easy thing to get hold of. These things Carter learned by degrees later.

The girl herself astounded him, drove all else from his mind momentarily. She was dark, capable, sun-touched to a golden brown, with dancing brown eyes which frowned just a trifle over Mr. Wing Fu's letter, then looked up at him with a gay comprehension which hardly jibed with her words:

"I thought you had a machinery business in Surabaya, Mr. Carter?" While she spoke, he felt as though she were laughing at him. "You see, I am personal—one has to be, out here. Also, I had you looked up upon getting a cable from Mr. Wing Fu that you were coming—"

"And you didn't understand why I wanted to buy a plantation?" Carter smiled. She had flung him off balance, and he took a desperate chance. "Well, to be frank, I don't want to buy any, Miss Bergen. I do want to have a look at yours, though."

She glanced across the water thoughtfully, then her eyes came back to his.

"Don't you think we'd better understand each other?" she said quietly. "I know very well what a friend Mr. Wing Fu was to my brother. I know that you come on behalf of Mr. Wing Fu, and I do not quite see why he should write what is not true."

Carter took heart. He had to fling aside in a moment all his preparations, and meet this girl on her own ground.

"He was not sure that you would receive me otherwise," was his grave response. "I think he feared lest you think him—and me also—officious in this. I had many things to see you about, and we had no time at all to discuss the matter before this steamer left Surabaya; in fact, I came at an hour's notice. So please be charitable toward Mr. Wing Fu!"

She laughed frankly and extended her hand.

"Thank you for that little speech—I do *so* hate to be kept in the dark about things! As for Wing Fu, I only wish that some white men I know were as thorough gentlemen as he is. So come along, please! I have a boat waiting, and we'll get home before dark. You'll stop at the plantation, of course—I'm frightfully anxious to hear what you have come to talk over!"

Her swift attack, adjustment of differences, and acceptance of his errand left Carter breathless, bewildered. Had she been a man, exactly so would she have greeted him, for she had smashed down his defenses and established a working basis between them with masculine directness and frankness.

Yet, Carter told himself, with vague delight, there was nothing mannish about her. A lissome, sure-footed figure of a girl she was, with cheeks deliciously pink in the sea wind, a mouth firm-lipped yet carved delicately, and her pongee gown swung to the lines of a lithe, trim body as marvelously close to perfection as ever a sculptor modeled. Like the great tender cameo shell that one finds on the beach at Ambon she was more delicate than any filigree, yet strong to withstand the rough sea surges.

Carter watched her, fascinated, as the boatmen ferried them across the Oostergat to the island of nutmegs. The authority that sat in her voice, the half-glimpsed coquetry that shone unaffected in her eyes, the *joi de vivre* and the vitality which her spirit wielded—these things went to make up a character as complex as it was charming. Carter thanked his stars that he had not lied to her about his errand.

She did not commiserate with him about the cockroaches aboard ship, or the other sad banalities of subtropical travel; she sat in silence, her brown eyes fastened upon the curving crescent of the shore ahead, her long, sun-browned fingers locked upon her knee. Carter noted that beneath the edges of her sun helmet her hair showed brown like her eyes—a rich golden brown, warm and radiant as the glowing brown silk weaves of Kedah.

The native rowers swung the boat in beside a low, long wharf. Landing, Carter picked up his grip and strode beside the girl along a shell-strewn walk that seemed to lead interminably through the greenery ahead. On every hand, beneath the magnificently towering kanari trees, shone the deep green of the nutmegs and their yellow fruit.

"Do you like it?" she asked quietly.

"It's—it's beyond words!" responded Carter, inhaling the spice-laden air. "I didn't know I would get here at bearing time."

"Oh, they bear all the year round!" she returned, smiling. "These are the government plantations. You have a two-mile walk to mine."

"I'm glad of that," said Carter. Her brown eyes came to his, then were routed before his frank laugh. "Honestly," he went on, with almost boyish enthusiasm, "I never dreamed there could be such a paradise as this! And to add real American girls as houris—well, I suppose you're used to it, but I'm not. The islands must be crowded with rich Dutchmen."

They were not, as she presently made clear. The chief traders of the islands were Arabs. While the Dutch had maintained a spice monopoly, the islands had been residential centers; but within the last hundred years all this had changed. The Bandas were now like one or two other islands which Carter had seen— whited sepulchers of past grandeur, their palaces peopled by bats, their native populations vanished, their streets tenanted by desolation.

And presently Carter saw before him just such a house as he had from the steamer seen on Banda Neira—a house of pergolas, of marble columns and marble terraces; a house built a hundred years previously, and now, in its decadent years, glorified with fresh paint and watchful care. This was the Bergen plantation house.

"We've made the old place comfortable—or at least half of it," said the girl, as two Chinese servants opened the massive front doors. "It was far too large for us, and—and after Fred died—my brother, you know—I've had enough to do to keep up the half which we occupied. Chang, will you show Mr. Carter to his room?"

Yielding his grip to the Chinese butler, Carter followed him up a huge staircase with a carved balustrade of rosewood; he glimpsed huge rooms, paneled with sandalwood and red teak; he saw for the first time some of that furniture which Solomon had mentioned; and he came to rest at length in a neatly curtained bedroom, one of several which had been partitioned out of the enormous chambers of a bygone day. Upon the wall hung a large portrait of a young man exceedingly like Miss Bergen, with a faded fraternity banner above, and Carter knew that he had been given the room which had been Fred Bergen's.

"Troubled waters ahead," he reflected, as he changed into a fresh suit of pongee. The swift tropic darkness was falling, and Chang had lighted a lamp in the room. "Just how she'll take my message is a question. According to first indications, she's already lined up with Wing Fu—but she's a woman, and therefore full of surprises."

Although unsummoned, Chang made his appearance at exactly the right moment, and led Carter downstairs. In a drawing-room where candles glittered from high sconces over shimmering pieces of old rosewood and mahogany, the American found Miss Bergen awaiting him. With her was a dumpy, pleasant-faced old Dutch lady, whom she introduced as Mevrouw van der Gelt, her companion and friend. The mevrouw was a quiet, silent old lady who knew not a word of English and who found Carter's Hollandsch gravely amusing.

Dinner was served in a great dining room paneled to the ceiling in red teak, and bearing huge silver-plated sconces, each holding a dozen candles. It was a good meal, well served; Miss Bergen explained that she was one of a very few hereabouts who could keep their Chinese servants, there being in the Bandas a pronounced lack of Chinese. Her ability to do this, conjectured Carter, was probably due to some wide-flung influence exerted by Mr. Wing Fu. Nor was the guess far wrong.

Dinner over, the three adjourned to the library, another huge paneled room where logs burned in an immense fireplace, for dampness had crept in upon the wings of the sea wind; the fire, as Miss Bergen explained, exerted little heat in the immense room, and was pleasant to watch.

Mevrouw van der Gelt picked up her knitting and reposed in the recesses of a great settle beside the fire. Miss Bergen and Carter sat in deep old chairs of carved rosewood, fetched from Holland a century gone, while Chang served coffee and laid beside Carter a small taboret holding cigars.

"Now," said Miss Bergen, gazing into the fire, "I am anxious to hear your message, Mr. Carter. The mevrouw speaks no English, and we need not consider her."

Carter reflectively lighted a cheroot. With every moment he found himself liking this girl more, admiring her more. Where her brother had failed through ill health, and had died, she had made this plantation, which was her sole wealth, a fruitful source of income. The great war, with its prohibitive freight rates, he had discovered, had led her to store her mace and nutmegs against a future day.

"I'll be quite frank with you," he said slowly, "but you mustn't mind if I ask some questions first. This affair is not straight in my own mind, Miss Bergen. First, do you know Mr. Wing Fu personally."

"No. I have corresponded with him, and my brother knew him."

"That explains his ignorance of your character," he responded, and she smiled at the words. "Now, then, is the plantation in the same shape as when your brother bought it?"

"Yes and no," she answered, frowning slightly until her delicate brows were like a penciled line above her eyes. "It was originally eighty acres; I have sold thirty-five of these in order to get money for current expenses. My crops have been stored for two years."

"Insured?" queried Carter.

"Of course. But I have made my smaller acreage do as well as any twice the size around here."

"I don't doubt it. Who bought that thirty-five acres, if I may inquire?"

"I do not know. They were sold through an—an agent, Mr. Stoppel, of Surabaya."

He was inspecting the end of his cigar frowningly, and did not catch the lightning-swift glance which she sent at him as she uttered Stoppel's name.

"And you got the money for the land you sold?" he asked.

"Again yes and no." A flush crept into her cheeks. "Captain Knowles, an Englishman who has resided here for thirty years and who acts as financial agent for Stoppel and others, gave me a Batavia draft for the amount. Two days later, when I went to bank the draft, it was gone, and it has never been found."

"What!" Carter's brows lifted. "Stolen?"

"No." She pointed to a small wall safe set into the paneling above the fireplace. "I kept it in that safe with my loose cash and personal valuables. It was simply gone, that's all. Nothing else was touched, so it was not robbery. I have often wondered if I were not careless enough to drop the draft into the fireplace without noticing it."

Carter was silent for a moment. He remembered how Solomon had told him that Stoppel had thieved half the Bergen plantation.

"I'm getting down to the end of my inquiries," he said, smiling apologetically. "I'd like to meet this Captain Knowles. What sort of a chap is he?"

"You may judge for yourself in the morning. He'll be over then to meet you and to inspect some of my furniture—he wants to buy some of it."

"I don't wonder," said Carter. "It's magnificent."

She laughed. "Oh, you haven't seen—but let that wait on the morrow. Now, what else can I enlighten you upon?"

He hesitated, then attacked openly:

"Is Herman Stoppel one of your friends?"

"Yes." With the word she shot another lightning glance at him. This one he caught, but could not interpret, except to know that she was upon her guard.

"May I say anything against him without offending you?" he asked coolly.

"Why should you say anything against him?" she parried. But her gaze met his with as firm and piercing a quality as his own.

"Because I wish to," said Carter, half angrily. "Because that is part of my errand here. Because three men are doing their best to save to you something of almost inestimable value, and because a fourth man is coming here to get that thing for himself."

He was startled by the effect of his words. The girl leaned forward, staring at him with distended eyes, her lips parted breathlessly. Tension had gripped her, and a tensed eagerness forced her next words into a whisper:

"Yes? And what is this—this thing of value?"

"Don't you know?" demanded Carter, almost roughly.

"No!" Her eyes shone at him like stars.

"Then, in Heaven's name, who does?" he exclaimed. She relaxed in her chair, and the color came back in a flood to her cheeks. Fearing lest he drive anger into her soul, and having sufficiently proved all that had been told him by Solomon and Wing Fu, Carter went ahead recklessly before she could speak.

He sketched that scene at the shop of Solomon, when he had first entered this game. He bluntly expatiated on the fact that Mr. Wing Fu was acting in an entirely disinterested fashion, as was Solomon. He laid before her all that had been said of Stoppel, all that he knew of Stoppel, and curtly chided her for claiming such a man as friend.

Half measures were not the choice of Ralph Carter. He said more than he had any right to say regarding her seeming carelessness in trusting Herman Stoppel and his friends, but to his surprise and vague uneasiness, his words sent no anger leaping into her eyes. Instead, he found there a hint of the same gay laughter with which she had greeted him at their meeting. And when she made answer, her words dumfounded him:

"This story might have been easily fabricated, Mr. Carter. Your letter from Wing Fu might have been forged. You might have come here as an agent of Herman Stoppel, with the intent of drawing me into some cunning trap."

She paused, meeting his astounded gaze with grave eyes.

"That," she went on steadily, "was my first impression. I suspected you. But your words have shown me that you are a very honest gentleman, Mr. Carter, and I apologize for my suspicions. Further, I must ask your pardon for doing something I had no right to do—for opening a letter which came here yesterday, addressed to you. It was posted here in Banda Neira, and the contents so thoroughly bear out your story."

She took from her bodice an envelope and extended it. Carter drew forth a sheet of soft rice paper, upon which was sketched a tiger's claw—but now with a difference. This was drawn with red ink, and the claws were outstretched as if to grip. A most palpable warning, sent by some local agent of Stoppel's!

"Please pardon me," she went on. "You do not know what tricks have surrounded me here, what attempts have been made to get this plantation away from me! I could trust no one. At times I have almost given up in despair."

"What!" Carter's gray eyes blazed out at her. "Then—you mean that you have not been deceived by Stoppel's protestations of friendship?"

"I was deceived at first," she answered, staring into the fire. "Then suddenly I began to see that there was something I had not suspected. Stoppel offered to buy this plantation and everything in it at an absurd price—far beyond its value. Captain Knowles has tried to buy my furniture collection in the same way. There's something here—something that Stoppel wants—something valuable! I hoped that you might know what it was, Mr. Carter.

"If I only knew!" She made a little gesture of despair and faced him again. "I am at the end of my string. I can ship no spices until the war ends, and meantime the expense goes on. I sold nearly half the plantation and carelessly lost the money. I owe my servants their wages—oh, it's terrible! And now Stoppel is coming here, and I know he'll make me a lucrative offer for the place."

Carter's lips tightened as he listened. In the girl's face and words he read that this was no momentary weakness, but the despair that comes of fighting a losing battle to the end. Wilhelmina Bergen had fought, and was close to the end, and knew it.

"How much money would carry you," he asked shortly.

"If I could get a shipload of my spices to Singapore, I would need no loan," she returned, flushing a little. For a moment Carter gazed into the fire, then his face relaxed in a grim, mirthless smile.

"You shall have the ship," he said. "Do you trust me far enough to appoint me manager of this plantation, with power to make such transactions as I see fit?"

"Yes," she said, her eyes on his.

"Then let's wait till morning and see what Knowles is after, eh? Good!"

CHAPTER IV

CAPTAIN KNOWLES

WITH THE following morning, Carter had formu-
lated a somewhat hazy system of campaign.

"It's fairly certain," he said to Miss Bergen, as they stood
together on the marble terrace and gazed over the Oostergat
at the white town in the hills, "that something on this place
of yours is worth about two million dollars—something that
Stoppel expects to market in the States, something that he can
carry off in his schooner, something that can't be very well stolen.
Otherwise, it would have been stolen before this! What, then, is
this 'something' of which only Stoppel knows the secret?"

The girl shook her head.

"I've asked myself that question a hundred times, Mr. Carter.
See—there's an *orembai* coming over; that must be Captain
Knowles."

Across the water they could see one of the native ferryboats
creeping toward the shore. Carter, however, reverted to something the girl had said the previous evening.

"This Captain Knowles—an agent for Stoppel, eh? And he
wants to buy your furniture? Well, that may be a clew. What is
this furniture?"

"Another of my dreams of wealth which the lack of shipping
dissipated," and the girl laughed mirthlessly. "You know, over on
Banda Neira are dozens of magnificent old palaces, built when
the spice trade was at its height and furnished from Europe.

To-day they can be bought for a few dollars—real estate is worth nothing here.

"Well, at home you may be aware of the absurdly high prices paid for old furniture, and the immense amount of faked stuff that is palmed off as antique? Here, however, was an immense quantity of the rarest, choicest furniture, genuine beyond all doubt—such furniture as New York or even New Orleans seldom sees! So when I first came out here I quietly bought up all the best of it. I have mahogany and rosewood and tulipwood and exquisite Adam and Sheraton—well, wait till you see it! If I could only get that stuff to San Francisco now, it would pay a small fortune in itself."

"It could not have been this regarding which Stoppel cabled to Frisco?" pondered Carter. "The American demand being heavy—"

With a flame in her brown eyes, the girl made a gesture of anger.

"Stoppel! When it comes to fine furniture, he is a vandal, no more!" she declared hotly. "Besides, even at Fifth Avenue prices, the stuff would bring only about twenty-five thousand dollars, I believe. That is enough to be considered a fortune by me, but Stoppel is well on toward being a millionaire and would not go out of his way after that sum. He is on the track of something larger."

"Right," and Cater assented. "We'll have to look farther than furniture to find that two-million-dollar stake. By the way, what craft is that over in the harbor—that schooner there by the wharf. You spoke of wanting a ship."

"That is the *Belial*, one of Stoppel's fleet. She has been under charter by Baodela Brothers, the big Arab merchants here."

"And isn't she now? Couldn't we get hold of her?"

The girl shook her head. "Knowles is the agent, but he tells me that the *Belial* is unseaworthy and is awaiting Stoppel's arrival with stores in another schooner. Another way of cutting me off from money, that's all. It's too expensive to ship by packet boat to Surabaya, then transship to Singapore; and, since the war broke, Stoppel has had almost a monopoly of the inter-island schooner trade. So there I am."

"Knowles again! By glory!" Carter's eyes widened. "Please introduce me to him as a prospective buyer, will you, and back up whatever I say? There was something tricky in the disappearance of that draft he gave you—it looks queer to me. H'm! Fate is playing into our hands, after all! Give me twenty minutes alone with him before he leaves, will you?"

She nodded, perplexed by his attitude. Carter puffed at his pipe suddenly elated by the idea which had whipped across his mind; elated by the game which was his to play, elated by the very presence of this girl beside him!

He had two weeks or less in which to work before Stoppel arrived. Stoppel was at sea and out of touch with Knowles, but had doubtless warned Knowles that Carter was coming; the red tiger's paw testified to that. Miss Bergen read his thought.

"Won't Knowles know who you are?"

"No! Stoppel had to cable him, and would not trust much to a cable. By glory, we'll win out on this!" Carter laughed outright, and impulsively his hand went down and closed upon the girl's slim fingers in a frank, swift grip of comradeship. "I'm going to get this Knowles up against the ropes—you watch him fall for my game, Miss Bergen! Now, give me an option on your plantation and stored spice—hurry!"

She stared at him, flushing a little beneath the eager flame of his gray eyes.

"An option? At what price—"

"No price at all! Hurry up, before he gets here—a ninety-day option!"

"All right. I give you a ninety-day option on my plantation and stored spice—so there!"

She rattled off the words, laughing the while. Carter's boyish laughter was infectious. He had given no hint of any scheme, and it appeared that his outbreak was due only to the optimistic self-confidence of youth and high spirits.

Ralph Carter, however, knew exactly what he was about.

Shortly thereafter, Captain Knowles appeared, marching up the shell-strewn pathway between the nutmeg groves. A thin man he was, shrunken by years of tropical sun. His right eye was gone, and his left flamed with a deep, deep blue—the exact blue of the great sapphire eyes in the image of Buddha under Tanggan Hill.

The leathery features of Knowles were old and wise and crafty. He walked like a soldier, and carried an ebony swagger stick which bore the silver crest of a forgotten East India Company regiment. He seemed like the relic of a dead generation, when laws were but made for the breaking and gentlemen adventurers thronged the Eastern seas.

Only that sapphire eye, that wondrously rich blue eye, spoke in eloquent betrayal of what vitality burned far within the dry husk of the man!

He removed his helmet and bowed. Miss Bergen introduced him to Carter—"a gentleman from Surabaya who is interested in the islands." The two men shook hands, and Carter found the captain's grip dry, curt, with unexpected power. A man evidently not to be wholly judged by appearances!

"Your first visit to our islands, Mr. Carter?" said Knowles, as they sat down. He took a cheroot from the box Chang proffered him, and mouthed it without lighting. His English was without accent, precise and dry. He had lived here thirty years. "I trust you are not disappointed in them, sir?"

"On the contrary, I am enchanted!" Carter glanced at Miss Bergen as he spoke. "In fact, if Miss Bergen and I can come to terms, I may remain here. A fine place, sir!"

Captain Knowles started slightly. His deep blue eye narrowed.

"Oh!" he said. "Then you—er—pardon the question—you are seeking to invest here?"

"That is my present thought," admitted Carter modestly.

"I hope you'll not regret it," said Knowles, and turned to the girl. "As I told you yesterday, Miss Bergen, I'd be very glad indeed to look at your furniture, in case you care to dispose of it in part. I—ah—I have a love of antiques—"

He paused, and Miss Bergen rose, with a smile.

"I'll be delighted to show you what I have, Captain Knowles! Mr. Carter is also anxious to see my collection, although much of it is crated for removal. If you'll come with me—"

At that mention of Carter, Captain Knowles dropped his cheroot. He stooped to pick it up, and stamped out stray sparks.

"Ah—most unfortunate! Clumsy," he grumbled. "Getting on in years—eh what? I'll be charmed to see it, I assure you!"

Carter followed them into the house, wondering, as he went, why that mention of his interest in the furniture should have startled Captain Knowles so perceptibly.

The three passed through into that half of the great house which Carter had not yet seen—a musty half, its great rooms thick with dust. Here was stored the furniture collected by Miss Bergen, and Carter found its value very apparent.

Nearly all of the collection was in rosewood, although there were a few Sheraton pieces in mahogany, and two or three with inlays of tulip and other woods. Massive sofas, highboys, buffets alternated with chairs and tables of all shapes and designs. Almost every piece was a master work of carving, for Miss Bergen had selected the best only; none were less than a hundred years old, while some possessed twice that age.

Captain Knowles priced two chairs and a table that were uncrated, and promptly bought them, although Miss Bergen very frankly stated that she charged New York prices, at figures which amazed Carter. Then, as the three came back into the huge hallway, Captain Knowles uttered an exclamation of delight:

"There!" He pointed behind the stairs with his swagger stick. "There is a piece I have always admired, Miss Bergen! I don't suppose, now, you'd part with that?"

Carter saw a monstrous piece of rosewood—a great hall seat, completely covered with carving. In surprise at its size, he went up to it and found that it was too heavy to be readily lifted. It had no particular lines, and this was explained by an oval amid the carving of the back; within the oval were cut three Chinese ideographs. The thing was of Chinese make, then!

"I'm afraid not," and Miss Bergen smiled slightly. "I really don't know the value of that, captain. It's an old piece which was here when we came—in fact, it was boxed, down in the basement. Yet it has an odd fascination, don't you think?"

"I like it!" declared the captain frankly. "Spacious—ah—large, you know! Well, if ever you care to part with it, let me know. I say, Miss Bergen, will you not come over to town—lunch with me, eh? And you, Mr. Carter. Delighted to show you around!"

Carter glanced at the girl and winked. She hesitated; then:

"If you'll give me time to get into street clothes, Captain Knowles, I'll be most happy to do so! Make yourselves at home on the veranda, and I'll have Chang bring you fresh cheroots and a drink."

Two minutes later, Carter and Captain Knowles faced each other, and the American smiled slightly as he caught that blue eye studying him.

He knew very well that Captain Knowles had been warned against him, but not in any detail. Therefore that fact could be twisted to his own advantage, as he soon demonstrated.

"I met a man named Stoppel in Surabaya," he said, without preliminary. "Quite a nice chap, although he intimated that I was cutting in ahead of him on this plantation. He didn't seem to like the notion—why, I can't imagine. Do you know him, Captain Knowles?"

"I am his agent here," said Knowles dryly. "An agent, no more. I have met him."

Carter repressed a grin.

"Well, he referred me to you," he went on smoothly. "Said you knew more about values than any man in the islands, and also that you would give me a hand wherever possible."

"Very glad indeed to do so," was the stiff response. "In the sapphire eye rose a warmer flicker of interest, and Carter's apparently idle glance did not miss it.

"Well," he said casually, "I've just acquired a ninety-day option on this plantation."

"You've what?" snapped Knowles, swallowing hard.

Carter raised his brows in surprise. "Acquired a ninety-day option on the place."

"How much did you pay for it?" rasped the Englishman, his blue eye narrowed down to a thin and gleaming line. Carter assumed a slight offishness.

"Oh, you'll pardon me for not discussing that, captain; I've not fully decided to purchase yet, you see. I'll ask your advice later, if I may impose on your good nature. Just at present there's something else you can do for me, if you will."

"Glad, very glad!" said Knowles, settling back in his chair. He had received a hard jolt, and his fingers were shaking as he poured a stiff drink from the bottle Chang had placed between them. "Here's how!"

Carter nodded and puffed for a moment.

"It's about the spice Miss Bergen has stored up," he went on calmly. "A couple of years' crops, I understand. My option covers them, and I got a long option purposely. You see, Captain Knowles, I'm taking no chances. Now, then, if I can get a ship to take some of that stored-up spice to Singapore and realize on it there, I'll know a blamed sight more about the quality of this crop and so on from the selling price, than I'll be able to depend on from the report of any experts. Money is the best expert on earth. Get me?"

"I—ah—apprehend you," assented Captain Knowles, and began to smoke in silence.

Carter forbore to interrupt the other's meditation. That wondrous blue eye had begun to glow and glow, just as the sapphire eyes of the great Buddha glow when the bonzes light the hidden lamps behind them. And Carter knew exactly what was passing in the man's brain.

Captain Knowles was getting an idea. A very obvious idea. An idea up to which Carter had been gently leading him from the start. An idea which, to all appearances, placed Carter wholly in the hands of Captain Knowles. An idea which promised to vastly benefit Knowles and Stoppel—to win everything for them at a single stroke.

"There is a scarcity—ah—of ships at present," said Knowles slowly. "Still, it might be—ah—managed, perhaps. Might I suggest that a better market than Singapore, because much closer, would be Thursday Island? There are plenty of traders there."

"Japs, however," put in Carter.

"Yes, but some white. However, either Thursday Island or Port Darwin would give you results in, say, three weeks' time. The prices would be slightly lower, but the Japs have no lack of pearling luggers, and their traders would be very glad to buy at close to market price and turn an honest penny by sending on the stuff to Brisbane by lugger. There they could get much higher prices, for everything is going up because of the war."

Carter nodded. He wanted, of course, to get hold of some ready money for Miss Bergen by his ruse; but he had still another purpose behind it all—a purpose which was much more important. It seemed as though Captain Knowles had swallowed the bait very neatly.

"I shall see what I can do, and shall let you know after luncheon, if possible," said Knowles, rising as Miss Bergen appeared with a demure apology for having kept them waiting.

They walked down between the fragrant groves of spice trees to the Oostergat, and as they went Carter asked within himself whether Knowles would have the requisite audacity to play the game as any average man would play it. It was a clever trap that Carter had conceived and sprung, and the hook was altogether hidden; only boldness and self-esteem would bite at that hook, however, and Carter rather doubted these qualities in the Englishman.

He was destined to find to his cost that in audacity and bold-ness the withered Captain Knowles had earned a reputation exceeding that of any man in the thirteen ports.

By luncheon time Carter had seen Forts Nassau and Belgica, the tjiemara trees, barracks, the native kampongs, and the ancient marbled mansions. Also he had stopped at the famous shop of Baodela and for a few shillings had purchased a fine bird-of-paradise skin for his niece in Boston. He wound up at the club, tired and hot; but he had not failed to remark that while showing them the fort, Captain Knowles had taken occa-sion to whisper a question to Miss Bergen, to which she had assented as quietly. Consequently Carter was grinning happily to himself—inwardly. Of course, Knowles had to make sure about that option!

"If you'll run over to my office after luncheon," said Knowles, as they were freshening up before luncheon, "I'll go into this ship business with you."

Carter assented. The trap was sprang!

CHAPTER V

THE *ZAMIEL* COMES

MISS BERGEN had gone to Baodela's for a bolt of pongee.

In the neat little office near the wharves which Captain Knowles called Headquarters sat Carter and Knowles. Both men were well satisfied with themselves, for different reasons.

"If I succeed in finding a ship for you immediately," said Knowles, "you might do me a small favor, Mr. Carter—a favor I would greatly appreciate."

"Anything in my power!" responded Carter blandly.

Captain Knowles looked out the window and toyed with a paper knife.

"I would like you to sign an agreement," he said slowly. "In case that cargo should be sold at a good price, thus proving the value of the Bergen plantation, I presume you would take up your option immediately?"

"Very possibly. The ninety-day clause is simply to cover possible delays," evaded Carter.

"I see. In case the result were cabled to you from Thursday Island, we might look for the message in a little over two weeks, dependent on the winds, which should be fair. Thus we will say three weeks at the outside."

In three weeks at the outside, as Carter very well knew, Herman Stoppel would be in Banda Neira. Captain Knowles was making things coincide very neatly. The American sat with stony features, however, and his gray eyes gave no hint of the exultation within him.

"I would like you to sign an agreement," went on Knowles, "to sell me whatever I choose to buy of the contents of the Bergen home. Some of that furniture—you understand—I have set my heart upon. And other things—things you would not value. I have been here for thirty years, and I love the old things."

His sapphire eye glowed and gleamed upon Carter, who nodded grave assent.

"Certainly, captain. What in particular did you have in mind, and at what price?"

The question was perfect in its assumption of carelessness. But it failed. Perhaps at this crucial moment some inner prompting warned Knowles away; perhaps his habitual caution was not to be drawn so easily. He merely waved his hand in air.

"Oh, nothing in especial. Merely in general. As to the price, let that be set by some third party—some equitable person—"

"Say Mr. Stoppel," put in Carter. "He told me he would be here before long."

The sapphire eye glowed like fire—glowed with sheer delight. Captain Knowles fell to jotting down the agreement, while Carter smoked and waited.

Thus it was agreed and signed. Captain Knowles discovered that the schooner *Belial*, then in harbor, could begin loading at once. Carter haled him forth to Baodela's shop, found Miss Bergen, and requested her to arrange with her warehouse people to have the *Belial* given a full cargo without delay. He was glad to note that she received the news without comment.

"Now," he said briefly, "if you'll excuse me for half an hour, Miss Bergen, I have one or two little personal matters to arrange. I'll rejoin you at the wharf. Glad to have met you, Captain Knowles. See you later."

He hastened away, leaving Knowles to explain as best he might to the girl of his sudden discovery that the *Belial* was seaworthy.

One more very essential detail, and his task was finished. In this detail he had to take some chances, for he was not at all sure of his ground. Striding past the shops, he found one which he had previously noted—that of a Chinese trader.

The only person in the shop was the owner, an elderly Celestial with spectacles and straggly gray beard. To him Carter advanced without hesitation and extended his card.

"You understand English?" he asked.

"Perfectly," smiled the old Chinese.

"Then I'd like to ask you," plunged Carter, "if you would recognize one of two things. The first is a knotted cord of silver: the second is the picture of a tiger's paw."

The inscrutable eyes of the Oriental searched his face for a moment.

"Am I a child that you ask such things?" came the guarded answer. "A tiger's paw has five points, which we call claws. A child could answer as much."

"Thank you." Carter smiled. "Perhaps you know Mr. Wing Fu, of Surabaya?"

"I am his agent here," and the Chinaman's eyes twinkled. "A letter came in by the packet boat yesterday, telling me to look for you. I am glad to see you. Whatever you may desire of me shall be done."

"Good! I want a sure man, or, better, two men, to act as agents for Miss Bergen, who is shipping a cargo on the *Belial* immediately. They must be faithful to our interests and act as agents in the sale of that cargo, and they must cable Miss Bergen from Thursday Island before returning here. They will handle all money involved."

"They will come over to the plantation at noon tomorrow," promised the old Chinaman. "I meant to have looked you up, Mr. Carter, and I am glad that fate led you to my door."

"It was a lucky fate," commented Carter, with the feeling that luck was playing on his side throughout the game—so far.

He rejoined Miss Bergen at the wharf, finding her alone. On

their way back to Banda Lontar he explained his plan in detail, and its consummation.

"Knowles, you see, thinks that he has won everything by my agreement to sell him whatever he wishes. Foxy dog! He almost told me what the mysterious 'something' was! We now know this much, however: It is something inside your house, Miss Bergen. What the deuce can it be?"

"The only theory that I can see is that it is the old furniture," she rejoined, her brows drawn into a frown. "But that is too weak to be tenable. Upon my word, there is nothing in that house worth two million dollars! I only wish there were! So you think that Knowles will let that cargo go in the *Belial* and be sold?"

"Sure! He'll have to. When the cable comes that the stuff is sold at a good price, you'll be fixed financially. Then he and Stoppel will come along and indicate the precious objects, and I will calmly say that I have no authority to sell 'em, having turned back the option. How's that for slick business—and everything legitimate?"

"You're a perfect genius!" She laughed merrily. "I was astounded when I found that Knowles had chartered the *Belial* for such a purpose!"

Captain Knowles had taken the bait, and he stayed happily within the trap.

In the days that followed, Carter worked hard. The old Celestial proved valuable, for he cabled to an Oriental friend at Thursday Island to look out for the *Belial,* and the friend promised by return cable a price of twenty dollars per picul—not a wonderful price for nutmeg, but a very good one.

The crew of the *Belial* was composed wholly of half-castes, even the skipper being a Dutchman of crossed blood. Knowles held them grimly to work, and Carter aided; at the end of a week the schooner cleared for Thursday Island with a full cargo, and with two Chinese agents of Carter's aboard.

Knowles was well satisfied with his supposed coup. Miss Bergen had been cornered, when this American buyer showed up, together with a warning from Stoppel. It was no longer a question of starving Miss Bergen financially; it was a question of prompt action, and Captain Knowles had acted. True, money would be put in the American's hand, but that was nothing compared to the signed agreement which reposed in Captain Knowles' safe.

In the week following the departure of the *Belial,* Carter left no stone unturned to discover what might be worth two million dollars in or around the Bergen house. He visited the Dutch resident and the old settlers, and one and all thought him mad. He tried to track down any legends which would lead to something, in vain. He went over the old house with Miss Bergen, in the effort to discover secret hiding places, and dug up the cellar floor in search of buried treasure. Together they spent hours over boxes of old letters that reposed in the attic, searching fruitlessly for some clew.

The result was nothing at all. In the course of his search, however, Carter discovered a fine gray ash in one of the drawers of the library safe—the same drawer in which Miss Bergen had thought her draft stowed for safe-keeping. Suspicious, Carter took this ash dust over to his old Chinese trader, who smiled and nodded knowingly.

"An old trick, Mr. Carter. There is an acid, in which paper can be dipped, which will destroy that paper within certain times, according to the strength of the acid. No, there is no proof, of course—we Chinese do not care to go into the Dutch courts."

So was the scheme of Stoppel and Knowles laid bare. The girl followed Carter's advice, and said nothing. Indeed, Carter had aroused in her a vast curiosity regarding John Solomon.

"Wait for the *Zamiel,*" counseled Carter. "Solomon will come in on her, and we'll let his clever head go up against this conundrum."

And at length Solomon came—but not as Carter had expected.

Carter, Miss Bergen, and Mevrouw van der Gelt were at

breakfast when the impassive Chang laid a folded note beside the American's plate.

"Me catchum chit befo' daybleak," he said quietly.

"A note?" Carter glanced up in surprise. "Who brought it?"

"No savvy. Me catchum befo' daybleak."

Opening the chit, Carter found it to be a brief note from his Chinese agent, asking him to come over to Banda Neira as soon as possible. Barely had Carter handed it to Miss Bergen when the knocker at the front door announced a visitor. This proved to be one of Captain Knowles' servants, bearing word that his master desired to see Mr. Carter regarding business, also that the *Zamiel* had been sighted from the hill and would be in port in an hour.

"Good!" exclaimed Carter, rising. "Will you go over to town, Miss Bergen?"

"No. That is, unless you want me—"

"You'd better come along. I fancy that my Chinese friend and Knowles have had word from our spice cargo about the same time. I'd sooner that you see the chink about the money."

The girl acquiesced, and they followed Knowles' boy down to the waiting boat.

Knowles fortunately did not come down to the wharf, and Carter hurried Miss Bergen to the Oriental's shop. There the old Chinaman made out Miss Bergen a check; the two agents with the *Belial* had received the money for the spice, and had deposited it with a Chinese friend at Thursday Island. Leaving Miss Bergen to settle finances, Carter hastened off to the office of Knowles. As he reached it, the *Zamiel* poked her nose through the Sun Gate.

Carter's guess had been accurate. Knowles had heard from the skipper of the *Belial* but did not discuss the subject, merely taking Carter down to the wharf to greet Stoppel. Signals were flying from the schooner, however, and they found the wharf barred by a file of soldiers. The *Zamiel* floated in and made fast, and Stoppel lifted over into the hands of the Resident the ironed figure of John Solomon, looking very woebegone.

There in the morning sunlight, with half the inhabitants of Banda Neira crowded at the wharf end behind Carter and Knowles, the case of John Solomon was tried and adjudged.

It was a very simple case, and Carter fortunately repressed his impulse to interfere. Stoppel handed over Solomon as a stowaway, and alleged that the little cockney had stolen money from his cabin on the voyage from Surabaya. The Resident was about to issue summary orders when Solomon mildly suggested that a British subject had some rights, and offered to pay any fine imposed, offering as an alternative to fight the case eternally.

"What have you to pay a fine with?" demanded the astonished resident.

Solomon named the old Chinese trader, who was sent for and who appeared with the information that Solomon possessed unlimited credit with him. Stoppel's cold smile vanished in savage consternation, while the Resident was staggered. Five minutes later the Chinaman signed a bail bond and Solomon walked away with him, free, giving Carter a wink and a sly nod as he went. The Resident and his soldiers departed.

"*Gegroet,* Captain Knowles! Why—if this isn't my friend, Mr. Carter!"

Stoppel came up to Knowles and Carter, brawny hand extended to the former. For some vague and undefinable reason it came to the American that here was a crucial moment, a moment fraught with grave possibilities.

True, Stoppel's powerful features were smiling, but his Mephistophelean eyes were cruel and piercing. Carter realized suddenly that the man stood at the crossroads of decision; did not know whether to pick a fight with Carter, and so come to open enmity, or to wait and not to assume the aggressive. Stoppel, of course, knew nothing of what had happened on the island. Because he had no wish to meet any crisis yet, Carter spoke up swiftly:

"I am very glad you told me to look up Captain Knowles, Mr. Stoppel! He has been of inestimable service to me—but I presume that you and he will have business to talk over, so I'll run along. Our private agreement, Captain Knowles, may be settled at any time you wish—we'll see you later, gentlemen! Adios!"

Leaving Stoppel gazing frowningly after him, Carter turned and walked away, thankful to have avoided any rupture. Stoppel would learn about the sale of the spice, and the signed agreement; he would come over to the plantation with Knowles, and would indicate whatever was wanted—whatever constituted the mysterious "two-million-dollar secret," as the American termed it—and that would be all. Carter chuckled as he thought of how the two precious rogues would look when he should tell them that he had thrown up his option and could sell nothing belonging to Miss Bergen!

It was by this time nearly noon. Carter betook himself to the old Chinaman's shop, where he found Miss Bergen conversing with John Solomon; both were laughing, and the old Celestial was grinning amiably.

"Hello! I see no introductions are needed," said Carter, shaking hands with Solomon. "Well, John, what's the meaning of that little scene on the wharf? Was Stoppel trying to put you out of the game?"

"Looks werry much like that, sir and miss," and the cockney chuckled wheezily. "We 'ad a werry pleasant trip all the way 'ere, as the old gent said when 'e buried 'is third, until we was a-coming into port. I'm sorry to say as 'ow Mr. Stoppel must ha' got a unduly exalted opinion o' me abilities, just like that, 'cause why, 'e was werry anxious to 'ave me kept in jail for a while."

"Did you find out what he was after?" demanded Carter.

"No, sir. Did you?"

"Not yet—but we'll know before long."

Miss Bergen interposed with the suggestion that, since it was nearly noon, they all cross to the plantation, where Solomon, she hoped, would be her guest.

"Thankee werry much indeed, miss," said Solomon, "but we'll be seen a-goin' there, and Mr. Stoppel will know as 'ow we're thick as thieves!"

"He knows it, anyway," said the girl calmly. "Come along!"

That Stoppel had discovered the dangerous ability in Solomon was to Carter ample evidence of that same ability in the half-caste. Herman Stoppel was diabolically clever. It had been clever to name his schooners after devils, because that had gotten him most of the Arab trade, and he had no reputable white trade, anyway. Everything Stoppel did was clever.

The three crossed the Oostergat and slowly made their way up to the plantation, John Solomon getting acquainted with things and events as they went. He chuckled hugely over the stratagem of Carter, and at his cautious compliments the American felt a righteous glow; he guessed that Solomon's compliments were rarely given.

Mevrouw van der Gelt was knitting on the veranda, and Solomon bowed ponderously as Miss Bergen introduced him. There was something comical, to Carter, about this placid old Dutchwoman eternally knitting, maintaining her unbroken calm amid a swirl of events which she did not half understand and which at any moment might break into a whirlwind of passion. She was the true center of the hurricane.

Not until after luncheon, which was the true Dutch *rijstaafel* and constituted a feast in itself, did Carter bring up the subject of Stoppel again. Then, being afraid lest Knowles and Stoppel might come upon them at any moment, he curtly recalled the situation to Solomon's attention and asked for advice.

"You know my plan, John," he concluded. "Is it good or not, to your mind? They'll give away what it is they're after, and then we'll show 'em the door."

"It looks werry simple, sir," replied Solomon, then turned to the girl. "Beggin' your pardon, miss, but if I might 'ave a look at that 'ere old furniture of yours, I'd be werry glad o' the chance. Then we'll make up our minds what to do, just like that. It's all werry fine to make 'aste, I says, but it 'adn't ought to be made in a 'urry!"

So, the mevrouw being placidly gone to her siesta, the three of them went over the house. Solomon heard of the search made by Carter, and approved with sage nods, but said nothing until they came back into the hall. Then he inspected that mammoth carved-rosewood seat and asked that Chang be summoned.

When the Chinese butler appeared, Solomon demanded that he translate the three ideographs carved into the seat.

Chang gravely shook his head. It was the ancient or classical writing, he explained, and only a student could translate it. Bidding him copy the characters immediately and take them to the old shopkeeper in Banda Neira, Solomon dismissed the huge seat as being "werry interesting," and returned to the veranda. With a huge sigh of relief, he pulled out his clay pipe and settled down in a chair.

"Now, sir an' miss, about this 'ere plan. O' course I 'aven't no right to interfere—"

"You have every right!" broke in the girl quickly, her brown eyes starlike. "You and Mr. Wing Fu and Mr. Carter have come into this affair like my guardian angels, and I can never express my gratitude in words! I can never tell you what it has meant to me—I don't mean the money end of it, but the finding of kind friends and helpers."

"Mr. Wing Fu and me, miss, we're only doing our duty, just like that," exclaimed Solomon uneasily. "Mr. Carter, 'ere—"

"Miss Bergen knows all about my end of it," interrupted Carter. "And I've thrown up that percentage business, Solomon. Whatever is found belongs to her, and I don't want any percentage. It's not right. By the way, Miss Bergen, what do her friends call the Queen of Holland?"

For a moment her perplexed gaze studied him, then her

face cleared in comprehension as he smiled, and she answered frankly:

"Oh! Why, I suppose—just Billy! That's what mine call me."

"Good! Billy it is, then, by your leave. Now—"

"Wait a minute!" she broke in. "I started to say, Mr. Solomon, that we'll follow your advice implicitly. I've heard enough about you to abide by whatever you say."

"Then I says to make it John, miss." The mild blue eyes twinkled at her, and Solomon chuckled wheezily. "Make it John and Ralph and—and Billy, beggin' your pardon, miss—just like that! And now we ain't got any time to lose. If I was you, miss, I'd go and wake up Mevrouw van der Gelt, and both o' you pack up some grips, 'cause why, we're a-going away from 'ere to-night."

The girl's eyes widened as she stared at the pudgy little dictator.

"Away! Going away!" she repeated. "Why, where are we going?"

"I ain't quite sure about that yet, miss," said Solomon apologetically. "But this 'ere is a-going to be a werry busy arternoon, so to speak. When so be as things 'appen, they're werry apt to 'appen all together."

With only a glance of frowning wonder toward Carter, Miss Bergen rose and departed.

"What the devil are you driving at, John?" exclaimed the American.

"No time to talk now, sir. About that 'ere plan o' yours, it's werry good in its way, but that 'ere Stoppel is danged artful, and 'e'd circumwent it mortal quick. That man, 'e could smell a rat where there ain't so much as a rat 'ole, Mr. Carter, sir!"

"H'm!" grunted Carter. "Well, what have you to suggest, then? If they come over here to buy that mysterious thing they're after, what shall I do?"

"Sell it to 'em, sir," returned Solomon blandly.

"*What!*" Carter straightened up, staring at him. "Oh, you mean to sell it, and then spring my little scheme—"

"No, I don't," wheezed the other. "I means to sell it to 'em, just like that!"

"And let them take it away?" asked the incredulous American.

"Yes, sir. And if I ain't mistook, they're a-comin' this blessed minute."

Carter turned. The veranda commanded a view of the Oost-ergat, and in the strip of blue water he saw one of the *orembais,* or native ferries.

"Oh, that's Chang on your errand," he commented. "Now—"

"It ain't Chang, beggin' your pardon, sir," struck in Solomon. "It's that 'ere Stoppel, and Knowles with 'im, and a lot more men. Now, Mr. Carter, are you a-goin' to obey orders or not?"

"Yes," assented Carter sullenly. Solomon leaned back in his chair and puffed his pipe alight. His pudgy face was quite devoid of expression.

"Werry good, sir. If I was you, I'd send one o' then chink serwants up to Miss Bergen with word not to come down while Stoppel's 'ere. I don't want 'im to see 'er this trip."

Carter obeyed, albeit with a bad grace.

CHAPTER VI

SOLOMON'S MAGIC

SOLOMON DEPARTED to his room, merely stating that he did not wish to be seen and had need of a bath.

Left alone to await his visitors, Carter's savage humor soon cooled down, as he began to perceive the reasons behind his orders. Stoppel probably knew that Solomon had gone to the plantation with Carter and Miss Bergen, and would be fully on the alert. He would be suspicious of just such a trap as Carter had prepared, and would reveal nothing until the thing he wanted was safely in his possession.

"John is a living genius," was the American's rather shame-faced conclusion. "That trap of mine might do for Knowles, but is pitifully weak for such prey as Stoppel. No, the only way out of it now is to sell him what he wants. Yet I've no right to sell anything, and there Stoppel will carry it off and laugh at us! Perhaps John has some scheme afoot to nab him after he starts away with his loot, however. I'll trust to Solomon and pray for luck!"

So, perplexed and frowning helplessly, Carter awaited the arrival of his visitors.

They came soon enough—Stoppel striding along with Knowles stiffly at his shoulder, and behind them eight men, the crew of the *Zamiel*. For a moment Carter entertained the cheerful hope that Stoppel was mad enough to try violence; but at a curt command from the half-caste the men halted a dozen feet from the steps. Knowles and Stoppel came on alone.

"*Gegroet!*" exclaimed the American hospitably, rising to meet the pair and shaking hands with apparent good humor. "Sit down and make yourselves at home. How do you like my plantation. Mr. Stoppel?"

"It's a good place," said the half-caste, his eyes dwelling on Carter's face. "So you've bought it?"

"What d'you suppose I got an option for?" Carter laughed and turned to Knowles. "I had a cable from those Chinese agents of mine aboard the *Belial,* Captain Knowles. The stuff was sold at twenty dollars a picul."

"Good price," commented Knowles. "I was glad to hear it— ah—got a cable myself."

Carter nodded. "By George, it *was* a good price!" He allowed open enthusiasm to show in his words and mien. "They've been talking three dollars and hard times and so on, and everybody's been holding off the market! I'll wager the price goes up to thirty in another six months! If Miss Bergen had anticipated such a market, she might not have given me that option on the place, eh. Knowles?"

"How much did you pay, if I may ask?" queried Stoppel. Carter laughed again.

"Can't discuss that—sorry, but it's an agreement. I tell you what, though—in ten years I'll go home a millionaire! Can't fail!"

Stoppel and Knowles exchanged an amused glance. They had heard many men talk like this many times. Everybody in the colonies would be a millionaire were it not for some strange and often unaccountable "if." Carter simulated very well indeed the delighted newcomer.

"Speaking of agreements," spoke up Knowles, "reminds me of our—ah—our little private transaction, Mr. Carter."

"Eh?" Carter gazed at him inquiringly. "What transaction?"

"The agreement between us," returned Knowles stiffly, "regarding one or two trifling articles in this house which I wished to purchase from you—"

"Oh, that! Why, it had completely slipped my mind," broke

in Carter, and waved his hand toward the waiting men. "That why you fetched those fellows along?"

"Exactly," assented Knowles; "and I brought Mr. Stoppel to act as arbiter, as per your suggestion. Of course, if the time does not meet your convenience—"

"No time like the present," said Carter cheerfully, coming to his feet. "If you'll point out what you desire, we'll not fight about the price."

Captain Knowles' beautiful sapphire eye roved swiftly about the place as though in search of some concealed pitfall, but the captain rose and followed Carter into the house. So did Herman Stoppel, who was plainly suspicious of this cordial reception.

For ten minutes the three men looked through the place, but not an inkling did Carter receive as to the object of the search. When at length Knowles turned to him and suggested that they go out to the veranda again, he frowned in perplexity.

"But you haven't picked out a thing, captain! If—"

"You will be quite satisfied with Mr. Stoppel's appraisal?" queried Knowles.

"Certainly!"

"Then we may sit down and settle the matter, if you please."

By the cold grin on Stoppel's face, and the sharpness of the Sapphire eye, Carter perceived that these twain had come prepared against any such trap as he had made ready, and again he blessed the foresight or John Solomon.

Seated once more on the veranda, Knowles produced a paper and a bag of coin.

"There are three articles in this house which I desire to buy, Mr. Carter. I believe you agreed to sell at Mr. Stoppel's price?"

"I did," said Carter curtly. Knowles handed him the bag of coin.

"There is the money, sir—five hundred gulden, as you will find. The articles are three pieces of furniture. Since the sale has now been consummated by your acceptance of the money, I will thank you to sign this bill of sale."

Knowles was undeniably nervous, and dropped his affable manner almost completely. Perceiving that he had been lawfully entrapped, Carter opened the paper and found it to be a bill of sale for two chairs, which then reposed in the library and the big rosewood seat in the hall.

"I'll sign certainly," he returned, taking the pen Knowles handed him and making good his words. "I don't quite understand all these precautions—"

Stoppel jumped up and signaled to his men, who hastened up the steps. As though it were now a question of getting away with their loot, Stoppel and Knowles paid no further attention to Carter, but led their men into the house. Carter followed, half tempted to ignore the orders of Solomon; but he resisted the temptation.

Three minutes later Knowles remembered his manners and shook hands with his host in farewell, then hurriedly stalked after the others. Carter watched them go, bearing nothing except the two chairs and the massive rosewood seat, which six of the men carried.

"I'm blessed if I can see any rhyme or reason in this!" he exclaimed aloud. "That big seat is not worth two million dollars, nor two hundred! But what the devil did they come after? What was Stoppel's game? If I've been tricked—then how?"

From the doorway behind he caught a wheezy chuckle, and turned to see Solomon.

"Yes, sir," responded the little man. "Mr. Stoppel is congratulatin' hisself this werry minute on 'aving tricked us, just like that. What did 'e take?"

Behind Solomon appeared Miss Bergen, her eyes bright with excitement.

"Two chairs and that big rosewood seat!" she exclaimed. "I watched them go—and was that really all, Ralph?"

"Even so," assented Carter, not without a trace of bitterness. "Stoppel must have suspected something—yet they went in a deuce of a hurry! Surely, John, that rosewood throne could not have any enormous value?"

Solomon stared at the American for an instant, his blue eyes very wide. Then he turned quickly to the girl; his usual placid manner was transformed into a burning eagerness.

"Now, miss, we've got to move sharp, and no mistake! Them 'ere two wagabonds are a-goin' out o' port in a mortal 'urry—"

"And you want to stop them?" put in the excited girl.

"No, miss, nothin' o' the kind! I want you to come along o' me—we 'ave to see the Resident, both on us. Mr. Carter, will you be so good as to bring Mevrouw wan der Gelt and the suit cases in an hour? We'll be a-waitin' on the wharf to meet you."

"What in thunder is the meaning of all this?" demanded the bewildered Carter. "Where do you think we're going, anyway? Why don't we stop those—"

"Mr. Carter, I ain't got time to stand 'ere talking!" cried Solomon in exasperation. "I'll explain in werry short order—but now we 'as to *act*. Come along, Miss Bergen, if you please!"

At this moment Chang appeared, returning from his errand to Banda Neira. As Solomon and Miss Bergen started down the steps, Chang handed the former a paper and received the latter's order to look after the house, then Carter watched his two friends depart rapidly.

With a deep sigh of resignation, he turned to fulfill his instructions. The meaning of Solomon's plan was absolutely unguessable; that the little cockney was not acting blindly was quite clear, but the purpose behind his orders was baffling. Irritated and even wondering if for any reason Solomon could distrust him, he resolved to await the promised explanations. What Solomon had meant by going away was hopelessly dark, since the packet boat would not be in port for another week, and the only ship in harbor was the *Zamiel*.

The mevrouw appeared, looking quite bewildered, and was followed by Chang, who bore her suit case, two of Miss Bergen's, and that of the American. Sharing the load, Carter offered

Mevrouw van der Gelt his arm and conducted her toward the Oostergat.

"Youth is a capricious thing," philosophized the old lady in Dutch. *"Mijnheer,* do you know whither we go?"

"Not in the least," returned Carter. "You must blame Mr. Solomon for this sudden move."

"Oh, Mijnheer Solomon! I like that man. He knows when to keep his mouth shut." With this firm expression of adherence, the mevrouw ended the discussion bluntly.

At the landing an *orembai* was waiting, and Chang loaded them aboard and toddled back to the plantation. But Carter sat staring in wild surmise across the stretch of water. The *Zamiel* was leaving the harbor!

Not only was she leaving, but she was well upon her way, her nose already poking into the Sun Gate, her sails fluttering aloft, and the chug of a motor signifying that she possessed auxiliary power. Before Carter was half across the water she had disappeared within the rocky passage.

Thus were Solomon's words corroborated; Stoppel and Knowles were certainly leaving port in a hurry, and as if they had secured their long-desired objective. More than this Carter could only conjecture.

Upon handing Mevrouw van der Gelt up to the wharf landing, he found it deserted. As the old lady was remarking that it was too hot to be standing here in the sun like a pair of fools, Carter observed Solomon stumping hurriedly down the street alone. The little cockney arrived, mopping his brow, and extremely out of breath.

"Dang it! This 'ere 'eat is frightful, I says!" he exclaimed, staring at Carter.

The American broke into a laugh, despite his irritation.

"Well, are we going traveling in an aeroplane, John? Where's Miss Bergen?"

"Up at the residency, settlin' of a few matters."

"Tell him that I am very warm," interrupted the mevrouw firmly. Carter translated, and Solomon's eyes twinkled.

"Tell'er to set down in the ware'ouse shade, then," and Solomon waved his hand toward the near-by godowns. The mevrouw correctly interpreted the gesture and obeyed it. Solomon gave vent to a wheezy sigh.

"Well, explain!" snapped Carter. "Do you know the *Zamiel* has gone?"

"I ain't blind, sir," was the dry retort. "Now, then, we'll get straightened out all shipshape an' proper, Mr. Carter. First off, what that 'ere Stoppel was after was that big rosewood seat in the 'all. We know it now."

"Then why didn't you stop his cursed schooner?"

"Dang it, sir, *will* you 'ave patience? You tell me why 'e wanted that 'all seat! Go on, now, tell me!"

Carter shrugged his shoulders. "How do I know why he wanted it?"

"Well, then, 'ow do *I* know meself?" demanded the cockney heatedly. "I don't. All I know is as 'e wanted it. What did 'e want of it?"

Regaining his usual phlegmatic manner, Solomon proceeded to expound himself.

The rosewood seat was doubtless a couple of hundred years old, but had no inordinate value in itself apparently. The secret of its value reposed with Herman Stoppel and Knowles alone, and they would certainly not impart it to Miss Bergen. Solomon was of the opinion that the thing might contain some hidden recess filled with valuables.

"Then why the devil didn't you keep it and examine it?" exclaimed Carter.

"Well, sir, that was only a guess, and guesses ain't neither 'ere nor there, I says. Now it's aboard 'is schooner, and you may be werry sure as 'e is workin' on it this blessed minute, 'cause why, there's two million dollars in that 'ere piece o' furniture! Where it is nobody knows but 'im, so the only thing to do was to let 'im find it for us!"

"And let him slip off with it?"

"I'm a-coming to that, sir, if so be as you gives me a chance. 'Ere was me plan."

Carter marveled that he had not seen through that plan, so simple was it. Solomon and Miss Bergen had gone to the Resident and demanded Stoppel's arrest, stating that certain stolen goods were aboard the *Zamiel*—but the *Zamiel* was already past being stopped and had left for parts unknown! All of which Solomon had apparently foreseen, as the bill of sale signed by Carter was of course illegal.

Therefore Solomon had proposed that he would settle the matter himself on being given the proper authority by the Resident. Now, Herman Stoppel was not highly respected by any Dutch official, and Miss Bergen was very much respected. Further, the Resident was only too thankful to have the matter taken out of his hands, especially—and here Solomon waxed mysterious—in view of some financial transaction not of a nature to be generally discussed.

"So 'ere we be, all shipshape," concluded the little man calmly. "Miss Bergen is gettin' 'er search warrant made out, and I 'as me papers as constable or whatever these 'ere Dutchmen calls it. All we 'as to do is to over'aul that 'ere *Zamiel*, see what Stoppel 'as done to the big chair, and recover the loot from 'im."

"I suppose you'll do it by submarine?" queried Carter sarcastically.

"No, sir." Solomon touched a match to his pipe, which he had been filling, and puffed very complacently for a moment. "There's Miss Bergen a-coming now. Oh, I clean forgot about them 'ere ideographs! You might see what you make o' this 'ere translation, Mr. Carter."

He handed Carter the paper which Chang had fetched, and which bore a neatly written translation of the three ideographs carved in the back of the rosewood chair. They stood for "heavenly seat," "good luck," and "Eastern-eye-shining." The connected meaning was not given, and was entirely problematical even to a Chinese mind.

"No help there," observed Carter frowningly. Miss Bergen joined them, waved a hand to the mevrouw, and met Carter's gaze with dancing eyes.

"So John has told you all his plan?" she exclaimed eagerly.

"All except the most essential part," returned Carter, his tone dry. "Unless he means to stand on the mountain and wave his handkerchief at the *Zamiel* to return so the papers can be served, I don't see how he expects to reach Stoppel in the near future!"

The girl laughed, but Solomon waved his pipe up the street, with a wheezy chuckle. At the gesture Carter saw that the town was disgorging its inhabitants, who were flocking down toward the water front.

"Look there, sir! They sighted 'er from the signal station a 'alf 'our ago—"

Even while the little man was speaking, an exclamation broke from Carter. Through the Sun Gate came slipping the slim shape of a yacht, at whose stern hung a flag not seen in the Spice Islands since the days of clipper ships—the Stars and Stripes!

"If you're all ready, sir an' miss," remarked Solomon calmly, "we'll go aboard. That 'ere is me own yacht, and a werry proper one she is if I do say it as shouldn't!"

Carter's jaw dropped in sheer, undiluted amazement.

CHAPTER VII

THE SECOND PHASE

THE YACHT did not drop anchor. As though she had been some magic vehicle summoned up by unholy wizardry, she gave birth to a small launch which darted in to the wharf and took aboard Solomon and his friends; the officer in charge, who was also the captain of the *Alcis* and was a Yankee by the name of Bingham, satisfied the Resident that the principles of pratique were inviolate, and the launch darted out again.

Behind her gaped the population of Banda Neira, from the thunderstruck Resident to the lowliest brown ferryman. Solomon had created a sensation this day, of a truth!

And at the top of the yacht's ladder stood Mr. Wing Fu, of Surabaya.

This was to Carter the crowning stroke. He was bewildered by the events of this multitudinous day. Since breakfast time he had been moving blindly in a whirl of things which seemed as silly as the boyish play of children. From morning until now, late afternoon, he had been a pawn in some game he could not understand. Solomon's explanation might be all very logical, but—

"Well, I'll be danged!" broke from the little cockney as the launch ran in to the ladder of the yacht. "If that ain't Mr. Wing Fu!"

Carter merely sighed. The amazement of Solomon seemed unfeigned, and this was the most surprising thing of all. Had not Solomon expected to see Wing Fu here on the *Alcis?* Evidently

not, for Captain Bingham touched his cap and stated that as
the yacht left Surabaya Mr. Wing Fu had hastily come aboard
and had demanded to be taken to Solomon at once. Captain
Bingham had known that the Chinaman was a particular friend
of his owner.

"Oh, it's all right," said Solomon. "We'll soon find out what's
what!"

Mevrouw van der Gelt was assisted up the ladder, Miss
Bergen followed, then Solomon and Carter went up to be
received by Mr. Wing Fu, who was promptly introduced to the
two ladies. Then, as the mevrouw demanded to be shown to her
cabin at once, Wing Fu turned to Solomon and spoke rapidly:

"I must have an explanation with you and Miss Bergen and
Mr. Carter—at once! Will you tell me quickly whether Stoppel
is aboard the *Zamiel*—we passed her just outside? And has he
with him any furniture from Miss Bergen's house?"

"Yes, 'e is, and 'e 'as," returned Solomon, staring.

"Then order your skipper to leave port and keep the *Zamiel*
in sight while we talk."

The little cockney obeyed with some signs of agitation, then
Mr. Wing Fu led the way to the after deck, where chairs were set
out beneath an awning. His manner was anxious and perturbed;
Miss Bergen frowned at Carter in dumb interrogation, but the
American could only shrug his shoulders resignedly. The situa-
tion was beyond his knowledge.

"I must be explicit, for details may be important," began Mr.
Wing Fu, addressing Miss Bergen. "So please pardon my questions to Mr. Solomon, madam. Now, Solomon, did affairs go as
you expected them to go with Herman Stoppel?"

The little cockney talked at greater length than Carter had
yet heard him; and as he talked, he laid bare what to Carter had
seemed inexplicable.

Solomon had weeks ahead decided on selling to Stoppel
whatever the latter wished to buy from the Bergen house,
although he had decided on no details. Carter had arrived at

Banda Neira and had managed this very thing himself, with somewhat different intent. It had been Solomon's plan to have the *Alcis* arrive on the same day as the *Zamiel*, and upon discovering what Carter had been doing in the meantime, Solomon had promptly utilized the presence of his own yacht in the project of pursuing the *Zamiel*.

Mr. Wing Fu arrived at a clear understanding of the situation before the yacht was out of the Sun Gate. He turned again to the girl.

"Miss Bergen, out of my regard for your brother and for your interests I entered this pursuit. I now find myself engaged upon it for more personal and for even more important reasons. We have been far at sea—aye, even you, my friend Solomon, have been outwitted! We have been like foolish children in this quest, but for that there is no help. That was the first phase of this affair, and we are now entered on the second and much graver phase—a phase which is to bring about the death of men, my friends."

In the Chinaman's air was an earnest gravity which did not fail of its appeal. Carter felt oppressed, weighted down by some communication of the spirit; glancing at Miss Bergen, he saw that she was watching Wing Fu with a frowning intensity, as though she, too, found in the man a serious and unwonted depth of foreboding. But Solomon, who was whittling shavings from a black plug of tobacco, nodded slightly and looked at Wing Fu with unruffled mien.

"So you 'ave found the secret, sir?"

Wing Fu started and bent upon him a keen look.

"Yes. How did you guess?"

Solomon sighed. "I'm a-gettin' old," he said gloomily. "Me mind ain't what it used to be, sir, 'cause why, this 'ere 'ole blooming thing 'as been a mystery to me, just like that! The 'and of time is a-laying 'eavy on me 'ead, as the old gent said when 'e kissed the 'ousemaid and got 'is face slapped."

"Console yourself, my friend." Wing Fu smiled thinly, almost cruelly. "No one except of my own race could have solved this mystery. Stoppel, as you know, has Chinese blood, and in past years has stood high among us. His men are half-breeds like himself. Now, may I see your copy of the ideographs carved in the back of that rosewood hall seat?"

Solomon searched his pockets and finally produced the paper. Mr. Wing Fu inspected it, nodded his satisfaction, and extended it toward Miss Bergen and Carter.

"Let me translate this fully," he said, his words slow, yet tinged with excitement. It was plain that eagerness spurred him hard. "It means 'The heavenly, or exalted seat of good fortune, dedicated to the omniscient or all-seeing eastern sky,' As you know, Mr. Carter, I am a member of a secret society, one of many which have existed among my countrymen for uncounted years."

A slight exclamation drew Carter's attention to Solomon. The little cockney was leaning forward, his blue eyes fairly bulging.

"You don't mean as 'ow that 'ere rosewood seat is the Chair of the Eye as was stole—"

"Yes," broke in Wing Fu. "But I must explain to these friends of ours. Many, many years ago, Miss Bergen, the society to which I belong possessed a very wonderful temple in Nanking, China. From this temple was stolen a chair—the most significant and marvelous chair which could then be produced in China."

"Excuse me," broke in the girl, voicing Carter's own unuttered thought, "but there was nothing at all wonderful about that hall seat, Mr. Wing Fu, if one excepts the carving upon it."

"I know," and the other nodded. "We have all been far astray, Miss Bergen. To return, then! Every initiate to our society is taught the story of this chair, which is called the Chair of the Eye. Stoppel, visiting your home, saw this rosewood seat and was able to read and appreciate the significance of the inscription upon it. The story of that seat we shall never know, but we do know what it is. One of Stoppel's friends, like himself an apostate from our society, died of fever the day I left Surabaya, and when on the threshold of the mystic world he sent for me and confessed. Do you know what Stoppel cabled to San Francisco? It was to inquire if there were a market in America for the finest specimens of chrysoberyl that had ever been produced!"

"Chrysoberyl?" Carter frowned in perplexity. "Isn't that some semiprecious stone?"

"Yes, but you will understand fully only when you see the Chair of the Eye, which is or was set with these stones."

"But really, Mr. Wing Fu, there were no stones at all set in this chair!" protested Miss Bergen, her brown eyes bent upon the speaker in puzzled wonder. Wing Fu smiled.

"Did you look *in* the chair, then?"

"In it?" she repeated, then laughed shortly. "I must confess that I don't understand!"

"Let me sketch its possible history, then. The Chair of the Eye was stolen, and was perhaps sold to some Dutch trader in these islands; indeed, we have a vague tradition to this effect. Now—and this is pure guesswork—the chair was seen by one who recognized it and who regained possession of it. Fearing to return with it to China openly, he concealed it by—"

"By covering of it up!" cried out Solomon, as one who sees the solution of a puzzle. "Dang it, we went an' give it to 'im—without thinkin' to tear off a bit o' that 'ere rosewood to see what was underneath!"

"How could you tell? How could any of us know, unless this man had confessed?"

"You mean, then," said Carter gravely, "that the stolen jewel-set chair was incased in rosewood?"

"Exactly," said Wing Fu. "And Stoppel wishes to tear out the jewels and sell them."

"But why"—and Carter frowned—"was not that very thing done long ago?"

"The intrinsic value of the jewels was not great long ago; the chair as a whole was a wonderful thing. Nowadays, however, chrysoberyl in certain forms is as valuable as a diamond of like size."

There was silence for a space. Mental adjustment to this information, realization of the depth of meaning that underlay the words of Wing Fu, was slow. Pregnant words had they been—aye, deeply pregnant and charged with the fates of men! No light thing was the Chair of the Eye, no mere furniture of some tong headquarters, but a thing for which men would fight with fanatic devotion. The second phase, indeed!

Carter followed the gaze of Wing Fu. There, over the rail, upon the unbroken horizon that stretched to the westward, was a fleck of white—the *Zamiel,* fleeing with engine and wind into the sunset. For now the afternoon was drawing fast to its close.

The immensity of the scene awed Carter and the rest; the great expanse of sky and sea, with the blue heights of Ceram to the north, and the peak of Banda behind. Here was the vastness of infinity, wherein little men planned and fought and plotted and staked their petty lives upon a wager of dross.

"And now it is man against man," said Carter, thinking aloud.

"Yes," Solomon assented, with a gloomy nod. "It's us against 'im. I suppose we'd better put on speed and catch 'im afore night."

"No," returned Wing Fu, with a glance at the sky. "In an hour the sun will be gone, and we could not catch him and recover what we wish in an hour. It will be better to stay at his heels through the night, then catch up with him in the morning. We need daylight for our work—we cannot take chances on the powers of darkness!"

Perhaps there was superstition in that thought.

"Then, as I understand it," said Miss Bergen, with quiet interrogation, "there is now no further need of my assistance, or of the papers we secured?"

"They will be useful," returned Mr. Wing Fu gravely, "but we are acting now above the law, dear madam. I regret that you are with us, except that it gives me an opportunity to assure you of my fair dealing with you."

"I need no such assurance," and the girl smiled.

"No, but now circumstances have altered all our arrangements. The Chair of the Eye is still your lawful property."

"But you just said that you were acting above the law!" she countered.

"Only so far as Herman Stoppel is concerned. The Chair of the Eye has an intrinsic value of something close to two million dollars, and this stake he is playing for. To me, as representing many thousands of my brethren, the recovery of that chair intact and uninjured is an object quite beyond monetary value. Therefore, I request that you sign over to me, here and now, your title to that chair. In return I will give you two million dollars."

"No," said Miss Bergen. "I have no right to extort such a sum of money, Mr. Wing Fu. Here is my chance to repay the debt of gratitude which I feel, and I shall do so by deeding you that chair freely."

Mr. Wing Fu waved his hand in the air.

"Extortion! Not at all," he said gravely. "The money must be paid you. It is only equitable and right that this be done, and I insist upon it absolutely. To those whom I represent the Chair of the Eye has a value far above its intrinsic worth, great as that may be; Stoppel dares not treat with us, dares not let us know that he even possesses the thing, so he is satisfied to ruin a great creation of art in order that he may sell its jewels. You must accept the sum which I offer."

"Very well." Miss Bergen yielded without further protest, for Mr. Wing Fu was firmly insistent. He produced papers, which he had evidently made ready beforehand.

"Won't this 'ere 'craft be suspected?" queried Solomon, puffing at his pipe. He was clearly much chagrined by his failure to pierce to the heart of things from the first; although, as Wing Fu had said, that had been an utterly impossible task. "Stoppel seen 'er comin' in, and seen 'er comin' out on 'is course again."

"Let him suspect," said Wing Fu grimly. "He will not dare destroy the Chair of the Eye. We will follow, and in due course end the affair. If he shows fight, we will fight. We have eighteen white men aboard here; he has but eight half-castes."

Carter leaned forward, his teeth gripping his pipestem.

"I'll tell you one thing," he said quietly. "This affair is not going to be an open-and-shut proposition. Unless I miss my guess, Herman Stoppel has some ace up his sleeve. It is not like that man to send warnings as he has done, to act as he has acted throughout, on a basis of bluff."

"Right," said Solomon. "You leave 'Erman Stoppel to me, just like that! Now, Miss Bergen, if so be as you wants to see your cabin, I'll be werry glad to point it out."

Solomon summoned his steward, who was an Australian of cockney extraction, and the party went to their staterooms before meeting again in the saloon for dinner.

The crew of the *Alcis* was composed of Americans all, except the steward and the second officer, who was a Dutchman. Carter prowled around and investigated the craft to his great satisfaction. She was not palatial, but she was comfortable; she was not new, but she was well found, and her crew were very proud of their owner for mysterious reasons which they did not explain. Also, the fact that they were chasing the *Zamiel* was a great tonic.

Solomon did not appear at dinner, sending word that he was busily at work.

And now began to draw in the threads set by men across the face of this infinity of sky and waters; all the hidden wiles of fate had wrought their will, and it remained but for the players in this game, which was now become a game of life and death, to battle with their wits and hands and hearts. Swift were the wits then at work—aye, and swiftly were the cunning thoughts of men being fashioned that night!

When the watch was changed at midnight. Carter was wakened by the stoppage of the engines. He slipped on deck. A seaman was pacing the deck beneath the bridge, and he pointed out to Carter, through a night glass, a fleck of white ahead. A dead calm had fallen, and the Zamiel, as though disdaining to use her puny six-knot engine against the propellers of the yacht, lay motionless under the stars.

"Orders are to hold off until daylight, sir," commented the sailor. Carter nodded and passed back to his berth. The *Alcis* rocked gently to the slow swells, and to the swinging motion Carter fell once more into sleep, while through his dreams danced the brown eyes of "Billy" Bergen, their laughing depths filled with golden gleams like the bronze lamps in the temple of the Sixteen Gods.

In the darkness that falls just before dawn, an unsensed, intangible something took hold upon Carter's mind, so that he found himself awake and staring at the dim gray outline of his porthole. He groped sleepily for his watch, and pressed the button which would flash on the electric lights. The button clicked—but no lights answered.

Then, sharp and unheralded as a thunderbolt, a revolver crashed out on the deck above, and was answered by the cry of a man in agony.

CHAPTER VIII

PIRACY!

CARTER TUMBLED out into the alley between the cabins and the ship's rail. He was clad only in his pajamas, and was unarmed, but it did not occur to him that anything of moment could have happened. That pistol shot, he thought hurriedly, might have been the fuses in the electrical circuits blowing out, which would account for the ship's being in darkness.

But as he stood beside the rail, gazing from the dark ship to the darker sea around, he remembered that man's scream; even on the thought, there came a second sharp crack, this time from the very bowels of the ship.

"By George, something *is* wrong!" muttered the American.

He started to run forward, but stopped short with fear clutching at him. Over the rail rose a silent, vague, naked shape, like some awful apparition risen out of the sea. Then it stood upright upon the rail, and Carter saw that it was a man. The man emitted a low, snarling sound and flung forward, hurtling bodily through the air as though flung by released springs, as indeed was the case, the springs in question being leg muscles like chilled steel.

Quite naturally, Carter went flat beneath the shock; but, having already realized that this was something entirely human and not at all supernatural, he had swung himself forward and down to meet the shock of that hurtling body. As a consequence, something made of steel and shaped exactly like a flame, that had been intended for Carter's throat, buried itself in the wooden cabin wall behind. As a further consequence, Carter rolled clear and aided himself to arise by means of a scientifically placed kick which left the naked shape completely hors de combat.

A second naked shape had materialized upon the rail at the same point, and now this body sprang forward and grappled with the American. Carter's hands gripped hard, but slid over a greased skin without effect; the keen edge of a second creese slithered through the coat of his pajamas, slightly burning his skin—and with that he struck out and struck hard.

The naked figure reeled back to the rail, where now a third shape was rising—even in that stark moment it reminded Carter of nothing so much as a chain of white ants running up a table leg. Things were growing more distinct now with each instant. Carter saw that these human ants of his were of Chinese features. On the ship's side under the rail appeared a fourth head, a flamy creese between its teeth.

All this passed in a flash of time. Although he did not in the least comprehend how naked men could be streaming aboard the *Alcis* in the middle of the Banda Sea, Carter did not waste any time on inquiries.

Before the second comer had reached the rail in his back stagger, Carter's fist took him under the chin and lifted him far enough over the rail so that the rush of the American's body sent him flying. The third man was poising on the rail, and his creese jabbed down—but the jab was too slow by half an instant. Carter butted square into his knees; and when you smash into the knees of a stooping man, that man is very apt to fall over with queerly jointed legs and a screaming throat.

The fourth boarder stabbed savagely under the rail, and nothing except a life preserver saved Carter's life from the slash. The life preserver was there, however, and it held the creese blade long enough to permit Carter's naked foot to drive out, heel first. The fourth man's head snapped back, and he fell with a thump into a boat that drifted below. Carter looked over the rail. There were no more ants left.

"What the devil!" ejaculated Carter, rubbing his knuckles. "Is this piracy? Then something's stirring up forward, sure enough!"

He stooped over the first comer, who was groaning, lifted the man, and without hesitation shot him over the rail whence he had come. Then, picking up the razor-edged blade dropped by the second man, Carter ran forward, his bare feet making no noise.

Unexpectedly a stateroom door swung silently open before him, and a pudgy figure emerged. Carter's fingers gripped down.

"Solomon! what's up?"

"Oh, it's you!" exclaimed Solomon agitatedly. "Take this 'ere gun, sir," and he shoved a revolver into Carter's hand. "Find Cap'n Bingham an' tell him to 'old the bridge for a matter o' ten minutes more. Move sharp!"

The little cockney ducked under Carter's arm and ran aft with surprising agility. Astonished, the American concluded hastily that Solomon must have lost his head with the confusion, and went on toward the bow at a run.

Another pistol shot, this time from the bridge, clarified the situation. In the gray light of dawn Carter was aware of naked yellow figures slipping about like ghosts. As he sprang for the ladder, one of them uprose before him. Carter pistoled him and leaped over the falling body to the ladder.

A knife slapped into the wood beside his ear and whanged with the impact of the throw. To pause now was death, and Carter went up to the bridge with a rush. Another revolver exploded over him, and a hand seized his, helping him up.

"Got that beggar, I think," said Captain Bingham coolly. "Hello, Carter! Good man!"

The bridge and wheelhouse stood well above the bridge deck, commanding it fully. In the wheelhouse was one of the seamen, and another was aft on the bridge deck. Thus for the moment

Carter could see that no peril threatened, save by way of the ladders.

"What's happened?" he asked hurriedly. "I found some chinks coming over the side—threw 'em back into a boat. Solomon popped out of a cabin, gave me a gun, said to find you and get ten minutes' more time, and rushed away as if he'd gone nutty."

"Hell's to pay!" said Bingham, reloading his revolver. "Get back under the windows of the house—watch that port ladder, now! I'll watch to sta'board. Why, it seems like a million devils came out o' the sea, slipped up on us in boats, most likely. Must ha' knifed the man on watch, then slipped down to the engine room. They bottled that up, bottled the fo'c's'le, and started to take the bridge. Ain't got it yet, though! But we're helpless."

"Chinamen! Where the devil did they come from?" Carter frowned. "Stoppel had only eight men on his schooner."

"Eight in the crew," interjected Bingham. "Prob'ly he had the hold filled with 'em."

"But Solomon came on his ship! Surely he would have detected their presence?"

"Nope. Stoppel is infernal clever. You ain't seen the ladies?"

The question was like a shock to Carter. For a moment he stood motionless; then he turned toward the ladder.

Bingham's hand gripped his shoulder hard.

"None o' that, Mr. Carter! They're safe."

"What do you know about it?" snapped Carter. Bingham chuckled. The man aft on the bridge deck fired twice, evidently at some one trying to get up by clambering over the side.

"Go slow, Mr. Carter—no use throwing away your life. This hooker was built for Mr. Solomon years ago—we were gun running up the Somali coast then. He told you to get ten minutes, so we'll give him fifteen; after which we'll join him. Trust me, Mr. Carter, there's no particular danger to the passengers now, and there are a few secrets to this craft that even Stoppel will slip up on. Ah—look out! The murderin' devils mean business this time."

Mean business they did. Doubtless Stoppel had gathered his men with the intention of landing at Banda Lontar and coolly carrying off the big rosewood throne; having easily guessed the business of the *Alcis*, perhaps even having discerned the figure of Wing Fu aboard her, he was acting with swift boldness. Having flung his men aboard at various points, and the yacht now being practically in his possession, he was consolidating his men in a rush for the bridge, which meant final control.

They came swarming up at all points, with revolvers spitting. The tropic dawn broke into red daylight, as though flames had leaped from horizon to zenith; to Carter it seemed that some old boyhood tale of piracy had blossomed into being, and he was amazed to find himself cool in the midst of this uproar, intent only upon ridding the port ladder of the crowding attackers. When they were gone, he glimpsed the bulky figure of Stoppel on the fore deck below, and aimed hastily; the hammer fell on empty cartridges, and Stoppel vanished again.

"Confound it!" exclaimed Carter. "One more bullet—"

He was surprised to discover that the affair was all over. The man in the wheelhouse was dead. Bingham was quietly binding up a bullet slash across the thigh. No yellow men had gained the bridge or the bridge deck, and the man who had been aft was coming forward, biting nonchalantly at a plug of tobacco and stowing away his revolver.

"Take some shells—right jacket pocket," said Bingham. Carter obeyed, and reloaded his weapon. The skipper glanced at the seaman and jerked his head toward the after deck. "Get that dummy ventilator ready, Loomis, then stand by—"

"If we could get our men out of the forecastle and engine room," said Carter, helping Bingham tie up his hurt, "we'd have a chance."

"We're all right," said the skipper calmly, and sheeted home his belt again. "That is, we might be a sight worse off. Those men below are battened down, and chances are they won't be hurt. The rest of us won't be found, at least until we're ready to act. Now, sir, kindly join Loomis and look sharp when I sing out."

Carter strode aft to Loomis, who was standing beside a ventilator. The *Zamiel* was still far away, but now Carter saw her heading slowly around, as if to creep across the windless seas toward them. Loomis glanced at her, shook his head slightly, then touched the high, red-throated ventilator; to his touch the funnel slid aside, disclosing a chute that seemed to lead slantingly into the bowels of the ship—certainly no ventilator shaft!

"What's this?" exclaimed Carter, staring at it. Loomis grinned.

"Little scheme o' Mr. Solomon's, sir. When the old man sings out, you hop in and let yourself go—she runs down to a secret cabin. Puzzled more'n one head, this old boat has! B'lieve me, we ain't through with these chinks."

Carter nodded tacit understanding.

Now was explained Solomon's plea for time, and Bingham's cool surety! Somewhere underneath, Carter realized, Solomon and Wing Fu must have stowed Miss Bergen and the mevrouw in safety; the comprehension came to him with a shock. It had been so easy to think that all was lost, so easy to lose all faith in the queer little man with the blue eyes! Yet here, caught wholly off guard as Solomon must have been, the very ship captured under his feet, the cockney gave fresh proof of his almost uncanny power of coping with emergencies!

But, thought Carter, of what avail was a secret cabin? It must eventually be found, for Stoppel would search the yacht with savage intensity—would go over every inch of bulkhead and hold space until the secret was located. After that, what? Counting Wing Fu and Solomon, there would be five men against Stoppel's possible thirty, for Carter reckoned the half-caste's force at about that number. And there could be but one end!

He was wakened from his musing by the robust voice of Stoppel from the forward deck:

"Ahoy the bridge! I'll give you a chance to—"

Bingham stepped forward, threw up his revolver, and fired—

then leaped backward with an oath of disappointment. He waved his left hand at Loomis in unspoken command.

"In with you, sir!" said the seaman quietly. "We must slip off before they rush again, or they'll get wise."

Without hesitation Carter sat with his feet in the chute, put up his arms, and let himself go. Blackness engulfed him.

After sliding forward for what seemed years, Carter emerged into space, felt himself caught and checked in progress, and found himself between Solomon and Wing Fu, in a small room dimly filled with daylight. He was hastily pushed to one side as Loomis and Bingham came after him.

"Oh—you're safe!"

Carter gripped the hands of Miss Bergen, and his heart thrilled to the anxiety in her voice. So, then, she had been thinking of him!

"Quite," he said, smiling slightly into her brown eyes and noting that she was pale but self-possessed. "I'm glad to see you all right—Ah, Mevrouw van der Gelt, *goeden dag!*"

This secret room held chairs, lockers along the walls, and a smell of coffee. Over the alcohol stove and percolator presided the mevrouw, dumpy, dignified, and unruffled as ever. She greeted Carter as if quite at home.

Glancing about, the American saw that the low-ceiled room was paneled to the top, and now there was no trace of the opening through which Bingham and Loomis had followed him.

"Where are we?" He turned to Solomon with the direct inquiry.

"Inside the for'ard coal bunker, sir," and the cockney chuckled wheezily. "Now, first off, 'ave a cup o' coffee and a biscuit all around. Then we'll 'ave a bit o' talk."

A false coal bunker—well, it was not a bad artifice, thought Carter, and turned back to Miss Bergen. At his quiet question, she said that Solomon had wakened her and the mevrouw and that they had arrived here in the same undignified fashion as Carter. Nor was any door apparent along the walls.

Solomon and Wing Fu were apprised of the situation, and the mevrouw passed around cups of coffee, then procured biscuits from one of the lockers. The place seemed well provided, even to rifles and pistols.

"Now, then," demanded Bingham bluntly, "what's to be done? There's six men in the engine room, though they've probably shot the chief. If we're going to show fight, we have to grab the engines, else they'll open the cocks and sink us in a jiffy."

"They'll not sink us," declared Mr. Wing Fu in his silky fashion. He did not explain himself, however.

"We'll not fight," said Solomon gloomily. "If we was alone, I'd say to 'ave a try, just like that; but we ain't alone, as the old gent said when 'e met the 'ousemaid on the street. No, we ain't goin' to fight."

Miss Bergen leaned forward.

"I understand what you gentlemen are driving at," she said coolly. "But let me tell you here and now that if it comes to fighting, I'll take a hand myself! I don't propose to have you change your plans in the least just because two women are here."

"Madam, we have no plans," said Wing Fu drolly. "It is Mr. Stoppel who has plans."

The girl flushed. Suddenly Carter understood what the Celestial had meant a moment previously. With the comprehension, he grew very cold. Heretofore he had not regarded Herman Stoppel as a particularly personal enemy, but now there flooded into his heart a bitter anger, a gripping desire to stand face to face again with Stoppel, a wild passion to punish the half-caste who dared to lift his eyes to this sweet-faced girl. An instant later, Captain Bingham made answer in his own fashion.

"What d'you gentlemen mean?" he demanded bluntly. "No use trying to back out of fighting; not a bit of it! 'Twon't gain the ladies anything to back and fill at this stage of the game, Mr. Solomon. The only way to get out of a half-finished fight is to get out on top!"

"Good for you, captain!" exclaimed the girl quickly. "Reverse your decision, John!"

Solomon stared blankly at her for a moment, then a twinkle came into his blue eyes, and a wheezy chuckle to his lips.

"I ain't werry spry in me old age," he declared slowly, "and me judgment ain't what it used to be, as the old gent said when 'e took 'is third. There's two of us 'ere as 'aven't 'ad a word to say"—he nodded toward the mevrouw, who was placidly knitting—"and you're the other, Mr. Carter. We'll leave it up to you, just like that.

"Shall we buy off them 'ere beggars, prowiding it could be done? Or shall we up an' fight? You 'ave your say, Mr. Carter, sir, and I'll abide by it."

Carter's gaze passed from the eager eyes of Miss Bergen to the cynical face of the Celestial; the bluff boldness of Bingham and Loomis; and back again to the twinkling blue eyes of John Solomon. With himself rested the decision, yet he conjectured that the little pudgy cockney had guessed that decision beforehand.

If Stoppel really wanted Wilhelmina Bergen, by fair means or foul, to temporize would be folly; bribery would be folly, negotiation at all would be folly. Stoppel must have planned, away back there in Surabaya, to carry off Miss Bergen and the Chair of the Eye at one blow, and then to run to some Australian or French port for shelter. Aye! Farther than this had gone the cunning of the half-caste! Stoppel had perhaps seen the *Alcis* at Surabaya or elsewhere, and knew to whom she belonged. Therefore he had tried to checkmate Solomon by having the little man arrested at Banda Neira; therefore, seeing a chance to get away with the Chair of the Eye sans trouble on shore, he had taken it, for he must have suspected the surprising quiescence of Solomon during that transaction. Therefore, seeing the *Alcis* entering the harbor as he had left, he must have outguessed Solomon's whole intent.

As these thoughts flashed across Carter's mind, the seaman Loomis spoke out in most startling antiphone:

"They may put it over on Mr. Solomon once or twice, all right, but when it comes to finishin' strong—Lord help 'em!"

Carter smiled.

"Fight!" he said briefly. "How do we get out of here?"

His decision had its reward in the girl's shining eyes, and Bingham growled swift assent. But Solomon drew out his clay pipe and prepared it for action.

"Werry good, sir! I 'opes as 'ow you'll take me orders without question?"

"Certainly," nodded Carter, his face stony as he searched the mild blue eyes.

Solomon cocked his head to one side, as if listening. In the silence, Carter noticed that the light was dimming in the room, and wondered at the cause; a moment later there came a perceptible shock, as though another ship had come alongside in the dead calm.

"Ah!" said Solomon, lighting his pipe with a nod. "That 'ere's the *Zamiel*. Now, Mr. Carter, sir, you'll 'ave a bit of a swim—and you'll 'ave to move lively, sir!"

For the first time Carter remembered that he was wearing only pajamas.

"I'm ready," he said, and laughed a little.

CHAPTER IX

KNOWLES TURNS UP

SOLOMON CAME to his feet suddenly, his eyes going from one to another; they stared at him in amazement, for a startling change had come over the little man. For the first and only time, Carter saw the round face glowing with exultation, the blue eyes blazing; it was as though Solomon were filled with some inner triumph, some glorious, laughing victory, which momentarily broke through all restraint.

"Put it over on me, 'ave they?" exclaimed Solomon. "Ho! Just you wait! 'Aven't I been a-prayin' for this werry blessed moment, as the old gent said when 'e buried 'is third? Ho! That 'ere Stoppel is a slick beggar, 'e is, but you just wait! 'Ere, Mr. Carter!"

From the locker he swiftly snatched an automatic wrapped in oilskin, which he shoved into Carter's hand.

What could Solomon mean? What, indeed, except that he had anticipated every move that had been made by Stoppel? So astounding was this conclusion that Carter could not accept it. Bingham stepped forward heavily.

"D'you mean," he demanded hoarsely, "that you've let our men be murdered for lack o' warning, sir?"

"No." Solomon stared at him, once more blank-eyed, expressionless. "No, Mr. Bingham, I 'ad no way o' knowin' what was a-goin' to 'appen—but I looked out for everything, just like that. Don't worry, sir; 'e'll pay for each blessed drop o' blood as gets spilled! Now, Mr. Carter, just you step over 'ere."

Carter followed to the far corner of the room, wonder still

gripping him. What game of wits was slowly revealing itself here? What incredible play of brains was involved in this affair? Stoppel was a man of wiles, pregnant with the cunning of Oriental and Occidental alike, and pitted against him was this blue-eyed little cockney—master against master! Or, on the other hand, was not all this mere imagination, and were not the coincidences of destiny being assigned to the cleverness of men? Surely this must be the case, for surely no man could possess such superhuman insight into the future as Solomon's words had suggested.

Thus Carter questioned—as other men had questioned when drawn into the affairs of John Solomon; and his answer, like theirs, was not to be had in words.

Solomon pressed a concealed spring, and a panel of the wood-work slid aside, disclosing a chute like that by which Carter had entered.

"I gambled on one thing," said the cockney quietly, "and if that 'ere schooner 'adn't laid up along this 'ere starboard side, I'd 'ave put me foot in it, an' no mistake, Mr. Bingham, sir! You slip out to the engine room wi' some guns, if so be as you can kill the chink what's there and arm the men, then wait for further orders, well an' good.

"Mr. Carter, you slip down this 'ere chute. I'll open the gate beyond, and you'll pop out into the water between the ships. Then you'll 'ave to climb up on the *Zamiel*—"

"You mean to our own deck," broke in Carter.

"No, sir, I don't! I means the *Zamiel*, just like that! Stoppel 'as every man aboard 'ere lookin' for us. Cast off the line what's 'olding the two ships together, sir, then stand by until Miss Bergen and Mevrouw wan der Gelt join you—"

"What!" Carter glanced at the girl. "Why, man, they can't slide down into the water and take chances."

"Dang it, will you obey orders an' stop askin' questions?" snapped Solomon. "Never you mind 'ow they're a-goin' to join you, sir. With 'em and you on the *Zamiel*, we'll 'ave a clear 'and 'ere—and mind you take care on 'em, sir!"

Carter nodded, put the oilskin between his teeth, and stepped into the chute.

In that instant of time, as he slipped downward and came to rest against some obstacle—the "gate" of which Solomon had spoken—he realized what a wizard this little cockney was. For some reason Solomon did not want the two women to remain in the secret room, and was planning to get them aboard the *Zamiel* with Carter. Then, with the two ships separated, Stoppel would be unable to carry out any maddog tactics such as sinking the yacht with all she held.

One person, however, had been completely overlooked by every one. This was the gentleman of the roving sapphire eye—Captain Knowles, of nowhere.

Carter felt the opposing obstacle slip away, and he plunged forward into daylight and water. He emerged, swimming, to find himself under the overhangs of the two ships, which gently ground together in the calm swell and gave him a half minute of terrible fear until he found that the yacht's overhang gave him three or four clear feet of space without danger from the swinging hulls. He struck out for the stern of the schooner, determining to obey orders and trust all to Solomon.

In two minutes he was under the stern of the *Zamiel,* and, seeing no means of getting to her rail—for she was in ballast and high in the water—he continued around to her starboard side. Aboard the *Alcis* he could hear the shrill tones of Chinamen and a banging of doors. Evidently the search was being pushed.

With a sigh of relief, Carter found the after boat falls hanging, where the *Zamiel's* boats had gone overside before dawn. He gripped the nearest rope and pulled himself upward.

A moment later his head came above the rail of the schooner. A cautious glance showed him that her deck was deserted, nor was any one in sight along the starboard rail of the yacht; so without hesitation Carter swung himself over and darted silently to the shelter of the after skylight, whose peak concealed him from those aboard the yacht as he crouched and hastily tore the oilskin from his automatic.

How Miss Bergen and the mevrouw were to get aboard was none of his affair, but he must get the two ships apart without delay. So, trusting to blind luck, he slipped out across the deck to the port side and cast loose the hawser that swung up to the yacht's rail, then ran forward and loosed the other binding rope. Luck favored, and no outcry arose from the *Alcis*.

Not yet certain that the schooner was deserted, Carter slipped down the forecastle companionway and found only a vile smell of opium, then cautiously returned to the deck. The fore hatch of the schooner was off, revealing the hiding place of the flood of pirates who had erupted upon the night. Carter raced aft, every instant expecting a shot to ring out from the yacht, but gained the after companionway in safety. He darted down, thinking to start the engines and head the ships apart, for they clung together as ships will in a calm sea.

As he came to the bottom of the ladder, Carter stood stock-still; from the deck above had come a thump of feet, as though some one had jumped down from the yacht's rail. And even as he glanced upward, Carter felt that he was not alone here, heard a shuffle of bare feet, and a door to his left opened to a half-naked, grimy figure—the half-caste engineer of this half-caste ship!

Before the man could cry out, Carter leaped. Fire he dared not, save as a last resort. His left hand closed about the oily throat and he struck out with the weapon in his hand; but the impulse of his fling carried them both on through the doorway into the tiny engine room.

If he had thought these men could not fight with their bare hands, the American was speedily undeceived. Fight?

The engineer developed a demoniac strength and activity; before Carter recovered from that lunge, he found himself backed over the engine, with a storm of blows battering him down.

Mindful of those sounds from the deck above, the American dared not fire, nor did he dare release the man's throat. He struck out with the weapon again, and blood spurted from the yellow brow, but the answer came in a smashing blow that bent Carter over until he lost his balance, and the two rolled to the floor. The American dropped underneath.

Then he realized that fate was tagging hard at his heels, for the engineer had slipped out a creese and was stabbing. Perforce, Carter released the man's throat, caught the wrist, and lashed out desperately below the descending arm. The automatic's muzzle went fair to the Adam's apple, and the yellow engineer groaned and rolled over.

Carter leaped to the door and closed it, whipped off his ragged pajamas, and securely gagged and bound the senseless engineer, then darted to the engine. Five seconds later he threw over the wheel and felt the schooner urge forward. After a moment he shut off the power, confident that she was well away from the yacht, and opened the door. The companionway was clear.

Being naked, Carter slipped across the passage to one of the cabin doors and entered. By good fortune he had struck Stoppel's cabin, and in two minutes was clothed and back at the ladder. That some one had come aboard he felt certain, and the shrill yells that drifted down to him signified that he had succeeded in separating the ships.

"I've got to get that beggar up above," muttered Carter grimly. "As to Miss Bergen—well, if Solomon has failed, I'll go back and take a hand in the fighting!"

He crept up the ladder, his automatic ready. A heavy footfall on the deck warned him that his prey was approaching, and he crouched flat against the ladder, his weapon thrust upward. What he did not see or hear was that behind him one of the cabin doors opened and then shut again, hastily but softly.

From the yacht came shots and the yells of men. Carter waited, and smiled grimly as he heard the footsteps approach the ladder with a rush. Then a shape appeared above.

"Hands up!" he snapped harshly. "Put 'em— Oh, Lord! *You!*"

The mevrouw frowned down at him.

"Put away that weapon, you fool!" she said in Dutch. "Let us down—hurry! *Gauw!*"

Beside her appeared Miss Bergen, and the two women broke into a laugh at sight of the disconcerted Carter. They descended quickly, and the girl seized his arm.

"You thought we were—oh, we didn't know where you were, Ralph!" Her brown eyes danced gayly at him, yet with a grave anxiety in their depths. "Mr. Solomon sent us through a secret doorway to the deck, and before any one could stop us, we had jumped down to the schooner, and she started off as Stoppel came to head us off—"

"And then the shooting began," concluded Carter. "Well, my job is to take care of this craft and you. Wait here a minute until I have a look-see."

"I intend to sit down," said the mevrouw firmly. "I shall not wait here. This shooting and conduct are disgraceful!"

She marched aft to the tiny saloon cabin. Carter ascended the ladder, but could make out little of what was happening aboard the yacht, for the excellent reason that a bullet nipped splinters from beside him. He withdrew hastily, having learned that the two craft were a hundred feet apart. Stoppel evidently held the decks of the yacht and was keeping an eye on his schooner.

"Looks to me as if the Dutchman were up against it," and Carter chuckled as he rejoined the girl at the foot of the ladder. "He has his boats, but if he sends his men off to capture us again, Solomon will certainly recapture the *Alcis!*"

"I see! Oh, I think John is wonderful!" said the girl softly. "If—"

She was interrupted by the appearance of Mevrouw van der Gelt.

"Come here!" ordered that commanding lady, her eyes very wide. "Come here and see what I have found! *Hemel!* Such a thing I have never seen, *nooit!*"

They followed her to the saloon. There, beneath the skylight, was a heap of wrenched and riven pieces of carved rosewood. Amid them, still incased from the seat down, stood the Chair of the Eye.

From Miss Bergen broke a little gasp of amazement. Carter, finding himself still holding her hand, gripped it a bit harder and stared at the chair which faced him from beneath the skylight. One had but to see it to recognize what it was, after hearing the tale; in its presence no explanation was necessary. The mevrouw, looking very satisfied with herself, dropped into a Singapore chair by the stern window, but Carter and Miss Bergen remained standing.

"Billy!" exclaimed Carter softly. "Look at those stones! Catch that gleam from the skylight?"

"It's wonderful!" she responded. "Wonderful! Yet two million dollars seems just as much of a dream—just as incredible!"

The Chair of the Eye, as it stood before them, was a very slender thing compared to the immense rosewood affair which had inclosed it from sight. It was a mass of intricate carving, and was completely covered by the magnificent royal gold lacquer which only old China could produce—lacquer infinitely more precious than its weight in gold.

Not the lacquer, however, nor the carving, held the three watchers in silent admiration. Set against the wondrous yellow lacquer, glowing from the carvings like sentient things, were the eyes of cats—hundreds of them! Green, shifty duplicates of the living eyes, with the deep, dusky green that never was on land or sea!

No synthetic, cheap "fixed" stones were these, such as flood the world's markets; no quartz, no cleverly cut and matched crystals. Royal chrysoberyls from the Brazilian mines were these, traded through Portuguese hands in the old days to Chinese markets, and cut as such stones were only cut in the old days— gracefully rounded to bring out every least shimmer of the simu- lated cat's eye.

"Whew!" Carter drew a deep breath. "Now I can understand the madness that has driven Herman Stoppel to such lengths!"

He realized that he still held his automatic, and after stepping to the stern windows and making sure that no boat was yet approaching from the *Alcis,* he tossed the weapon to the corner table. The clatter aroused the mevrouw from her contemplation of the wondrous chair, and she rose.

"I shall find something to eat," she announced.

"Eat!" Miss Bergen glanced at her with a ripple of laughter. "Why, we've just had breakfast—"

"We have not had *rijstaafel,*" broke in the mevrouw firmly. She could not get away from the tremendous meal of the Dutch colonial. "There are Chinese, or were, aboard this horrible ship—ugh, how filthy it is! Therefore there must be rice. Those men on the yacht will not shoot at me, so I shall go upstairs and look for the kitchen."

Carter grinned.

"Go ahead," he said. "They won't shoot either of you, right enough. We may be here for a long time before the deadlock over yonder is broken. Solomon has the engine room and Stoppel has the bridge and decks, so neither can control the yacht. But if you see any boats coming, you'd better skip down here. We may have to repel boarders."

"Let them try it!" said Mevrouw van der Gelt.

With a laughing glance at Carter. Miss Bergen followed the majestic figure to the deck above, leaving the American alone.

For a space he stared at the Chair of the Eye, marveling at the thing. As he moved about, the eyes followed shiftily, uncannily, after the nature of the royal chrysoberyl and the cat. They seemed alive, sentient, weirdly impish. No wonder that they had been chosen as symbols by Oriental minds; no wonder that in these later days they could command their own price—stones rarer than diamonds or fine pearls of Sabara!

Wakening suddenly to the responsibilities of his position, Carter strode over to the stern windows. An exclamation broke from him. A boat was putting off from the *Alcis,* with two Chinese rowers! And in the stern sheets of the boat was Herman Stoppel.

"Here is where friend Herman gets his!" said Carter, with a grin. He reached for his revolver—and a voice stayed his hand:

"Not yet—not just yet, I believe, Mr. Carter! Please do not move!"

Carter turned his head to see a man standing in the doorway, with a revolver cocked and aloft. Over the weapon's ugly mouth shone the deep sapphire eye of Captain Knowles, brilliant as the flaming eyes of the great Buddha under Tanggan Hill!

CHAPTER X

STOPPEL'S HOUR

THERE WAS no mistaking that sapphire eye; Captain Knowles was entirely willing and ready to bring down the trigger.

Carter observed the behest and stood motionless while Knowles advanced and appropriated the automatic. On discovering Stoppel's approach, he had exultantly thought to rid them all of that archenemy; the appearance of Knowles was a bitter surprise.

"Sit down!" Knowles closed the door and stood to one side of it. Carter sat on the edge of the table, wondering if the other man knew of Stoppel's approach. "Thought you had—ah—played a very pretty little trick, Mr. Carter—eh what?"

"Why are you in with this gang of cutthroats, Knowles?" demanded Carter bluntly.

"Money." Knowles nodded toward the Chair of the Eye. "Going home and—ah—to be a gentleman."

"You damned dog!" snapped Carter. "Don't you know that Miss Bergen and Mevrouw van der Gelt are aboard here—"

"Certainly." The blue eye roved swiftly about and then fastened upon Carter with a mocking deviltry. "That is all arranged, my dear chap. The mevrouw will be sent home unharmed a bit later. My friend Stoppel will marry Miss Bergen. I trust you'll see that there is nothing—ah—indiscreet in our plans."

Carter's muscles tautened; he was half minded to throw

himself across the cabin at this renegade—but the revolver flecked up and gave him pause. Knowles smiled.

"You should have searched the cabins in the—ah—first instance. Then circumstances might have been altered. As it is—ah—be quiet!"

The blue eye flamed out with sudden savagery. From the ladder outside sounded a light thud of feet, and Carter knew that the girl was coming with news of Stoppel's approach. Before he could act upon that thought, or even cry out to give her warning, she had flung the door open and darted into the cabin.

"Ralph! You'll have to come—"

Her voice died, for he was staring over her shoulder at Knowles. She whipped about, and from her lips broke a single word:

"You!"

At her evident fear, at her white-faced shrinking, the evil lips of Knowles twisted into a thin smile, a smile of utter cruelty.

"Yes, it's your old friend, Captain Knowles, madam," he mocked her. "So sorry to see you in this position—ah—Mr. Carter is a very nice young man, no doubt."

She gave Carter a single glance, then turned to Knowles, her cheeks burning.

"Careful!" he went on sharply. "Stand still, or I'll put a bullet into Carter, even if it breaks your pretty heart."

"You cur!"

Like a flash the girl stepped in front of him, seized his pistol in both hands, and pointed it upward. Carter was off the table in a leap.

The situation was desperate, but if they could down Knowles, Carter hoped to keep Stoppel off the ship. With a swift thought of blessing for the girl's bravery, Carter threw himself across the cabin.

Captain Knowles was an old bird, however, and exceeding tough. With a single startled oath, he wrenched the girl's hands around, drew her off balance, and literally flung her against the charging Carter. Then he slipped to the door.

Insensate with anger, the American staggered, pushed Miss Bergen aside, and leaped out into the passage. He went at Knowles in a headlong dive. That surprised gentleman fired wildly and in vain, then Carter's arms took him above the knees and pulled him down. In the rage that gripped him, Carter utterly forgot Herman Stoppel.

He wanted only to punish this renegade—and he had his wish. When, fifteen seconds later, two brawny Chinamen slipped down the ladder and bore him to the deck, Carter yielded to the flame-bladed creeses that touched his throat; he sat up in the grip of the two men, and grinned with some satisfaction at the groaning Captain Knowles.

Over the prostrate men Herman Stoppel stood and looked at Miss Bergen, his powerfully lined features set in a smile.

"Wars and rumors of wars, my dear lady!" he exclaimed, as genially as though they were meeting at her plantation house. "I welcome you to my little schooner."

She did not reply, but turned her back upon him and walked to the Chair of the Eye and sat there, waiting. Stoppel glanced after her.

"Spirit—aye, wastes no words, asks no banal questions," he said reflectively, as if to himself. "But we must have an under-standing."

Captain Knowles sat up, feeling his facial bones and cursing luridly in Dutch and English. Stoppel paid him no heed, but looked down and locked eyes with Carter.

Then for the first time Carter really began to feel fear of this man. In the gaze of Stoppel he comprehended something of the man's inner nature; a diabolically clever, brutal, masterful, cold nature, and at the bottom utterly ruthless and without scruples. That was the Oriental blood in him, thought Carter, the terrible taint of Asia which knows no pity and holds life the cheapest thing in life.

But the American forgot his fear in rising anger, and his gray eyes blazed back at Stoppel until the latter laughed cruelly.

"You shall be tamed soon enough, my American—ah!" Stoppel whirled upon the rising Knowles, who had clutched a revolver and was flinging it up toward Carter. With a swift movement Stoppel knocked the weapon away and jerked Knowles upright. "Damn you, don't you start any murder— until I give the word! Get into the cabin!"

He flung Knowles into the saloon, and, beckoning to the two Chinese who held Carter, strode in toward Miss Bergen. Carter was propelled after him, and was halted inside the door.

"Please, Miss Bergen," said Stoppel suavely, "remove the pistol which is in your waist and throw it out of the window! I refuse to submit you to the indignity of a search; besides which I must remind you that the fate of Mr. Carter is very apt to depend upon yourself. Ah, thank you!"

White with her anger, Miss Bergen silently took a small revolver from her bosom and tossed it through the window. Stoppel smiled. He seemed to radiate an infernal geniality, and his force of character was dominating.

"You are sitting upon a throne worthy only of you, Miss Bergen," he said softly. "But may I request a few moments in private conversation?"

The girl looked up at him, and her brown eyes were starry with repressed anger.

"If you have anything to say, say it here," she returned curtly.

"Very well." Stoppel paused, then continued reflectively: "It seems that at last we have played this pretty little game almost to the end, Miss Bergen. The chair upon which you are sitting represents a fortune, which Captain Knowles is to share with me. Besides that, I have converted most of my other possessions into ready money. There is one thing, however, more important to me than all else, upon which I have long set my heart. That, Miss Bergen, is yourself. I ask you now to marry me—"

"You cross-bred hound!" cried Carter furiously. "Go pick a mate from your own kind, instead of—"

Stoppel turned and struck him with a lashing blow to the cheek. The half-caste was livid with rage.

"Be silent until I address you!" His voice was like a deadly snake. "You have no say in this affair."

Carter, who had been standing passively beneath the yellow hands that held him, flexed his muscles and for one moment tore himself free. His fist cracked into Stoppel's mouth and sent the man reeling—then Captain Knowles deftly tapped him with a pistol butt and as Carter staggered, the two Chinese fell upon him and lashed his wrists at his back.

Drawing himself up despite his whirling senses, in that moment Carter expected no less than death. But Stoppel wiped the blood from his lips with a slow gesture, and then spoke very slowly:

"Later, Mr. Carter, you may repent that hasty action." He swung about to the girl, who had risen, watching the scene with fear in her eyes. But the fear fled out of them as she met Stoppel's gaze, and they grew hard and tense.

"Miss Bergen, I was asking you to marry me," continued the half-caste calmly. "Although I do love you, and have loved you from our first meeting, I realize that at present you cannot reciprocate this feeling." The poise of the man, his cold finality and deliberation, were terrible.

"Therefore I make my plea on the grounds of expediency," he proceeded. "You are poor; I am wealthy and powerful. Those who have befriended you are in my hands. I ask only your promise, and am content to wait in the surety that before a great while you will share the feeling which I—"

"Do not flatter yourself," cut in the girl coldly, with such contempt in her voice and eyes that Stoppel flushed darkly as though a whip had lashed over him. "Sooner than mate with you. I would marry the lowest wretch in Banda Neira who could still call himself a white man!"

A bitter word was that, and it drove the flush from Stoppel's face and left there an unnatural pallor. In that moment the man's Mongol blood showed very plainly.

"It is a great temptation to be melodramatic," he returned evenly, keeping a tight rein upon his passions. "Yet I must impress you with the clear light of reason, Miss Bergen. See, now! Here is Mr. Carter; yonder on the *Alcis* are Mr. Solomon and Mr. Wing Fu, who will shortly be in my power. Shall I, then, free them? Or shall I hang them and sink that yacht and take you away?"

For a moment he paused, his heavy jaw clenched; at his temple throbbed a hot pulse, and then he burst forth with a tensed passion in his words:

"Will you drive me to the farthest lengths, my girl? Force me to it, and not a man of all these shall remain alive—and what will you have gained? Nothing! Nothing! For I shall take you with me, and presently you shall be glad indeed to marry Herman Stoppel the despised! Have you I will, my girl, and if you think I cannot break your will with mine, you shall find out differently!"

The girl shrank before him, her hands clenched upon the curved back of the jewel-studded chair; and against the whiteness of her face stood out the scarlet line of her lips.

Yet ever her eyes blazed at him defiantly, and she did not lose the self-possession which had carried her so far and well.

Stoppel choked down his passion and forced a smile.

"Now answer me!" he concluded hoarsely, "if you dare to answer no, your will shall be broken like a rotten stick!"

"No, you cur!" she flung at him.

For a moment he gazed down at her, a cruel admiration flaming in his evil eyes. Then, with a little gesture as though dismissing the subject, he turned to Captain Knowles.

"I shall return to the other ship alone, leaving these men with you," he said in Malay, not knowing that Carter understood it. "That little fat man is a devil incarnate, but now I have him fast.

Still, it is probable that I may make a bargain with him, in which case I must let them all go alive."

"Don't be a fool," snapped Knowles in English, his blue eye staring at Stoppel. Then he started and laughed suddenly. "Oh, you mean to promise anything, eh?"

"I keep my oaths." And Stoppel's face hardened. "Solomon and Wing Fu keep their oaths, and I am not less than they! I think that we shall call truce until I can fetch the fat cockney over here and settle matters. By the way, what has become of that cursed big woman who was with this girl?"

"I haven't seen—" The response of Knowles was cut short by a heavy tread upon the companion ladder outside. Stoppel moved lithely to the doorway and stood beside it, waiting.

A moment later the mevrouw appeared, beaming, quite unconscious of what had transpired. Evidently she had found the galley, for her two hands supported an immense platter, heaped high with steaming rice, whose whiteness was marred by curry and tinned supplies. She had prepared a worthy *rijsta-afel,* had Mevrouw van der Gelt.

As she came within the doorway, Captain Knowles grinned and made her an elaborate bow. She stopped short. Over the heap of rice her horrified eyes slipped around the cabin and widened in comprehension.

"You!" she gasped at Knowles. "You English *hond—schaap— konijn—*"

The flood of epithets ended in a deft movement. Captain Knowles, rising from his bow, received the rice and platter squarely in the face, and went over backward with a howl. The irate mevrouw was about to complete her work when Stoppel fell upon her from behind, one of the Chinese sprang to aid him, and between her they spun the mevrouw about and propelled her from the cabin. A moment later there came the slam of a door, and Stoppel darted back with a key in his hand. Nor could he repress a grin as he aided the cursing Knowles to rise.

"A clever woman, that!" he commented, while Knowles wiped

his face. "She's locked in your cabin—here is the key. Now, my friend, keep these two prisoners safe until my return, and keep them apart also! Allow them no communication, although you may keep them both here with you for safety's sake. Farewell for the moment, Miss Bergen; I shall not yet accept your answer as final, for I shall return with your friend Solomon in my power. *Tot weerziens*, my girl!"

With merely a glance at Carter, he turned and left the cabin.

Knowles followed him, and after a moment returned with the Chinese engineer whom Carter had overpowered. The three yellow men rescued the *rijstaafel* and crowded around it on the deck; Knowles appropriated the Singapore chair and stretched out comfortably, his revolver in his lap and a cheroot between his teeth.

It was a time of waiting—intolerable and weary. No word was spoken save among the three yellow men. Their naked torsos, the creeses that swung in their belts, the evil that sang from their faces, formed a dread menace of what the future might bring forth.

Miss Bergen sat motionless in the Chair of the Eye. She met Carter's gaze, and a wan smile lighted her eyes with warmth—an unspoken message between them that set his pulses to leaping madly. Then she looked at Knowles, and presently, under her level eyes, the malicious satisfaction died from his leathery face and his splendid sapphire orb was veiled. She smiled again, a little scornfully.

Carter fell to watching through the stern windows, for the ships had drawn a bit closer together, and he had a clear view of the *Alcis*.

Hope in the wizardry of John Solomon still stirred within him. The evil genius of Stoppel held the whip hand, of course, but it was not beyond possibility that Stoppel might be slain; in which case Knowles would prove a very different adversary. So, as he watched the powerful figure of Stoppel swinging the long oars of the boat and slowly coming to the side of the *Alcis,* Carter hoped against hope.

"Our only chance is that John or Bingham will disregard everything and put a bullet through Stoppel," thought the American, as he saw the half-caste go up the side of the yacht. "If they stop to argue, they're lost. John and Wing Fu will give up everything once they know that Stoppel holds Miss Bergen as hostage!"

Three minutes later he saw some of Stoppel's men piling into a boat. They were followed by Stoppel himself, and then by the pudgy figure of John Solomon. Carter turned away with his last lingering hope destroyed. Solomon had capitulated.

Once more he met the eyes of the girl, and she read despair in his face. This time she did not smile.

CHAPTER XI

MR. SOLOMON DELAYS

AS HE searched the girl's face, so stirringly sad in that moment, yet so beautiful, Carter strained fruitlessly at his bonds. The movement brought the three Chinese about him; he was helpless. Knowles rose, went to the window, and, seeing the approach of the boat, passed out to the deck above to greet Stoppel.

Miss Bergen rose and crossed to where Carter stood bound. At her smiling gesture the slant-eyed breeds, although watching her closely, offered no objection. Her hand rested on his shoulder for an instant like a caress.

"I am sorry, Ralph," she said quietly, a wealth of meaning in her words.

Carter's face whitened.

"Billy, I swear before Heaven that—that while I live he shall never win!" His voice was low, tense, vibrating with the emotion that shook him. "Oh, my dear girl—I would give my life gladly if you were but safe at home again!"

"You would?" Suddenly she smiled, and her heart was in her eyes. "Why?"

"You know why, dear heart—because I love you!"

"And I you, dear Ralph." She laid her palms against his cheeks and touched her lips to his. Then, drawing back, she spoke very swiftly: "Don't give up hope—John told me the last thing to warn you that whatever happened you must do nothing rash until he mentioned his 'old gent.'"

One of the three Celestials roughly caught the girl's arm and pushed her back. Carter's foot snapped out and laid the man groaning on the deck; the other two sprang upon him with a low hiss of rage, and steel flashed.

At that instant the voice of Stoppel filled the cabin, and before his presence the two shrank away. He came forward alone and caught the creese from one of them.

"Truce has been declared, and Mr. Solomon is up above," he said curtly. "If you assent to the truce, Mr. Carter, you may go up freely."

Carter nodded assent, and Stoppel hacked at his bonds with the creese. Miss Bergen went to the door and disappeared from view, but Stoppel paid her no heed other than to motion his men away from her.

Those final words of the girl bred a riot of conjecture in the American's brain, as he slowly took his way to the upper deck, following Stoppel and the Chinese.

What had John Solomon meant by that warning, transmitted through Miss Bergen? The natural supposition would be that Solomon had prepared some final coup—but if so, this had been brought to naught by Stoppel's recapture of the schooner.

There could be nothing left save defeat, thought Carter. To think how Solomon and Stoppel, masters of cunning play, had pierced the heart of each other's inmost plans and had parried each sudden thrust and riposte was staggering. Carter wondered if Knowles had been left aboard the *Zamiel* to defeat some such scheme as Solomon had formed, and concluded that this had indeed been the case. A clever man was Herman Stoppel! And now he had brought Solomon to utter defeat and ruin.

In this opinion Carter was confirmed upon reaching the deck. None the less, Solomon's warning remained with him, for so deep was his respect for the pudgy little man's wizardry that when he was tempted to let himself go and at least save Miss Bergen by dying with his enemy, cold caution settled upon the American. And through all that passed he found himself watching, for some mention of that "old gent" from the lips of Solomon—watching and waiting with agonizing fear as the sequence of events bade him nay.

And now the deck of the *Zamiel* was set as a stage for the final grim scenes of this master game.

Carter found Stoppel's men banished up forward, where they grouped in sullen watchfulness. Mevrouw van der Gelt was in security below. The two ships had drifted a little closer in the dead calm that prevailed, and the only sign of life upon the yacht was a slow stream of smoke from her funnels that wended straight up and up into the heavens like the thin stream of incense that ascends eternally from the great bronze bowl of Ermya.

Near the wheel, on the after deck, stood Knowles and Stoppel. A small, hastily rigged awning of canvas sheltered the space from the sun, already burning down upon the glassy sea with tropic glare. Upon a high-coiled line, careless of tar, sat Miss Bergen. Solomon was standing beside the rail, sucking his clay pipe and staring at the horizon.

"Smoke?" Stoppel produced cheroots, and Carter took one and lighted it. "Well, gentlemen and Miss Bergen, I believe we shall now reach an amicable settlement. There is no occasion for any rancor to be displayed. I am in control of the situation, and you, Mr. Solomon, will, I trust, accept defeat in good part."

"Yes, sir." Solomon sighed wheezily, but to Carter it seemed that the faintest shadow of a wink flickered at him from one of those mild blue eyes. "I only 'opes, sir, as you ain't a-going to be too 'ard on us. About Miss Bergen, now—"

Stoppel laughed.

"Miss Bergen shall of course be honorably treated, Solomon—but she does not enter into this matter at all. I claim her and shall make good my claim!"

"I take it," said Carter quietly, addressing Solomon, "that you have given up because of Stoppel having taken this ship from us?"

"What else could we do?" returned Solomon. "Dang it, sir, Stoppel was ready to shoot you an' the mevrouw, to say nothin' o' them 'ere men of ours shut up in the fo'c's'le! Fair got the upper 'and of us, that's what 'e did!"

"Then you were a cursed fool for your pains," said Carter, his face stony. "Stoppel does not intend to release Miss Bergen at all. Your surrender won't help her in the least, so you may as well go back and fight. That's my vote!"

Stoppel darted him a furious glance. Solomon, however, shook his head.

"No, sir, I'm afraid as 'ow you're outwoted, so to speak. Now, Mr. Stoppel, sir, we may as well be settlin' terms. First Miss Bergen. What about 'er?"

The girl sat and watched Solomon with narrowed, puzzled eyes. Carter said no more but withdrew to the rail and perched there, smoking. He was angered by the demeanor of the little cockney, and could not fathom it.

Stoppel was brutally frank. "Miss Bergen is to marry me later," he said calmly. "We may leave her out of the argument. It is now a question of saving your yacht, yourself, and your friends. I can afford to be magnanimous. Your word and that of Wing Fu are perfectly good with me, and I have no particular desire to commit wholesale murder."

"Especially," put in Carter dryly, "as that course would cost you dear before the end."

Stoppel nodded assent. Suddenly his eyes narrowed as he glanced over the rail, and his gaze fastened on the yacht.

"What's that smoke?" came his sharp demand, and he gestured toward the slowly streaming funnels of the *Alcis*. "Solomon, is this some cursed trick?"

Solomon was engaged in carefully whittling tobacco into his pipe. He glanced up, his pudgy features quite expressionless.

"Trick?" he repeated blandly. "What—that 'ere smoke? Why, sir, I s'pose as 'ow Mr. Wing Fu is a-getting up steam, just like that! If there's any trick there, sir, just you up an' tell me!"

Stoppel frowned, but did not recur to the subject. But Carter
could not help feeling angered at the passive submission of the
little cockney. He knew very well that Solomon could have sent
out his engine-room force via the passages from the secret room,
with most favorable chances of overpowering Stoppel's men.
Why, then, did Solomon refuse to fight, since Miss Bergen's fate
no longer depended on his actions? A moment later Solomon
himself gave answer to that question, as though he had read it
in the minds around him.

"We ain't licked, so to speak, Mr. Stoppel," he said slowly. "You
might bore 'oles in the blessed yacht and sink 'er, but we could
fight werry 'ard while you was a-doing of it. But it's a werry bad
job to be a-fightin' prowidence, as the Good Book says. I don't
'old with no silly wasting of life, Mr. Stoppel. If so be as you
wants to make fair terms, then we'll lave a bit o' talk, as the old—"

He checked himself suddenly. The clay pipe fell from his
fingers, but struck against his boot and did not break. Solomon
picked it up and his face was white.

"Dang it!" he said softly, staring at Carter. "I nearly went and
did it that time!"

"Have a light—you're nervous." Stoppel grinned as he held
out a match. Solomon thanked him politely and lighted his pipe.

But in those words and in that look Carter had read something that reminded him of the mental leash which for a
moment he had forgotten. So, then, there was still some vague
plan in Solomon's mind!

"He wants me to act in some way," reflected the American,
frowning to himself, "when he gives that signal. And he blamed
near gave it by mistake just then! H'm! There's something queer
behind all this, and I'd like to figure out what the devil it is!"

Now, however, Solomon turned to Stoppel with a blunt
demand for terms. The half-caste nodded complacently and
proceeded to set forth his ultimatum:

"You might show fight, but, as you say, it would be senseless,
Solomon. Now, then, I have the Chair of the Eye and Miss

Bergen, and I'm satisfied. I'll turn over to you that big Dutch-woman and Carter, here, and, instead of sinking your yacht and finishing off the lot of you, I'll sail away in this schooner and leave you in peace—on two conditions."

"Let's 'ave them," said Solomon, staring reflectively at the northern horizon.

"They are very simple. I might require a good ransom, but I'll not do it, in a financial sense. I merely require assurances from you and Mr. Wing Fu that this entire affair shall be forgotten—in other words, assurances of complete immunity. This, of course, includes your friends, for whom you can answer."

Solomon emitted a cloud of smoke. "It'd be a werry great temptation to break such a promise as that, Mr. Stoppel. You don't mean to say as 'ow you'd trust us?"

"Yes. It's either that, or kill you." Stoppel smiled suddenly. He could be gracious when he chose, this big half-caste, and for a moment the better side of him showed plainly. "I know Mr. Wing Fu very well. I looked you up before leaving Surabaya, Solomon, and I found out enough about you to trust your word absolutely. Now, is that condition fair?"

"It looks werry much so, sir," returned Solomon. "What's the other one?"

"That you allow us to smash your engines—simply as a precaution against any of your men talking, or other such untoward circumstances over which you might have no control. Before you get back to Banda Neira, I'll be in safety."

For a moment Solomon puffed reflectively, his placid features giving no hint as to his thoughts. Then he removed his pipe.

"I can say yes to that, Mr. Stoppel, 'cause why, that 'ere yacht belongs to me and not to Mr. Wing Fu, just like that. But about that first condition, now, you'll 'ave to get 'is consent. I was thinkin', now—"

He paused for a thoughtful puff at his pipe, and his eyes wandered to the horizon.

"Yes?" prompted Stoppel.

"Oh, I was just thinkin', sir, as 'ow you might be willing to go a bit farther in them 'ere concessions, besides savin' a lot o' trouble for yourself, so to speak."

"What do you mean?" Stoppel frowned suspiciously. He was plainly watching the pudgy little man very cautiously. But Solomon's blank, wide-eyed gaze met his with frankness.

"About that 'ere Chair of the Eye, Mr. Stoppel. Did you find it all shipshape?"

"Yes. Carter and Miss Bergen have seen it."

Carter nodded assent. Solomon drew a wheezy sigh.

"Well, Mr. Stoppel, you know as 'ow that 'ere chair means a great deal to Mr. Wing Fu. You expect to break it up, and get two million dollars out o' the stones, which same is a-going to be werry wasteful and also werry slow business. Now, if you was to turn over that 'ere chair to Mr. Wing Fu and take 'is check for the money, I 'ave a notion 'e would be werry glad indeed. You'd 'ave the money in 'and and everybody would be 'appy."

"H'm!" Stoppel pondered this with suspicion. "Not a bad idea."

Carter glanced at Miss Bergen and nodded slightly in response to the warning in her eyes. He was very certain, now, that Solomon was up to something—was evolving some scheme of wizardry.

Miss Bergen had Wing Fu's check and had deeded over the Chair of the Eye. It was extremely unlikely that Wing Fu would calmly hand out another two million dollars like so much car fare. In the girl's silent glance Carter read that she, too, was hanging upon every word of the cockney's utterance with anticipation of some surprise.

Herman Stoppel himself, although ignorant that the chair had been bought and paid for, pitted suspicion against the phlegmatic mien of Solomon. The cockney won.

"No, not a bad idea," repeated Stoppel musingly. "I don't want to push Wing Fu too far, and his check indorsed by you would be satisfactory. See here! We'll send Captain Knowles over to the yacht to fetch Wing Fu. You give Knowles a note to your men, and let him smash your engines before he brings Wing Fu back—eh?"

Solomon accepted this test with a nod and drew forth a little red notebook and pencil. He tore out a page and scribbled a curt note. Stoppel took it, read it, then gave it to Knowles, who called four of the men from the forward deck and got into the waiting boat. As Stoppel leaned over the rail with brief instructions to Knowles about the engines, Carter saw a peculiar gleam flash into Solomon's blue eyes—the momentary gleam of a master player who sees his opponent make the fatal move.

CHAPTER XII

THE NET OF SOLOMON

A S KNOWLES was quickly pulled over to the *Alcis*, where the pirates waited at the ladder to receive him, Stoppel and Solomon fell into a mild discussion of the island trade. The half-caste did not neglect to watch the progress of Knowles, however.

Carter watched, also, and for a space believed that he had fathomed Solomon's plan. Was it to be a desperate battle, after all, with Knowles caught in the bowels of the yacht?

This thought passed again into perplexity, for Knowles passed out of sight aboard the *Alcis,* and Solomon went on chatting and cleaning his pipe with the utmost sang-froid. Yet still Carter watched and waited, confident that some deep-laid scheme was forward.

Captain Knowles reappeared. With him was Mr. Wing Fu, immaculate and frock-coated. They descended into the waiting boat, and put off for the schooner. The American watched in moody silence. Had Knowles been allowed to work his will upon those delicate engines? If so, to what end?

"And John deliberately worked it to have Wing Fu brought here—why?" Almost upon the thought Carter struck an answer. "By George—he means fight, after all! Wing Fu may be able to hold those pirates in check with his Chinese jabber; I take care of Stoppel; John himself takes Knowles, and Captain Bingham recaptures the *Alcis!* Can that be it?"

His gray eyes keen with eagerness, Carter waited. He was

still far from fathoming the intents of John Solomon, however, although this final guess of his contained more than a hint at the secret had he but known it.

The morning was by this time far advanced. Upon the glassy, windless ocean the brazen glare of the sun was terrific, and those aboard the schooner were thankful indeed for the stretched canvas that gave them some measure of protection. The vapor from the yacht's smokestacks had dwindled to a thin trickle that wound straight up into the heavens, unbroken by wind. As the boat approached. Stoppel leaned over the rail.

"Did you smash those engines?" he called.

"I just did!" returned Knowles, with vindictive satisfaction, his sapphire eye glowing up at his partner. "They won't be repaired this side o' Macassar, my lad!"

"Good!" Stoppel turned to Solomon with visible relief. "I was a bit suspicious of you, to tell the truth. Now you're safe, however."

Solomon sighed, but Carter caught a twinkle in his blue eyes.

"Yes, sir, werry true—we're safe. What would you 'ave done, now, if so be as we'd 'ad a wireless aboard?"

Stoppel grinned. "I'd have changed my plans, Solomon. But I had that craft of yours thoroughly examined at Surabaya, and knew you had no smell of a wireless outfit aboard. That might have saved you, I'll admit."

"Yes, sir, it was werry thoughtless o' me," meekly admitted Solomon. Then, thumbing the pages of his red notebook, he began to write with a preoccupied air.

Mr. Wing Fu came aboard, bowed smilingly to Miss Bergen, and crossed to where Solomon stood. Then he spoke rather sharply, to the evident amusement of Knowles, who had also come to the deck:

"I hope, Mr. Solomon, that I did no wrong in allowing Captain Knowles to tamper with our engines? Your note was—"

"You did werry right," asserted Solomon, looking up from his writing. "Mr. Stoppel, 'e 'as us 'ard and fast, Mr. Wing Fu, and I 'opes as 'ow you'll see fit to meet 'im 'alfway in the proposition 'e's a-going to make."

Wing Fu turned and met the sardonic gaze of Stoppel.

"I am sorry," he said blandly, "that you did not take my advice in Surabaya. I do not think this cruise is going to benefit your health very greatly, Mr. Stoppel."

"You may well be sorry," and Stoppel laughed. "But come, now! A truce to compliments, for I do not intend to stand here talking all day. Solomon has suggested that you might care to pay me two millions for that Chair of the Eye. By so doing I would be prevented from destroying it in order to sell the stones, while you would be performing a very meritorious action in the eyes of your ancestors."

"Undoubtedly," assented Mr. Wing Fu. He pursed his lips, glanced meditatively at the horizon to the north, and nodded. "Yes, undoubtedly. But, my dear friend, I never buy anything without having inspected it."

"Naturally. Now, if you agree to buy this object, and give me your check, may I have your word that it may be cashed anywhere without question or protest?"

Wing Fu directed a swift glance at Solomon, but the latter was still engaged in writing. He nodded assent.

"Certainly, Mr. Stoppel. *If* I find the Chair of the Eye to be genuine, and *if* I give you a check in purchase of it, you need have no fears. You and I, sir, know each other very well. Whatever may be our private feelings, our given words are inviolate. When I give you the check, my honor passes with it."

"That is quite sufficient," said Stoppel. "The chair is in the cabin below. You may inspect it at once, if you so desire."

With a tiny bow, Mr. Wing Fu stepped to the companionway and went below. Stoppel, who appeared to at last show signs of nervousness, looked at the little cockney.

"What are you writing, Solomon? Articles of agreement?"

"No, sir," returned Solomon, without glancing up. "Makin' up me accounts, sir."

Knowles laughed nastily, but said nothing. They waited in silence until Mr. Wing Fu returned up the ladder. Solomon put away his pencil, sighed wheezily, laid the notebook on the rail, and began to whittle tobacco into his pipe.

"Well?" snapped the half-caste.

"The Chair of the Eye is undoubtedly genuine," said Wing Fu calmly.

"Ah! Then you accept?"

"No."

"What!" From Stoppel and Knowles the word broke simultaneously. Stoppel took a step forward, his powerful features darkening in a flush. "What do you mean?"

"Simply that I do not care to buy it." Mr. Wing Fu waved his hand gracefully.

A snarl broke from Knowles; but Stoppel, repressing his own evident rage, curtly repressed that of his partner also, and faced Wing Fu. Carter, leaning against the rail, gathered his muscles for instant action. Solomon, however, quietly lighted his pipe.

"Very well," said Stoppel, in cold anger. "You have then the choice which I set before Solomon. Either fight this thing out or else promise me immunity and I shall go my way in peace."

"I shall leave the choice to Mr. Solomon," returned Wing Fu, with a bland smile. "His judgment is far better than mine, and I shall be content to abide by it."

With a gesture of relief, as though he had sought some guilt in the Celestial and had found it not, Stoppel turned to the cockney.

"Well, that clears up the atmosphere, although I am sorry that your plan did not go through. Then you accept my terms?"

"Why, sir, I don't see as 'ow we can 'elp ourselves, so to speak." Solomon took his notebook from the rail and extended it to Stoppel. "If so be as you'll glance over them 'ere accounts and find em all shipshape, sir, I'd be werry greatly obliged."

With a gesture of impatient assent, the half-caste accepted the little notebook.

Carter had a swift impression of some impending denouement; yet it was a sensation which sprang from no visible cause or reason, save that Solomon seemed to him to have been sparring for as much delay as possible.

Although he began to read with an expression of half-amused tolerance, suddenly the Eurasian's face changed. He stared at the writing as though something which he read there had stricken swiftly into his heart; then, his countenance livid, he glanced up at Solomon.

"What is this?" he cried in a terrible voice. "What does it mean?"

Solomon looked extremely apologetic.

"Why, sir, it's wrote down plain enough, though I don't say as 'ow me 'and didn't shake a bit."

"Curse you! What do you mean by it?" Stoppel demanded furiously.

"Just what it says, sir!" Solomon stared blankly at him, as though astonished by his rage. "John Solomon, retired, in account with 'Erman Stoppel, just like that! I 'opes, sir, as 'ow you don't find nothin' wrong with it?"

Stoppel gazed at him with incredulity, suspicion, and a helpless wonder in his eyes. Then, with an obvious effort, he mastered himself and regained his cold poise, disregarding the question that Knowles flung at him.

"But—you confounded idiot! What do you mean by it?" he demanded again. "What is the meaning of those items?"

"It means this, Mr. Stoppel, sir!" Solomon drew himself up, and his blank blue eyes became suddenly stern. Mr. Wing Fu was gradually moving forward, smiling a little to himself as if in anticipation.

"It means, sir," went on the cockney, "as 'ow you've forgot the one thing as was most important—prowidence, Mr. Stoppel! You've went and forgot prowidence, and werry sorry I am to say it. 'Ere prowidence 'as made you what you are, a big 'earty man with unusual good brains—and what do you do? You goes an' makes yourself into a werry wicked man and forgets prow-idence entirely!"

"Thanks for the sermon." With cold contempt, Stoppel flung the notebook at Solomon's feet and turned to Knowles, smiling grimly. "Pay attention, captain, and it may be that your innocent youth may yet be reclaimed from the wiles of Satan."

Through Stoppel's words and through the cackle of Knowles there pierced a sudden shrill yell from the yacht that was echoed from the Chinese on the schooner's fore deck:

"Tch'ouan!"

"What!" Stoppel whirled, and every eye followed his gaze.

Over the schooner's stern rail Carter saw against the northern horizon a tiny smudge of black—smoke, betokening a steamer where no steamer had any business to be! From the Eurasian broke a hoarse shout, as he pointed to the smoking funnels of the yacht:

"Knowles! Get over to the *Alcis* and cut off those damned fires—flood them if—"

"Beggin' your pardon, Mr. Stoppel," broke in Solomon mildly, "it ain't no use. She's been and seen us long afore this."

Knowles halted. Stoppel stood as if petrified, his gaze boring into the cockney.

"She?" he repeated. "What do you mean?"

"Why, sir"—and Solomon chuckled wheezily—"that 'ere is the Dutch gunboat from Anabon. Werry lucky it was that I found 'er at Anabon, when I cabled yesterday just afore we left Banda Neira."

"Oh!" said Stoppel, as though stunned. "And that's why the yacht's fires were smoking!"

"Yes, sir." Solomon knocked out his pipe against the rail.

Stoppel's face was livid, and he spoke in a lifeless voice:

"You devil let loose! That's why you've been wasting time with me! That's why you let me break down your engines—"

"Prowidence, I calls it," said Solomon. " 'Cause why, if you 'adn't done that werry thing, sir, you could 'ave run clean away from that 'ere gunboat in the *Alcis!*"

Something like a stifled groan broke from Captain Knowles. His splendid sapphire eye left the growing smudge of smoke, roved about the deck, and settled upon Miss Bergen. To her he made a wordless bow, then set back his shoulders and marched to the companionway, and so passed below decks and out of the story.

Mr. Wing Fu, meanwhile, had stepped forward, speaking very softly in Chinese to the gathered pirates, and producing two automatics from beneath his coat. Whether it were the hissing syllables or the menacing weapons, the sullen Chinese abode motionless.

Stoppel, heedless of these things and all else, stood with his gaze riveted upon John Solomon. In that moment he must have known that he was beyond all help now. The *Alcis* might have saved him had he not broken down her engines.

"You devil!" he said slowly.

"Beggin' your pardon, sir, nothin' of the kind," objected Solomon. "Just the werry same prowidence as I was a-tellin' you about, sir. It's a mortal queer thing, Mr. Stoppel, 'ow prowidence does let a man run on and on in 'is wicked ways, and then all of a sudden rises up and 'its 'im over the ear, so to speak—"

"What do you mean to do?" said Stoppel.

"I'm werry much afraid, sir, as we'll 'ave to 'ang you and Cap'n Knowles, unless 'e 'as went and shot 'is 'ead off by this time, as I think 'e's a-doing. Mr. Wing Fu is tellin' them 'ere men o' yours as they won't be prosecuted unless they makes more trouble, and I thinks it's werry likely they've give in. But you've been an' murdered men last night, Mr. Stoppel, and now you've got your blooming 'ead in a werry tight trap, just like that!"

"Don't talk to me of providence!" said Stoppel harshly. "This is your doing, you infernal devil—I did well to be afraid of you from the very first!"

For a moment he lifted his eyes toward the smudge of smoke

that spelled his fate, then he half turned to face Miss Bergen, and his powerful features lightened in a smile.

"Be thankful that Mr. Solomon was your friend," he said quietly. "Yet I think that you might have been happy with me, my girl. Well, no matter now."

One swift glance showed him that Wing Fu was in control up forward, and he shrugged his shoulders. Then, with no warning, he put his hand to his pocket and whipped out a revolver and stepped toward Solomon.

"You've won, Solomon," he said. "But you're going with me— savvy? Damn you, you're not bullet-proof! That boat won't be here for twenty minutes, and when she comes you'll be cold."

"Why, sir"—Solomon faced him, unmoved—"there ain't no gettin' around fate, as the old gent said when 'e took 'is third to the altar—"

Carter, silent in his bare feet, threw himself forward. As he did so, from somewhere below came the hollow crack of a pistol, and he realized vaguely that Captain Knowles had chosen the easiest way out.

Silent though the American was, Stoppel sensed his approach and whirled—but not quickly enough. Carter seized his revolver wrist and the weapon spat its deadly message upward at the heavens, as though the half-caste still denied the supreme power he had denied. Locked in a fierce embrace, the two men reeled against the rail.

Unleashed now, Carter pitted every ounce of his wiry strength against the power of Stoppel in mad fury. The schooner's rail was hip-high, and, getting his adversary against it, Carter bore forward savagely. One glance Stoppel shot over his shoulder, then, with a snarling curse, gripped hold of Carter's shoulders and flung himself backward.

The two went over the rail, and as the American plunged down at the water he heard Wilhelmina Bergen's voice rising in a wild cry. Then the warm sea engulfed him.

As he sank, he strove savagely to free himself from Stoppel. That savage, powerful face was close to his, magnified a hundredfold in its deviltry by the green water. Vainly Carter struck at it; vainly he drew up his knee and tried to pry the other man away. They sank, and then came to the surface again, still locked.

But, gasping in the blessed air, Carter heard Solomon shouting from overhead—shouting in a wild frenzy of alarm—and a rope flicked down across the heads of the two. With one hand Carter caught it, and found himself against the side of the schooner. With this purchase, he drove home one savage blow that sent Stoppel backward—and then gripped tight to the rope as hands above jerked it up.

And as he rose, Carter perceived the reason for all this, and turned his face away, sick with sudden horror and fear. For Herman Stoppel had disappeared, but across the surface of the water below was cutting the black, triangular fin of a shark.

CHAPTER XIII

"PROWIDENCE"

"YES, SIR and miss, I calls it prowidence, just like that! You needn't look so at me, Mr. Carter! I 'adn't nothin' to do wi' that 'ere shark's coming!"

Carter laughed faintly. For a moment he had felt wild fear of this little man's wizardry—fear that was incoherent and foolish.

Dripping, he rose to his feet.

Solomon and Miss Bergen had hauled him up, and the three stood alone on the quarter-deck. Silently Carter caught the girl's hands and drew her to him, gazing into her eyes. With a sudden sob, she hid her face against his sea-wet shoulder; wordless, he held her close. For them, the earth was not; and Solomon, with a stifled sigh, picked up his notebook and turned his back.

Wing Fu, who had sent the yellow men overside into their boats, slipped below and came up hurriedly.

"Knowles shot himself," he said quietly to Solomon, and looked over the rail to where the gunboat was now plain against the horizon. "I have promised these pirates immunity. What will you tell the Dutch?"

"The truth," returned Solomon. "Lay the blame on Stoppel an' Knowles, sir; and we'll not appear against these pirates, who'll go free. But if I was you, sir, I'd get that 'ere Chair of the Eye out o' this in a mortal 'urry, afore them 'ere Dutchmen claps their peepers on it! Take it aboard the yacht, and back to China it goes, just like that!"

"Good!" Wing Fu hastily departed.

"I know it's terribly foolish!" Miss Bergen drew away from Carter, wiping her eyes and smiling shakily as she gazed at him. "But—but the strain—"

"It's all over, I think," said Carter, all the grimness vanished from his face. "It's over, dear. Er—John!"

"Yes, sir—just one minute, sir!"

Solomon was writing in his notebook. He closed it and put away his pencil.

"Account wi' Mr. Stoppel closed—prowidentially," and he chuckled as he joined them. "Now, sir, what was it you was a-wanting?"

"I want to thank you"—Carter smiled as he spoke—"for bringing me to Banda Neira, John—and to the greatest treasure of all! It's been—"

Solomon shuffled uneasily and lifted a protesting hand.

"There's one thing I'd like to ask you, sir. You mind 'ow we come together, so to speak? Well, did you ever get them 'ere presents off to that 'ere niece of yours, if I may make so bold as to ask?"

"No." Carter laughed. "They're still in Surabaya, packed and waiting. How about those for your godson?"

"They're gone long ago," returned the little cockney. But Miss Bergen turned to him and seized his hand in hers, and her brown eyes danced glowingly as the bronze spirit fire glows above the hill of the Ninety-nine Steps.

"Oh, John, you shan't escape so blunderingly!" she cried. "I want to thank you, too, for bringing Ralph to the Bandas—and for bringing yourself!"

"Don't thank me, miss," said Solomon hastily. "You can't never tell what's going to come of givin' thanks, as the old gent said when 'e kissed the 'ousemaid. No, miss, don't you go a-thankin' of me. If you wants to give thanks, why, you just thank prowidence, I says!"

"And so say I also," added Carter, and brought the girl's hand to his lips.

ABOUT THE AUTHOR

H. BEDFORD-JONES is a Canadian by birth, but not by profession, having removed to the United States at the age of one year. For over twenty years he has been more or less profitably engaged in writing and traveling. As he has seldom resided in one place longer than a year or so and is a person of retiring habits, he is somewhat a man of mystery; more than once he has suffered from unscrupulous gentlemen who impersonated him—one of whom murdered a wife and was subsequently shot by the police, luckily after losing his alias.

The real Bedford-Jones is an elderly man, whose gray hair and precise attire give him rather the appearance of a retired foreign diplomat. His hobby is stamp collecting, and his collection of Japan is said to be one of the finest in existence. At present writing he is en route to Morocco, and when this appears in print he will probably be somewhere on the Mojave Desert in company with Erle Stanley Gardner.

Questioned as to the main facts in his life, he declared there was only one main fact, but it was not for publication; that his life had been uneventful except for numerous financial losses, and that his only adventures lay in evading adventurers. In his younger years he was something of an athlete, but the encroachments of age preclude any active pursuits except that of motoring. He is usually to be found poring over his stamps, working at his typewriter, or laboring in his California rose garden, which is one of the sights of Cathedral Cañon, near Palm Springs.